THE RUINS OF CRESTFALL

GRYPHON INSURRECTION BOOK 5

K. VALE NAGLE

STET PUBLISHING, LLC

Cover art and map by Jeff Brown.

Interior artwork by Brenda Lyons.

Interior graphics by Crystal Gafford of Crafty as a Coyote.

Published by STET Publishing, Denver

WWW.STETPUBLISHING.COM

WWW.KVALENAGLE.COM

10 9 8 7 6 5 4 3 2 1

Trade Paperback
ISBN: 1-64392-026-X
ISBN-13: 978-1-64392-026-9

To R. Kent Nagle, who responded to my barrage of animal questions as a young child with road trips to visit experts in other cities.

BELAMURIA

ALABASTER EYRIE

REEVESPORT

WHITEBEAK

CRESTFALL PALACE

DUCKBILL

ABYSSAL NAZE

ARGENT HEIGHTS

CRAC S

NIGHTSKY

NEW EYRIE

ALWREN

CRA RA

JADEBEAK MOUNTAINS

EMERALD JUNGLE

FLOWER OUTPOST

SUNKEN EYRIE

STORMTAIL

RAFTWORK

KING'S REACH

SUBMERGED FOREST

BLACKTALON

BLACKWING
FYRIE

MOTHFEATHER
FYRIE

GLASSWORKS

GLACIER
PRIDE

PITOHUI
EYRIE

POISONMAW

KLING
EA

CRACKLING
SEA EYRIE

REDWOOD VALLEY
EYRIE

OVER
NCH

KJARR
NESTS

TAIGA

KJARR

WEALD

STRIX
PLATEAU

LUMINAIRE

NIGHTHAUNT

Mally watched as his latest experiment coughed its last breath and gave out. It had been an opinicus once, and not one in favor with the Seraph King. He'd run it through the changes as many times as the body would take until its heart gave out.

Treating someone with the salts without adding in blood made them regress, as though there were attributes of past birds and gryphons hidden in their very essence. Had opinici really evolved from seraphs, Mally hoped that essence might still be hidden somewhere far enough back.

At least thus far, his hypothesis wasn't bearing fruit for anything except the graves outside of Whitebeak. The nearby jail was starting to run low on prisoners, and he didn't want to go back to experimenting on gryphons. They were always unruly, and the local varieties were prone to holding a grudge.

His assistants came in to remove the corpse for examination. The newer ones avoided looking at his strange, twisted body, but the older ones had grown accustomed to it. While he valued his assistants and their input, they were still learning what to look for and relied upon him to make sense of their observations.

Eleven. He scribbled in his notebook. The number varied a little. Some subjects gave out at seven, others made it to thirteen. He wasn't as interested in the number of times he could dose someone with the essential salts so much as the signs that the body was starting to give.

He grabbed a cloth and wiped sand off of a mirror sitting on a workshop bench. He could see the markers of strain around his black eyes. His joints ached, and the gape of his beak sometimes bled without provocation.

Some of his issues came from the disease that had haunted him his entire life. Some came from having used alchemy to reset his biology so many times.

By the reflection, he had two treatments left before his organs would fail. If he hadn't found a cure by the second treatment, it would be too late.

While his assistants cleaned up the mess, Mally wandered through the holding pens. Several northern quarter Redwood Valley opinici regarded him with trepidation. A parrot opinicus who had once been blue, red, and green cowered. Mally wasn't sure what the Seraph King had promised them. Wealth and land for their loved ones, perhaps?

Little did these opinici know they owed Mally their lives, after a fashion. His research had served as the basis that allowed Headmaster Neider to come up with a cure that only worked on eggs. Mally had tested all of the refugees from New Eyrie. The ones in his pens tested positive for the iron disorder, but they weren't dying of it. Whatever Neider had done with Mally's research, it had worked—on eggs.

Perhaps I was a little too hasty in killing the headmaster.

A cough came from behind him. Mally ignored it,

assuming it was someone trying to get his attention, but one of his assistants collapsed.

The beautiful peafowl had once been a vibrant green and blue. Now, his feathers were leached white by disease, his talons and beak stained red.

"Prepare the chamber." Mally's voice came out in clicks and hisses, echoing throughout the pen and startling the Redwood Valley opinici. The experiment that had granted him his black eyes had taken his speech. And, when the gryphons of the Abyssal Naze had found out what he was doing with their captured pridemates, it had cost him his favorite workshop and a reeve's ransom of purple elixir.

He reached down to his peacock assistant. They intertwined red talons.

"Thank...you," the assistant whispered.

Mally looked into the peacock's face. There was no sign of darkening around his eyelids, no other signs that his body was giving out from treatment. "What number is this?"

"Four," the assistant said.

Rather than help him up, Mally began to drag his body towards the chamber where his other assistants were unpacking the last of the crates from Crestfall. Unlike Mally, the peacock should live long enough for a cure to be found.

"Nighthaunt." A voice echoed from the entrance of his workshop, where blinding light spilled in.

Mally squeezed the peacock's talons, then left to see what his patrons wanted.

THE NIGHTHAUNT SQUINTED in the harsh daylight. Silver and Hi-kun were waiting for him.

Hi-kun, high commander, wore his ceremonial armor

even in the summer heat. It was hard to look at him through the glare. If Whitebeak were an eyrie, he would be its reeve. Instead, as a military outpost along the edge of the desert, he served as the king's shield against invasions from the blackwings and their allies. Soon, if all went according to plan, Hi-kun would get to be the king's talons.

He already carried himself as such, having no problem wandering through Mally's workshops, knocking over all manner of important vials. No, the squeamish one was Silver.

She still wore bracers on her forelegs because of her run-in with Rybalt, the blackwings' top assassin. The Nighthaunt reeled at the thought of losing the seraph in the bog to such rabble. She flinched when Mally's peacock assistant screamed in the background as the blood solution was heated and the salts added.

"How are you recovering?" Mally asked.

She winced at the bestial, echoing sound of his voice but didn't pull away when he inspected her wounds. "I'll be fine. I didn't come for a check-up."

Despite her tone, Mally liked the silver hawk. She wasn't as pretentious as most of the Seraph King's reeves, and he owed her his life after the assassination attempt in the swamp.

The feeling wasn't mutual.

"There's been some sort of outbreak north of here, at the prison camp," Hi-kun said. "We need you to investigate."

They both knew Mally wouldn't be going out on his own. He was worth too much to the Seraph King to risk him becoming another casualty of something so unimportant as a war.

Mally's sounds echoed back into the dark of his workshop, and a dozen pale opinici with red talons came out.

"Quite the cult you have going here," Silver said.

"Not a cult," Mally clicked. "Just opinici with a common purpose—find the cure or die trying. I find the more opinici who are incentivized to search for a cure, the faster it's found."

Hi-kun pointed to two pale assistants who'd once served under him before they'd become too sick to fight. They bowed and went to fetch their things.

"How long until the next shipment from Crestfall?" Mally asked.

Hi-kun looked down at him. "The pink reeve is stalling, asking for assurances and wealth before the full might of the king arrives. The desert isn't kind to goliaths. Padfeet attack the caravans at night and thunder birds during the day."

The thunder birds, with their thirty-two-foot wingspan, were much larger than opinici. Having fed on the dead and been harried by both sides, they'd become antagonistic towards any creature that stepped foot into the high desert.

"Fine," Mally said at last. He didn't have enough essential salts to continue both curing his assistants and experimenting. If he had to travel to Crestfall to make that happen, he'd do it. Unlike Hi-kun and Silver, *he* didn't fear the things that stalked the dark. He was one of them.

FAMILY PORTRAIT

CHERINE, NINOX, MARSHMALLOW, SQUIRRELBANE, AND
SOUND OF SNOW

1

CHERINE & NINOX

Cherine tossed Sound of Snow into the air with a squeal and caught her on the way down. Marshmallow was napping on Ninox's front paws, and Squirrel-bane chirped angrily at a squirrel that had run up a tree to get away from him.

"He will be ferocious when his feathers come in," Ninox assured Cherine. "Squirrels are only hard to catch when you cannot fly or climb. You should not judge him based on his performance. I am teaching him how to be a good hunter."

"I know you are." Cherine had become accustomed to Ninox's reassurances on the hunting prowess of their three children. It had taken him a while to find the appropriate responses, but he'd come to realize she thought of their offspring as a group project. She was in charge of teaching them to hunt; he was in charge of teaching them *opinicus thoughts,* as Ninox called them.

Sound of Snow pulled one of his quill pens out of a harness pocket and started chewing on it.

"Hey now, that's one of my favorites," Cherine scolded. He grabbed a stick and put it into her tiny talons as a replacement. Snow was the only opinicus of the bunch, and she would mature slower than her gryphon brothers.

"Who can show me the glyph for owl?" he asked.

Marshmallow got up with a yawn and began to trace the letters for owl into the dirt. Squirrelbane, not to be outdone by his brother, rushed over to do the same.

Sound of Snow started using a talon to trace the letters, but Cherine put the stick back in her grip. "Use this. It'll make it easier when you have to do anything complicated later."

Sound of Snow whined but gave in. "What's something complicated look like?"

Cherine considered, then pulled out one of his favorite pens for art. Instead of the sand, he used some of the paper Ninox had brought him. She'd scavenged cases of it from the Redwood Valley ruins while searching for Reeve's Nest. The edges were warped and brown from the heat, but it was still usable—preferable, even, when dirt was the alternative.

He was in the middle of sketching out a drawing of Ninox and the children when a chirp from above alerted him to the arrival of Kia and Zeph.

"Hello!" Zeph called down. "How're things?"

Kia landed near Cherine and examined his drawing. "That's pretty good! Here, you go stand over there, and I'll add you to the picture."

Cherine stood next to Ninox, who was trying to groom Marshmallow's fluffy down, while Kia finished her sketch of him.

Zeph and Squirrelbane made eye contact, and Zeph crouched down like he was going to pounce. Squirrelbane mimicked the hunter's stance and prowled towards Zeph.

The copper hawk backed up, the gryphlet advanced.

Squirrelbane pushed Zeph towards the edge of the grove until his back was against a Redwood.

Squirrelbane began shaking his tail, but Zeph just backed up farther, using his dewclaws to climb the tree upside-down.

"Mom!" Squirrelbane shouted.

Ninox looked up from her grooming. "Do not cheat, Zeph."

The copper hawk gryphon pounced, catching Squirrelbane in a tumble. Then, from his back, Zeph lifted the chubby gryphlet into the air with all four paws.

"I win!" Zeph said.

"Snow, Mallow!" the gryphlet squealed. Both of his siblings attacked, jumping on top of Zeph.

"Okay, okay!" the Reeve's Bane said. "I give up."

Ninox purred her approval. "It is better to hunt as a group than alone. This is why Zeph is so bad at it."

Zeph pulled himself out from under the pile of gryphons. "I'm not bad at hunting. I catch more than my fair share."

"That is not what Pink Paw says," Ninox countered.

Zeph puffed up, but Ninox slow blinked at him. While there was still a rivalry between the two, it had turned friendly as their territories now bordered each other, and both spent a good deal of time visiting Cherine in his comfortable exile.

Since Reeve Rybalt and Iony had retreated and Ninox's Owlfeather Highlands had opened up for Ashen Weald use, there'd been a push to explore farther north. When Ninox sent word that the blackwings were using the old saberbeak pride grounds at Poisonmaw as a base of operations, Hatzel showed up to reclaim her birthright—with a little help from her allies to clear out the monitors.

Though, in fact, Hatzel was no longer the last saberbeak. Several of the gryphlets born in the spring had the same fang-like sabers on their beaks. Cherine hadn't discovered a polite way to ask if the eggs were hers or if the interbreeding between the copper hawk, magpie, and saberbeak prides meant *saberbeak* was a recessive trait.

While Hatzel's pride kept Poisonmaw Valley safe, the Strix Pride guarded the mountains around it. Together, Pink Paw and Ninox coordinated to watch the land north of the Redwood Valley Eyrie. It had been several months since the Seraph King and Blackwing Reeve's forces withdrew from the area, but it was only a matter of time before their lackeys returned. Already, there had been several sightings of the glacier pride scouting the new borders.

Kia put down the pen. "There we go. What do you think?"

She turned the sketch around so everyone could see. Ninox looked on with curiosity. Cherine lifted up Snow so she could inspect it.

She made a chirp-meow of delight. "I want to do that!"

"Keep practicing!" He rifled through his harness pockets to find an old, worn pen. "Your mother will find some charcoal for you."

A hoot came from overhead. The owl gryphons and opinicus looked up.

"It is time," Ninox repeated in common for the sake of the non-owls. She hooted a message into the trees, and Grax arrived with more of the Strix Pride to carry Ninox's children back to the Owlfeather Highlands.

Once the escorts were gone, she looked at the two scholars and Zeph. "What is your plan?"

"Crestfall," Kia said. "It's been quiet for too long."

"The Ashen Weald says it is empty," Ninox said. "They see no one flying around it."

"The glassworks is empty," Cherine corrected, "but the eyrie is farther north. I think if we search around the glass-works and buildings along the Crackling Sea, we might find a clue or two on what's happening with the eyrie."

Ninox sized up Zeph. "You should bring owls. Zeph will not be able to protect you."

The copper hawk stuck out his tongue at Ninox. "We're not fighting; we're sneaking."

She turned to look at Cherine. "If you are captured, I will not rescue you again."

"It's a quick flight," Cherine reassured her. "Nobody's been spotted there in a while. I'm sure we'll be fine."

Ninox tilted her head to the side to show her doubt. In the distance, her owls disappeared into the highlands.

"What're you up to while we're gone?" Zeph asked. "Still searching the northern mountains for Iony?"

No opinicus had been more surprised than Cherine to see gryphons working alongside the Blackwing Eyrie's forces. That their top assassin considered Iony, the pride leader of the glacier gryphons, as close friend had caught everyone off guard.

"No, I know where he is." Ninox licked a paw to groom her whiskers. "The glacier pride is on a large mountain far to the north. We will know if they send more gryphons or opinici against us. We will see them in plenty of time."

Kia finished adding a few lines to the sketch. "In plenty of time to do what?"

"Evacuate Poisonmaw and notify the Ashen Weald," Ninox said. "All of the pride leaders are meeting north of the Crackling Sea Eyrie to discuss military matters. Satra would like us to be able to work together when the next invasion comes."

"At Sailfin Point? That's not far from here," Zeph cautioned. "Is Cherine's hideaway going to be safe?"

Ninox stretched her wings. "I am working on securing his freedom. Daytime diplomacy is hard. I ask for one thing, another pride asks for something in return."

Nighttime diplomacy, as Cherine understood it, involved more killing than talking.

From the forest, Grax hooted that Ninox's children were safe. Twenty owl gryphons appeared around the grove.

"It is time for me to go. You three do not get into trouble," Ninox commanded. "Come back here when you are through. Do not go exploring."

She addressed all of them when she spoke, but her ears never left Cherine. Only after he'd promised they'd try not to do any exploring and wouldn't go over the water did she gather her owl gryphons and head to the meeting of leaders.

"Sorry about that," Cherine apologized. "She likes having me stuck here teaching math and writing to the gryphlets and Snow. I suspect she's dragging her paws just so I'm stuck in this grove a while longer."

Kia unpacked her harness, pulling out one of the scorched maps found at the headmaster's study. "While we're checking the glassworks, Piprik and Lei are headed up the western bank in search of Mally the Nighthaunt. Piprik thinks that he'll be located near the refugees from New Eyrie who went with the Seraph King. If everything goes well, we'll meet Piprik and Lei here."

She pointed to the northwest corner of the Crackling Sea on the map. There was an old, abandoned raftworks along the edge of the water they could use as a meeting place.

"The blue opinici say the reeve's pet has been growing more aggressive," Zeph said, "so don't fly over the water. Stick to the land. If something bad happens, fly towards Poisonmaw or New Eyrie, whichever's closer."

"Why does Piprik think the Nighthaunt will be near the refugees?" Cherine grabbed a spare journal and a few more quill pens and finished securing his harness. While Kia and Zeph had gotten to know Piprik for their time on the shore, Cherine had yet to spend much time with the strange opinicus.

Kia folded up the map. "Didn't say. But he's the only one who knows anything about Mally, so I trust his hunch."

"So Piprik is searching for Mally, and Lei is looking for the Redwood Valley opinici to make sure they're okay," Zeph said. "What're we looking for, exactly?"

"Scholar stuff," Cherine replied.

Kia's answer was longer. "Anything that can tell us what happened to Crestfall without us actually having to go into the desert. Satra and Grenkin would love to turn the desert reeve into an ally, but any sign of Ashen Weald troops might spook either side. Failing that, we want to know whom they're allied with."

"We can talk about it on the way," Cherine said. "We'll stick close to the mountains until we reach the end of the sea. Let's head out."

2

BLACK MASK

Along the southern mangrove coast, a small raft made its way west. Piprik and Lei managed the stormcloth sail while Soft Paws and Blinky helped them navigate.

Piprik's goal was to head north and look for Mally the Nighthaunt, but first, he had a few things to check out in the south. The mummy at the dig site and the refugees hadn't been the Seraph King's only goals in the bog. He'd also taken a goliath bird caravan's worth of *something* out of here, and Piprik wanted to know what that was. Thankfully, Soft Paws had been willing to humor him—and convince Blinky to come along. There was also the issue of the missing Fantail Pride leader.

"It would be faster by air," Lei complained. Ever since his recovery on the shore after the events of New Eyrie, he'd been keen to show off how well he could fly. A winter and spring of good nutrition and flying between Ashfoot Isle and Luminaire had turned him into quite the aerial acrobat.

Of course, showing off wasn't his only reason for learning to fly. Since being separated from his family and subjects at New Eyrie, he'd become obsessed with making sure they were okay. Having heard Piprik's stories of the Seraph King, he'd expressed a growing sense of dread that his fisherfolk mentor shared.

"The skies aren't safe," Soft Paws said. They were actually using the same raft that had brought the bog witch and expedition from the Raftworks to Sandpiper's Dune last autumn. "We haven't cleared the infected starlings from this section yet."

"Why not?" Lei asked.

Blinky tried to catch a small fish off the edge of the raft, nearly falling in. "Satra wants what is left of Vitra's bog gryphons left alone. She hopes they will rejoin us if we show we are peaceful."

Where most of the members of the bog expedition had sworn never to return to the accursed place ever again, Blinky seemed at ease among the mangroves, hanging moss, spike palms, and cypress. What's more, she claimed she had a contact who could give them the information they were after—someone who wouldn't talk to anyone except her.

Blinky hooted to draw Soft Paws's attention to a marker along the shore. Where the bog pride's traditional markers were bog blossom blue, this one had a violet tint to it, as though the blue paste had been mixed with red.

"Land along the stretch of sand by the river. Any farther inland and we risk upsetting them." Soft Paws's blue paint was caked thick on her fur and feathers. On most of her body, the paint hinted at her skeleton underneath, though the bone markings on the underside of her wings more closely resembled a bat's than a gryphon's. The tops of her wings were decorated with bog blossom drawings, allowing her to hide in the underbrush.

She ruled Bogwash, sometimes called the Village of Lost Gryphlets, and had convinced some of the bog wingtorn loyal to Satra to come south and teach the old ways to the young bog witches growing up among the mangroves. With Urious's help, they helped root out the remaining infected starlings.

Piprik secured the boat. Offshore, he could make out several small islands to the southwest, just below the hill-like end of the Jadebeak Mountains.

Blinky flew atop a broken pillar and let out an owlish cry, both soft and haunting.

Soft Paws examined the glyphs on the stone. "I was born atop this same pillar. Erlock's explosion and flooding nearly took it out to sea."

From the tall grass lining the river came a response in owlish.

Lei stretched his long neck to look around. "What was that?"

"My name," Blinky replied.

From the reeds, a bog wingtorn with exaggerated mask markings stood up and limped over to where they were waiting. He wore an old sailor's harness with the needles of a spike palm woven through it to protect himself from flying assailants.

Soft Paws bowed her head. "Black Mask. I'm glad you're alive."

While he only nodded to acknowledge Soft Paws, he let Blinky groom his facial feathers. "I got your message. What brings you back to the Heart of the Bog?"

Where the harness was torn and spines broken, Piprik could see bite and claw marks on the wingtorn, several infected. "Can we patch you up while we talk?"

Black Mask started to protest, but Blinky hooted something to him, and he relaxed enough to let them remove his armor.

"What happened?" Lei asked. He started preparing the aneda poultices like a good assistant while Piprik examined the wingtorn and Soft Paws gathered some kashow sap.

Black Mask looked from Lei's flippers to his necklace of shark teeth before answering. "Starlings."

"You should let the Ashen Weald take care of the infected starlings." Soft Paws rubbed the numbing sap over his cuts and bruises. "Even if it's just myself and Bogwash."

"Not infected starlings, just normal starlings, testing the borders." Black Mask winced as pus was drained from one of his wounds.

Piprik finished sewing the wounds closed and applied the poultices. "We'll see what we can do. Figuring out the starling problem is our next stop, if you can get us safe passage up the Jadebeak River."

Black Mask's ears showed his skepticism. "If you really think you can get the starlings to back off, I can get you up the river. Is that what you came here for?"

"No, we wanted to know what the Seraph King took when his forces came through the bog," Blinky said. "They were the white opinici who look like Pip who came in the spring. Urious saw eight goliath birds pulling carts of something."

Black Mask tensed when Urious's name was mentioned. "We had a stash of Crackling Sea supplies we'd stolen over the years, including most of the stormcloth from the raftworks, enough to build an armada with. They took all of it."

"But why?" Soft Paws shook her head. "That's still not enough to turn it into a barrier like the Crackling Sea Eyrie uses."

"Maybe they're building rafts?" Lei suggested. "The fisherfolk turned their stolen stormcloth into sails."

Piprik looked out past the Jadebeak Mountains. The end

of the mountain range blocked his view of the Emerald Jungle. "Have you seen any boats?"

Black Mask stood and let the others re-secure his armor. "A boat is what the fancy rafts are called, I assume? Sure, I've seen them. They come by all the time. But they don't make it past the emerald coast. The starlings fly out and kill everyone on board."

"War boats?" Blinky asked. "Like the blue opinici's floating city?"

"Just small ones," Black Mask replied.

Piprik had once ridden on a small raft off the same coast when he fled the Emerald Jungle years ago. It sounded like he wouldn't have survived the same trip today.

"Soft Paws, Blinky, can you take our raft back to the raftworks on your own?" Piprik wasn't sure if gryphons could work the sails. "I'd like for Black Mask to take just Lei and me the rest of the way in."

Soft Paws shrugged. "If he is correct and he's cleared the infected out of this section of the bog, we can fly back and return with a fisherfolk opinicus to fetch the raft."

Blinky's face was very close to Black Mask's.

"It's true," he said. "You should watch yourselves along the mountain range, but it's been a month since the last infected starling came through."

It seemed burning the seraph had stopped the spread of the parasite, at least for now. There were still several species that served as carriers. The Ashen Weald's bog witches and medicine gryphons had begun testing animals trapped in the kjarr. There were a few that tested positive without silver eyes, particularly the red-spine sailfin monitors, but the number of infected was declining.

"There were stolen clay jars with the parasite," Blinky

said. "I saw them when we escaped. What happened to them?"

"His lot didn't get them." Black Mask gestured at Piprik, whose white plumage and black circles around his eyes resembled those of the Seraph King's home eyrie. "We buried the jars carefully, thinking that's what they were after. But as soon as they found the stormcloth, they took it and left."

"Satra would like those clay jars back," Blinky said.

Black Mask shook his head. "No chance there. The crone says she's holding onto them as insurance. She appreciates that Satra hasn't tried to reclaim the Heart of the Bog, but Satra's the fourth Kjarr in the crone's lifetime. She feels fairly certain Satra will get killed one day and wants some protection against the next Kjarr."

"I understand. Come, Soft Paws. You are needed north." Blinky groomed Black Mask's feathers one last time, then they took flight and headed east to let the raftworks know to pick up the raft first.

Black Mask led Lei and Piprik north along the river. "There's some climbing up by the Heart, and the turtles have reclaimed a few sections, but otherwise, it's fairly tame now."

"Are we safe from your pride?" Lei looked away from Black Mask's scars.

"I apologize for my apprentice," Piprik said. "If Blinky trusts you, that's enough for us."

They'd gone several feet before Black Mask spoke again. "No, he's right. I suppose everyone knows what I did to the last Ashen Weald expedition. You're safe enough with me. And if you run into Urious, tell him I'm sorry."

Piprik wasn't sure what that meant, but he promised to do so if he came across Urious.

3

URIOUS

Urious patrolled the rocky outcroppings that formed Sailfin Point. Normally empty, the stretch north of the Crackling Sea Eyrie was looking crowded. Both wingtorn and bog witches followed him around. Soft Paws would be joining them later, but he was in charge of the wayward boglings until she arrived.

He walked along the rocky beach, looking for any signs of the serpentine whale that stalked the sea. When two splashes came from right offshore, one of the red-plumed wingtorn next to him tensed. In response, the rest of the witches and wingtorn did the same.

Urious laughed. "You survived falling off two eyries and you're afraid of getting wet?"

The red wingtorn bristled and was about to give him a piece of her mind when two fisherfolk exploded out of the water and landed next to Urious.

Without thinking, both Tresh and Quess shook as hard as they could, spraying the bog and kjarr gryphons with water.

"Oh... oh," Quess said, finally opening her eyes. "I'm so

sorry; I didn't see you all here!"

There was a grin to Tresh's beak that told Urious that, unlike her sister-in-law, she'd known exactly where she'd landed.

"How's the water, Sharkbeak?" he asked. Many of the wingtorn were still afraid of Tresh. When they'd served on opposite sides of the war, she'd made quite the entrance, erupting out of the water and pulling down several of their opinicus jailors.

She'd later joined his expedition into the swamp to save Quess. The stories of Tresh from that time were no less impressive—she'd evaded bog armies, silver-eyed starlings, and giant turtles. She'd swum twenty minutes through an underground river to liberate the Ashen Weald prisoners.

"I prefer the ocean, but it was a nice change of pace." She flicked her tail, missing Urious but hitting his crimson-plumed second with water. "No sign of your sea monster. It is a pity. Rorin brought his favorite fishing spears."

Tresh and Quess flew off to join their kin. Fifty fisher-folk, a mixture of crane sentries and petrel divers, had taken the beach for their own.

"They're odd birds," the red wingtorn said. She was still staring at the shark tooth-like scarring on Tresh's beak. What she really meant was that it was strange to see them among the wingtorn.

Urious had several regrets. One of them was leading the charge to destroy Crane's Nest and all eggs in it. Both Tresh and Quess had nearly killed him in the last few years before finally forgiving him as best they could.

Overhead, Ranger Lord Mia's peregrine falcon opinici played tag with the Fantail Pride. Owls and copper hawks carried out their own games in a lost grove of redwoods breaking the flow of the aneda forest. Magpies and harpy eagles were gathered around Carru and Xavi, who were in the middle of telling some sort of story, complete with Askel and Triddle adding their own sound effects. After being reunited, the co-consorts always stayed within touching distance of each other.

Several of the taiga pride had agreed to come down from their mountains and set up an embassy at the Crackling Sea Eyrie. They were currently having their massive coats shaved down to help them survive the heat.

Urious led his retinue past all of these groups to meet Orlea's goliath bird caravan. She'd sent a letter asking to meet with him ahead of the official proceedings. She'd said she wanted to return something to the wingtorn.

Urious chirped a greeting.

"Look at all of this!" Orlea exclaimed. "Is the eyrie housing everyone? Or should we set up nests along the forest?"

"Ranger Lord Grenkin has opened the eyrie to all who feel comfortable staying there," the red wingtorn said.

"Pride Leader Grenkin," Urious corrected. It was taking some getting used to. "Most of the wingtorn who were held along the Crackling Sea have opted to nest in the forest. With the summer nights, we probably won't need the cover of the trees."

"It's those exact wingtorn I'm interested in talking to," Orlea said. "Didi, if you wouldn't mind?"

The splotchy blue merchant poked her head up from the back of the caravan and chirped a few orders. She opened one of the crates to reveal metal claws.

Unlike the manufactured talons used by the Redwood Valley's army, these were designed for gryphon use. They wouldn't work for just any gryphon, however.

The wingtorn held inside New Eyrie by self-styled

'Grand Reeve' Ivess had faced horrors of their own, including being declawed—a process by which the last bit of the toe was chopped off. It was a barbaric practice, and it had made life and hunting hard for them.

These new claws were designed to slip over the severed tip of the toe.

"I fought against using the metalworks to make weapons for most of a year," Orlea said. "In the end, I decided that there were some we needed back, the ones that brought a sense of dignity with them."

One of the bog wingtorn who'd been declawed came forward, and Didi slipped the claws over his front and back legs.

"We have about twenty sets," Orlea explained. "I'm sure there are uses or problems we didn't predict. Test them out. See if you can climb, hunt, and run in them. If anything needs to be changed, we'll fix them before the next run."

"Make sure you can get them on and off on your own, too," Didi added. "We tried to make sure you wouldn't need opinicus help to secure them, but we probably forgot something."

Urious turned back towards the kjarr camp and trilled out the names of nineteen more declawed wingtorn, who came running over.

"Thank you for your gift, Pride Leader," he said. "I believe Satra's waiting for you by the spines. She'll want to thank you personally."

Orlea bowed her head and left Didi to secure the claw prosthetics and manage the goliath birds.

Urious walked alongside Orlea. At least so far, the first gathering of the southern prides was going off without a hitch. All that remained to be seen was what happened after they'd spent a week together.

4

JADEBEAK

Piprik and Lei made their way up the Jadebeak River from the ocean and into the bog proper. Piprik had been very careful to stay away from the cypress trees during his original escape south to find the fisherfolk years ago. Now, he kept one wary eye towards the Jadebeak Mountains.

Black Mask warmed up to the two fisherfolk, something Piprik credited to Blinky's influence. Lei tried to pry into Black Mask and Blinky's past, but all the wingtorn would say was that they'd bonded over a misadventure involving a wasp's nest.

When it came time to skirt around the Heart of the Bog, Lei asked if they could explore. While some of the walls lining the old eyrie were outlined with moss and lichen, all that remained of the forgotten city's core were the tops of towers sticking out of the water in a giant hole in the ground.

"It's too dangerous, little fisherfolk," Black Mask said. "It's all turtles in there now."

Lei was excited by getting to see one of the locations Quess and Tresh visited on their own bog adventure. "I don't see any turtles. Can we toss a fish in there or something to make them come to the surface?"

"We're not on vacation, Lei," Piprik scolded, but Black Mask was considering it. The fish here were notoriously large.

"See that pool across the way?" The wingtorn pointed to one of the pools northwest of the colossal sink hole. "It's safe to fish there. If you can catch two fish and cook one for lunch before I catch up to you, we'll toss the other down to the matamata."

Lei cheered.

"Contingent upon you having salt for the fish," Black Mask added.

"Have you ever heard of fisherfolk traveling without it?" Piprik asked. "Okay, let's get to work. Are we safe to fly across the hole?"

Black Mask nodded. "I'll meet you over there. It'll take me some climbing and walking. Just don't fly too high."

A short flight and a bit of luck later and Piprik got to work setting up a fire for the first whiskerfish while Lei used a bamboo spear to try to catch a second to drop on the turtles. This section of the bog cascaded down as acidic rains ate more and more of the calcium underpinnings away, collapsing it to a gentler slope. Where Erlock and Ellore had destroyed a dam to flood the Jadebeak River, the heavy waters had washed away a large section of moss and vegetation here to reveal an old system of canals that used to lead into the city.

Just as Black Mask made his way on foot to their pool, Lei managed to snag a second whiskerfish with an "Ah-ha!" It was so large, the small peafowl had trouble getting it out of the pool.

"Sorry about the delay," the wingtorn said. "The crone

and rest of the true bog pride aren't happy you're here. I told them about the starlings, and I think they'll let you pass. I wouldn't stay any longer than you need to."

Piprik nodded. "The fish is just about ready to eat. Is Lei still okay to toss his in?"

"There's a pillar in the center." Black Mask settled down to watch the cooking fish. "You can drop it from there. Just don't get close to the water. Matamata have long necks."

It took Piprik and Lei working together, but they got the whiskerfish down to the pillar and then rolled it over the side.

At first, nothing happened. The fish swam down and disappeared from view.

Then the mossy, grass-covered edges of the city detached and revealed themselves to be turtles. Several were large enough to fit two gryphons on their backs, but none were as big as the ones in Tresh's waterfall story.

Still, Lei's excitement was palpable. "It's one thing to hear about these places; it's something else entirely to get to see them for myself!"

Piprik took the fish from the spit and cleaned the scales off before dividing it into three.

"I imagine fisherfolk don't get to travel much," Black Mask said. "What's the coast like on the other side of the taiga?"

"Lots of sand and rocks," Lei said. "Someone planted bamboo generations ago, and it's gotten out of control. Oh, sand dunes! And salamanders as big as a gryphon. They're getting out of control, too."

"We've traveled a bit to trade salt," Piprik lied. "We heard about the trouble with the Seraph King and the starlings, so we were asked to lend a helping talon."

Black Mask finished his meal. "It's not much farther.

Once you're north of the waterfall, you're the Ashen Weald's problem. Don't come back."

"We understand," Lei said.

Piprik looked at the large, cooked whiskerfish. "We've only eaten about half the fish. Can we leave the rest for your pridemates?"

"Too much salt," Black Mask said. "They'll assume you're trying to poison them. Wrap it up and take it with you. There's not much to eat in the bog that's safe for outsiders."

"Right, I'd forgotten," Lei said. "No birds or capybaras or sailfins, right? Just fish and plants?"

"That's about right," Black Mask replied. "And don't venture too far into the Jadebeak Mountains. The starlings have no problem crossing into our territory, but turtle forbid anyone puts a paw near their emerald trees."

Piprik thought back to his expedition with Mally. He didn't need any reminders about being careful around starlings.

They packed up the fish and headed north, following the river as it turned west towards the mountains and waterfall.

BLACK MASK SAID his goodbyes when they came to a bog blossom glyph marking territory reclaimed by Soft Paws and Urious. They continued on to the edge of the bog.

Piprik watched the Jadebeak Falls for an hour. No one came or went.

"I'm sure Erlock is okay," Lei said.

Piprik didn't respond. They'd never run any tests on how far green wing altruism extended. It was possible she was too much weald, too little starling, and they'd torn her apart.

Lei poked Piprik's leg. "I never met the Fantail Pride leader. What was she like?"

"Grumpy," Piprik said. "She didn't like us poking and prodding her. Didn't like being around the sick starlings. By all accounts, she was a fierce fighter and excellent flyer before her tailfeathers burned off."

"Tresh likes her." Lei nibbled on some of the cold fish. "Says she has a lot of personality. I'm not really sure what that means."

Things were still quiet on the falls. Piprik decided it was about time to head in. "Rorin also has a lot of personality. I'm going to fly up there and look around. There's a cave near the top of the falls. If anything happens, I want you to stay hidden, okay? If I don't come back out, head to New Eyrie or the Flower, whichever seems closer and safer."

Lei nodded. He found a hiding place, his long train of green feathers blending in with the summer foliage.

Piprik flew up to search the cave. He didn't know if his old friends would recognize him in this body or kill him as another white eyrie scout. He'd promised to bring Piprik's badge to prove his identity, but he'd sent that along with Erlock, rightfully predicting the Fantail Pride leader would seek out the healthy starlings.

It took some time to locate the cave after all this time. It wasn't precisely behind the waterfall, as he remembered from his first trip to the Emerald Jungle. At least he didn't have to go through the water to find it this time. Instead, there was a break in the rocks only visible from the south side that led back into the mountain itself.

Inside were several nests and an old journal sitting on top of a pile of crates. All of the nests were dusty, though some more than others. Woven into the edge of the nests was a mixture of sweet vine, cassia blossom, and citrus peel.

He twirled the vine in his hands. One hadn't finished drying out, suggesting it was only a few days old. The cassia bloom gave it the scent of vanilla and cinnamon, but the citrus peel and sweet vine kept the most pesky nest vermin away. It had been a common practice among the goliath bird herders where he'd grown up.

When he'd first stumbled upon the cave with the initial scouts looking for a way into the Emerald Jungle, Piprik had remembered it as damp and hard to see unless an opinicus was right on top of it. There'd been puddles of water and even an angry lace monitor guarding it.

Since his fateful flight from the jungle, someone had added in a packed dirt floor covered in dry reeds. It sloped down towards the entrance, keeping water from pooling inside.

He touched the bottom of one of the boxes. It was dry. He looked at the journal atop the crates. It had his name on it.

Khalim, fill the cauldron with the recipe in this journal and leave it cooking. Do not stay in the cave overnight. Return in the morning.

He turned the page, dislodging dust. It contained a strange recipe. The notation and measurements were blackwing, and it took his old mind a moment to remember the weald conversions.

The formula was long and involved. He called down to Lei, and they got started using pitchers to half-fill the cauldron with water from the falls and get a fire going underneath it. He transcribed the recipe into Lei's journal in Redwood Valley measurements and had his apprentice check the crates.

For the other ingredients, he flew down to search the bog.

The timing was close, but they'd just located a stray craneberry bush and added juice when the sun disappeared behind the mountains.

"It's time to go," he told Lei.

The peacock looked down at the mixture. "Are you sure this'll be fine? We don't need to tend it? How's anyone going to know it's cooking here?"

"I don't know," Piprik admitted. "Those were our instructions. Like good apprentices, ours is not to question why. Let's find a tree to sleep in while we wait."

5

ERLOCK STARTAIL

The next morning, Piprik woke up early to watch the cave. His joints ached from the cool air.

Lei rose just after the sun. "Hey, look. Is that your friend?"

He didn't recognize her at first. In the six months since she'd borrowed his badge, Erlock's tailfeathers had finally grown back.

Piprik flew above the tree tops and waited to be noticed. Erlock let out a caw and motioned for him to fly up to the cave.

He brought Lei with him this time, afraid to leave his apprentice in the bog unsupervised. The cave, empty the previous evening, now housed Erlock, a starling gryphon, and a starling opinicus.

The opinicus embraced Piprik without shame. She had gryphonic ears and a tail. "Khalim! You look so old. I thought for sure you'd been killed. Even when your strange messenger arrived with your badge, I didn't believe it."

Piprik returned the embrace and found his eyes watering. It had been a long time since he'd seen any of the scholars he'd gone into the Emerald Jungle with.

"If all of your friends changed into the same starling," Lei asked, "how do you know which one of them this is?"

Before the starling scholar could answer, Piprik spoke up. "It's Wendl. She hugs with her wings."

The starling scholar laughed, revealing the truth. "You caught me! The others are easy to spot, once you know what to look for. None of us reacted the same way to the elixir. Gryphon tails, opinicus tails, talons, forepaws, ears. We all drank the same mix, but no two of us look the same."

Piprik turned his embrace from one old friend to a newer one. "Erlock, I'm glad to see you live. Why have you been away for so long?"

She returned his gesture, but something troubled the large gryphon, something she wouldn't speak of in front of their one starling gryphon guest.

"You're not green," Lei said to the starling. "You're... pretty."

Lei was right. Where Wendl, and to a smaller degree Erlock, shared a deep green plumage with white stars, the starling herself was a deep purple with a white stomach.

"This is Nighteyes, leader of the Nightsky Pride," Erlock said. "She's the reason I've had to stay. There were things she needed to show me, but the starlings' pridelord wouldn't let me deeper into the jungle until I'd molted."

The Nightsky pride leader looked over Piprik. She swayed a little and held onto the cave wall with a forepaw. Her eyes had white spots in them, a disorder more common in owls. Despite the sway, her eyes focused, suggesting that someone, perhaps Wendl, had saved her eyesight.

"You'll have to forgive her," Wendl said. "I've been

working on figuring out an elixir that inhibits the starling's altruism—that was the recipe I left for you to make yesterday. I've been trying to perfect it, but since we don't meet many non-starlings, I haven't figured out the correct dosage."

Wendl had always been good at taking someone else's recipe and modifying it. It was one reason Piprik had suggested Mally bring her along on the expedition. Had he known what lay ahead of them in the Emerald Jungle, Piprik would have spared his friend this fate.

"It's fine." The true starling sat down to steady herself. "Your friends speak highly of you. We have a problem. Tell the new Kjarr the pridelord is willing to renew your treaties and stay out of the bog, but we need something in exchange."

"What's that?" Piprik asked. They weren't here on behalf of the Ashen Weald, but he figured Erlock could handle anything official, assuming they'd let her leave.

"Do you remember our last days as blackwings?" Wendl asked. When Piprik nodded, she continued, "Remember how Mally infected the starlings with his affliction, then they escaped into the wilderness when our camp was razed?"

Piprik started to see where this was going. "They went back and bred with the rest of the pride?"

The Nightsky starling nodded. "It took several years to manifest, but we have sixty gryphons who've lost their starling colors as the sickness takes hold."

He thought things over. "Enough of the Redwood Valley's research remains that we can show you how to treat the eggs to keep new gryphlets from being born with it. As for those who are already sick, there's nothing I can do. If there were a cure, Mally would have found it. When he attacked the bog in the spring, his talons and beak were still red."

"I have some ideas." Wendl rifled through the empty crates.

Piprik recognized his own writing and the seal of Crestfall carved into the wood. "Are those... did you go back and get our research?"

"Yes," Wendl admitted. "Our eyrie and the Seraph King's forces cleared out most of the wreckage, but they left some of our notes."

Piprik wondered at the adventures his former colleagues had gone through since they parted ways.

Wendl pointed to one of the Nighthaunt's old journal entries. "Look here. Mally had a hard time giving his disease to some of the gryphons. The starling population is huge, ten thousand strong divided among the different prides. I'm convinced there *must* be starlings who have a resistance. Our friends are already out searching for gryphons who match the description in Mally's notebook of those who seemed immune to his attempts. I think we could use them to cure the others. I just need—"

"More of the purple salts," Piprik finished. "How do you expect the Ashen Weald to get those for you?"

Wendl's ears, a feature she hadn't had when they'd first met, went backwards. "Khalim, it's not the Ashen Weald I'm asking this of. You're Piprik now, Eyes of the Seraph King. You can walk into one of the white eyrie's strongholds and take it."

Piprik was quiet. It was a lot to ask of any opinicus. But his plan was to hunt down Mally. Searching for the elixir would help him find his old master. And Wendl was hard to say no to. They'd grown up in the same village, and she was like a sister to him.

"I'll see what I can do," he said. "I don't know that it's possible. How much do you need?"

"As much as you can find," Wendl said, but Nighteyes seemed to have her own ideas.

The pride leader traced several glyphs into the sand. "For the pridelord and Kjarr to reach any sort of agreement, we need this many vials."

Wendl looked at the starling's eyes. A clarity was returning to them and with it, a hostility. "You should go. The altruism suppressor is wearing off. She refused to drink too much of it, just a taste. Come back once you have the elixir. You know where to meet us."

"I'll walk you out," Erlock said.

"Do not go past the waterfall," Wendl commanded.

The fantail ignored her warning. Once they were out of the starlings' hearing, Erlock returned Piprik's white eyrie badge to him and opened up. "I'm sorry I didn't come back. They're willing to give those of us with starling heritage a little leeway since we don't trigger their altruism, but they don't like us near the capital. Once I leave, I don't believe they'll let me return.

"I've been pulling favors looking for word on Merin's son. It sounds like a massive, hook-beaked weald gryphon did come through here a few years back. I've traced his route as far as Stormtail, but that's it. I'm going west for a few days to ask around there, then I'll be done here. Let Merin know, okay? He's been worried sick for years."

Piprik didn't know what to say, but Lei did.

"Merin's dead," the peacock stated.

"Zrim, Strix, and now Merin." Erlock sat down. "I suppose it's just me and old Parrotface, now."

"He fought bravely," Lei began, but Erlock interrupted him.

"I don't want to know," she said. "I came out here to make sure the starlings knew how to cure the parasite. With the last of my time, I'm going to finish my search for Merin's son, then I'll head home to lead my pride. You just make sure you find what they're looking for. We can't afford to antagonize the pridelord."

Piprik put a talon on her shoulder. "We'll do what we can. Is there anything else you need?"

"Pumpkins," she said. "They're still sending expeditions into the swamp to get the bog blossoms to make paste with, but it's not a cure. We can't risk one of those scouts bringing the infection west of Jadebeak."

"We burned the seraph in the swamp," Lei said. "The mummy at the dig site. So there shouldn't be more parasites."

Wendl called out for Erlock from inside the cave.

"Don't tell the starlings that," the Fantail pride leader warned. "Most of this treaty is based around the idea that they *can't* go into the bog without going insane."

With another cry, Erlock flew back inside, leaving the two fisherfolk to consider their next move.

"Should we go back?" Lei asked.

Piprik shook his head. "Let's continue on to New Eyrie and see if we can find Foultner or Mia. I don't want Kia and Cherine to have to wait for us too long. We have a lot of flying ahead of us if we want to catch up."

Lei snorted. "They have Zeph watching over them. Nothing bad ever happens while he's around!"

6

NOTHING BAD

W hen late morning arrived, Cherine and Kia had to wake their guard gryphon, who'd chosen to sleep halfway up an aneda tree near the bank of the Crackling Sea.

Zeph listed, partially upside-down, and snored softly, prompting Cherine to ask, "Why doesn't he fall?"

"Dewclaws?" Kia guessed. "After listening to him and Hatzel argue, I'm afraid to go near either of them while they're out cold. I think they *both* probably bite in their sleep."

"He looks like a bat," Cherine said and immediately knew he shouldn't have.

"One of your imaginary bats that don't exist?" Kia teased.

"Hey, until you show me a bat, I'm going to assume they're extinct," he protested.

Kia tapped her beak, her way of teasing his scholarly skills. "Ninox and Grax spend all night outside. What do they have to say?"

"Grax is with me. She's never seen a bat," Cherine said.

"Ninox says she hears something echolocating out there, but that could be anything! Bats aren't the only animals that echolocate."

"Mm-hmm," Kia said. "What about your old prison buddy, Neider's pet forger? Didn't he say bats were stealing his food in the cave?"

"It was probably squirrels." Cherine was willing to admit —privately and only to himself—that his bat theory had some holes in it. He'd definitely heard clicks in the Ashen Weald's underground prison.

"Squirrels who echolocate. With big ears. And wings." Kia picked up a small rock and threw it at the branch Zeph was on, finally waking their companion.

The gryphon dropped down, landing on all fours. "Oh, hey, you two. Is it time? You should sleep more. If you sleep until you need to act, you'll be better rested."

"Tell me, Zeph, have you ever seen a bat in the weald or taiga?" Kia asked.

Zeph looked back and forth from one scholar to the other. "A smart gryphon knows when to keep his beak shut."

"That's only something someone would say if they've never seen a bat," Cherine chirped.

"The *Nachlass Mal* says that pregnant opinici shouldn't eat bats or squirrels," Kia countered. "Why would it say that if bats weren't around when Mally wrote it?"

Their flight took them to the salt marsh and sawgrass fields outside the glassworks, where Zeph finally shushed them and forced everyone to walk the rest of the way on foot.

Cherine wasn't sure how stealthy they would be. He was much taller than the reeds, and Kia was brightly colored, but they humored their guide as best they could. Despite his admonition, even Zeph had trouble being stealthy. The sawgrass obscured pockets of saltwater, and they all splashed as they walked.

Once they reached the salt flats, the reeds thinned. Terraces here were designed to flood, creating a series of pools that evaporated into salt. Some of the clay used to build up the different levels had broken. Other pools had run dry. It was obvious no one had given any thought to salt in some time.

Round and lopsided like an overfed ground parrot, glassworks loomed high in the distance, situated along the coast. While the glass it produced was beautiful, the building itself was an ugly clay structure. Even from the salt flats, they could see scratch marks all over the outside of it.

A village had developed around the glassworks. The change from salt marsh to dunes was abrupt, but where some of the sand had blown away, Cherine saw wooden planks used to provide dry ground to build on. More planks formed pathways through the sand. No buildings stood as tall as the glassworks itself, but each squat building had a single tower entrance. Judging by the holes, many of the towers had once housed stained glass windows.

From here, he couldn't tell what the structures were made of. Several buildings looked like coquina, a compacted, shell-like material. Others were clay and already starting to give way. All had long scratches down their sides.

"Claw marks?" Cherine asked. "A starling attack, maybe?"

Zeph hushed him.

Dunes and red rocks, precursors to the desert, rose to the north. South, the preternaturally calm Crackling Sea kept watch on the intruders.

There were no sailfins along the salt marsh, leaving Cherine to wonder if the reeve's pet had eaten them all or if they didn't range this far north. Perhaps they needed easy access to fresh water, or perhaps they faced heavy competition from any of the types of desert lizards. If they had a free moment, Cherine was hoping to sketch out a sand swimmer or gritmaw monitor.

The gryphon and two opinici slipped past a collection of rain barrels outside a small saltworks. Without anyone to collect the evaporated salt, it was beginning to pile up in the clay pools. The smell brought him back to his years working the butchery after his brother's death.

A northern wind shook the grass, dislodging several small crabs that skittered into the water to find new hiding places. Most of the water and sand was pocked by tiny burrows, and he counted at least six species and twelve colorations.

The gryphon and opinici reached the outskirts of the small town and decided to approach from the docks. Cherine helped the smaller members get up top without flying. There were still a few rafts adrift on the water, but none of those tied to the shore were in one piece. The buildings had strange marks on them, as though a gryphon had reached up with its claws and raked them down the sides.

They worked their way from dock to sand to reach the main glassworks building. They'd gone twenty steps before Zeph suddenly leapt back and clutched his bloody paw.

Kia pulled out an aneda bandage and started wrapping his paw while Cherine investigated the scene of the wounding. He grabbed a pair of thick leather talon-protectors, a necessity with so much glass around, from one of the crushed rafts and sifted through the sand until he found the culprit.

Not glass, as he'd initially assumed, but metal. He held it up for Kia and Zeph to see.

"It's just a spike," Kia whispered. "Did they toss them in the sand like caltrops to keep wingtorn from sneaking up, maybe?"

Zeph nursed his paw. "Would they expect wingtorn this far north? It wasn't the Ashen Weald that attacked them."

Cherine examined it further. One end of the metal spike was sharp. The other end had four little fin shapes. *Maybe for throwing?* He considered. It seemed a little far-fetched. He put it in his harness pocket, and they moved off the sand and onto the packed earth of the goliath bird path.

More spikes littered the roads and building tops.

"I think they fell from the sky," Kia suggested. "They punctured some of the roofs here, see?"

Cherine nodded. He wasn't sure why it had happened, but it explained the markings on the buildings. He felt exposed out here in the open and missed the slight protection the sawgrass had provided.

They were nearly to the primary glassworks when he heard a caw to the north. In the distance, a vulture flew overhead.

"Perspective is a funny thing," Cherine said. "I can't tell if that's a tiny vulture close to us or a giant vulture far away."

Spikes, but little blood. Broken glass. Cherine was reminded of his old apprentices. They'd say they were no closer to figuring out what had happened here or if the Crestfall opinici were still alive. But he knew that to find the path to answers, the first step was having the right set of questions. With any luck, the inquiries raised inside the glassworks would set them off in the right direction.

They located a door, and Kia got to work getting it open. The problem wasn't the lock, which she quickly dismantled; it was debris that had been pushed against it.

Inside, the floor was covered in broken glass. Stained

glass windows, baubles, telescopes, magnifying glasses, trinkets—nothing was in one piece. They found more paw and talon protectors.

Kia and Cherine slipped theirs on, but Zeph had a problem.

"The talon ones don't fit my forelegs," he said.

Kia laughed and tossed him an extra pair of back paw protectors. His nares blushed red when he realized the obvious solution.

The ceiling and the tops of the walls were black, which was strange. The entire top of the glassworks was dark, which was even stranger as Cherine was certain he'd seen windows on their approach. It took his eyes a moment to adjust to the darkness. Despite being inside, the bodies of a dozen flamingo opinici had been picked clean by crabs.

He shivered.

They walked through the main workshop, pushing aside a divider. A long warehouse was connected to the main building, and they began to explore it. The ground crunched as they walked on it, and Cherine was grateful for the thick hide on the boots.

"No sign of the Seraph King or the blackwings." Zeph slipped a paw out of its boot for a moment and stuck a claw into a hole in the clay wall, angering the crab hiding inside.

The crab latched onto the tip of his claw, and he used it to gesture at the broken glass and bones. "Any of this help either of you?"

"It's just chaos to me," Kia said. "Someone smashed this place to bits and neither side tried to hold it."

They turned to leave the shattered glass warehouse when they heard the sound of the door opening.

"In here!" a blackwing opinicus shouted.

Zeph, Kia, and Cherine scrambled to hide behind

several dilapidated crates in the back of the warehouse. Cherine's first thought was that the blackwing opinicus had been looking for them, but that proved incorrect when twenty more came into the building.

"Watch your step," a blackwing said. Cherine caught a glimpse of him before ducking back into his hiding place. That blackwing had the natural red markings on the tops of his wings, but several of his feathers had also been painted red.

A captain, perhaps?

"Looks like there's one pair of boots left," the captain said. "Wait, it's just four of the front boots. That's strange. Well, figure out a way to make do."

Cherine and Kia both looked down at Zeph's feet.

"Someone go search for clean water," the captain continued. "Blacktalon was supposed to have someone here to meet us."

"Probably Rybalt," one of the others complained. "He's never on time."

"I don't care who rescues us just as long as *someone* does," a third blackwing whined. "I'd grab Iony by his whiskers and kiss him on the beak if he'd show up. White-beak's forces were right behind us. We can't stay here."

From their hiding place, Cherine heard the sound of a water barrel being pushed through glass towards the entrance they'd come through, followed by the slurps of several loud drinkers.

"What do we do, Captain?" came a wet voice.

In the silence between question and answer, Cherine thought he heard another opinicus whispering about silver eyes and a lost outpost. He made a mental note to ask if infected starlings had been seen going north. He'd thought that problem behind them.

"There's still time to get east," another prompted. "We could hide in the mountains, fly north tomorrow."

The captain cleared his throat. "No, we wait. The Seraph King's goons weren't far behind us. I'd rather fight them fresh with reinforcements. We stay here. Blacktalon's scouts are watching the sea."

Next to Cherine, Kia was working on another door. She carefully removed a crushed box. Crabs rushed out of the crates when she lifted them, startling Zeph, who barely kept his beak shut. He slipped his boot back on.

"We should spread out and see if there's a place to hide in here," the captain said. "We don't want a scout catching sight of us through the broken windows."

Cherine watched one of the displaced crabs start to climb a wooden pillar. He'd never known crabs to climb, but he admitted that crustaceans were a blind spot in his edible fauna research. He wanted to ask Kia or Zeph about the critter, but they were too busy getting the door open.

Across the warehouse and great hall, the blackwing wearing the mismatched set of four front boots they'd left behind began to clean a pathway through the glass. In front of Cherine's eyes, a small crab climbed up a wooden pillar towards the beams in the ceiling.

"I don't see any windows back in the storage area," the mis-booted blackwing called. "I'll start clearing a path that way."

There was little chance they'd stay hidden if the black-wings made their way into this part of the building. Kia and Zeph worked harder, but Cherine's attention remained firmly on the crab. It was like a husky, armored spider. It settled onto a beam directly above his head. What he'd taken to be shadows or burn marks on the wood moved over to make room for their fellow crustacean.

Cherine tapped Zeph on the shoulder and whispered the words *tree crabs* to the gryphon.

Zeph shook his head, not understanding what Cherine was trying to say.

Cherine mimed crab pinchers, then pointed up. Zeph continued to look confused.

Cherine grabbed Zeph's head and pointed his eyes at the direction of the dark beams overhead.

At first, Zeph didn't see it. Then the blackwing searcher, still awkward in his strange footwear, knocked something over, and the beams seemed to ripple as over a thousand crabs all shifted. Small pinpricks of light danced across the storage room's floor as the crabs on the windows skittered back into formation.

Zeph's eyes got very, very wide. He and Cherine tried to get Kia's attention to warn her, but she gave the door a heavy push, shaking the wall, beam, and rafters.

Dozens of crabs fell from their perch onto the hiding weald denizens. Zeph let out a small scream, catching the attention of the blackwing scout just as crabs fell atop his head, too.

CHERINE, Kia, and Zeph made a mad dash into the sand, leaving a trail of angry crabs behind them. Cherine could feel the metal spikes press against the hardened leather of his boots, but there were no punctures. The blackwing opinici spilled out of the other door and chased after them.

Cherine's natural instincts were to take flight as soon as the hard ground of the docks was below him, but there were thirty white gryphons above them. The Seraph King's forces had the glassworks surrounded.

"Do we risk the water?" Zeph asked. The boots on his front paws had come loose, and he pulled another metal spike from between his toes with his beak and tossed it on the ground. The blackwings were gaining on them.

Cherine didn't think that was a good idea. A swell of water had moved the wrecked boats, and he wasn't sure what that meant yet.

Five of the blackwings were nearly upon them when the sky began to sparkle.

Kia shoved Zeph and Cherine under a canoe just as the rain of iron struck from above. A hundred of the spikes —*flechettes,* Cherine realized by the way they were used— peppered the area they'd just run through.

At the Redwood Valley University, flechettes were part of the metalworking courses. They were the right combination of crude and still useful while small to make for a handy first assignment. By the end of the course, basic metalworkers had progressed to buckles, which was where Cherine had come to the conclusion that metalworking wasn't for him. He'd never seen so many flechettes in one place before now, never even considered what they looked like in action.

By the sounds outside, the blackwings behind them hadn't fared well. They lifted the canoe up a bit so Zeph could peek his head outside.

"They've seen us. We need to fly!" the copper hawk shouted. They left the safety of the canoe and took to the air.

Four of the Seraph King's opinici started to descend towards them, then stopped and turned away. Cherine looked back at the water, which appeared to be growing. His suspicion had been correct.

"Reeve's pet!" he shouted.

A spray of water caught a fleeing blackwing and knocked her out of the sky. The massive serpentine whale inhaled more water and began shooting streams at any of the opinici near the coast.

"Not south," Kia said. "We should head west to the abandoned raftworks and meet Pip."

Cherine wished he'd heeded Ninox's warning. As the white opinici tried to pull the blackwings out of the glassworks and the snake-like whale used its clawed flippers to pull itself onto land, one last burst of water split Cherine from Zeph and Kia.

Cherine flew between fighting opinici. The buildings had been designed to house large, stained glass windows. With the windows mostly shattered, he slipped in and out of towers and buildings to try to get away from the worst of it.

He pulled himself out of a fancy nest, brushed off some crabs, and looked for his companions. To the east, Iony and the glacier pride were soaring in to help the blackwings. To the south, the reeve's pet filled the sky with jets of water. To the west, more of the Seraph King's forces appeared in the distance, chasing Zeph and Kia.

There wasn't much of a choice left for Cherine. He went north, towards the desert, and prayed he reached Crestfall Eyrie before he ran out of energy.

BELATEDLY, Cherine realized he hadn't brought any water with him. Kia had an extra flask, just in case, but they planned to meet Piprik and Lei at the abandoned raftworks by nightfall. They definitely did not plan to be out over the desert.

He looked back a few times but couldn't tell if he was still being chased.

He'd never flown in such heat before. He couldn't tell if he'd been flying for an hour or an afternoon. He could feel his skin burning through his feathers and fur. The heat sapped his energy and left him disoriented. He thought he was still headed north, but he wasn't entirely sure. He risked a look back, but he couldn't see the Crackling Sea anymore, just the endless, blinding white of sun on sand. To the north, what he hoped was north, he thought he could make out a canyon of red rocks.

He followed lines in the sand below that seemed to be an old, dry river bed hoping it would bring him to water. Sun sickness overcame him, and he looked for a place to land, spotting a cave mouth.

He nearly reached its entrance before his wings lost their strength, and he dropped to the sand below. Sand felt a lot harder when he fell onto it than it had when he'd had to walk through it earlier.

Somewhere on the flight, he'd lost one of his boots, and the ground burned the pads of his back foot. He crawled farther, trying to get out of the sun, but his body had reached its limit. He lost consciousness just as his talons scratched the stone entrance of the cave.

7

OASIS

M ally the Nighthaunt uncurled from his covered wagon and slithered into the sunlight to drink from the oasis when the desert caravan stopped for a rest. As much as he'd like to retrieve his salts from the depths of Crestfall sooner rather than later, the desert was an unforgiving place.

It was impossible to go straight to the palace. The thunder birds owned the northern desert. There was no water or shelter. Instead, they were forced to lead the caravan to an oasis east of Whitebeak, spend the night, then head north. Even this relatively straightforward route had its own perils.

One of their goliaths and its handler were forced to turn back when the bird stepped on a hidden scorpion den and suffered a multitude of stings. Whether that had been an accident or the desert-dwelling gryphons playing a trick on them was unclear.

While they had antivenom, the domesticated goliath birds were resilient beasts. Given a few days' rest, they usually recovered without using up precious medicines.

Two silver hawks pulled themselves out of another wagon. If the desert was hard to cross for goliath birds, it was even harder for messengers in a hurry. They wore special harnesses designed to carry water and rubbed oils on the tops of their head, wings, rump, and tailfeathers to keep from burning.

If nothing went wrong, they had a nice, relaxing ride to the palace and back. Being on the front lines of the war, it was a coin toss whether they'd be needed.

A flash of grey feathers coming from the west suggested the coin had not fallen in their favor.

Silver backbeat her wings on the landing, kicking up sand and startling the goliath birds, but letting her settle onto her back paws and then lightly put weight on her forelegs. It was what Mally called a *Redwood Landing*, and he'd taught it to her while she healed up. There was a corresponding *Redwood Takeoff* that didn't put as much weight on the forelegs. Most of the military leapt into the air from all fours like a gryphon, but the wounded had to make do.

She looked around but missed Hi-kun splashing in the water without his reeve's ransom worth of metal armor.

While the high commander rinsed off, Mally made his way to Silver, his long form winding between the palms. "Everything in order at Whitebeak?"

"Your apprentices we sent to check out the prison outbreak are dead," she said. "A group of twenty blackwings were waiting outside our prison camp. Most of the guards and prisoners had been torn apart; the rest appeared to be afflicted with a new type of poison. No one is to land and look around until we know what it is. I've come to consult with Hi-kun."

The lost prison camp was a logistics problem, not something Mally concerned himself with. Though he worried at the small teams of blackwings that crossed the desert from time to time, the fact that both prisoners and guards had been torn apart is what caught his attention. Particularly since the prison camp was north of Whitebeak, along the road to Reevesport.

The high commander shook water out of his feathers and padded over. "Did you send a force after them?"

She nodded. "We killed all but four at the glassworks before their reinforcements arrived. We caught two reds poking around and tossed them in a cage while we figure out the prison situation."

Hi-kun frowned. "I must be missing something. We kill the blackwings rather than capture them, so what were they after at the prison? Were we holding someone they wanted? Did they break anyone out?"

"No one, as best we can tell from our flyby," she said. "We heard word of an outbreak or poisoning of some sort and were ambushed on our way over."

"The jailors and prisoners had both been torn apart, you said?" Mally slithered up a palm tree and pulled down a hard fruit. "And how many blackwings did this?"

It was Silver's turn to frown. "Twenty."

"You should quarantine anyone who flew over the prison," Mally said. "Then burn it to the ground."

"It's situated along the supply line," Hi-kun said. "If we raze it, we risk lowering morale and lose a key outpost for catching any blackwings trying to sneak across the desert."

Silver looked up from taking a drink. "You think it might be the southern sickness?"

"Perhaps. Or something new." Mally hadn't been given an opportunity to inspect any of the infected starlings that plagued the south. Concerns about spreading disease was one of the reasons they'd sent so few forces to New Eyrie to search for the seraph.

"Fine," Hi-kun said. "Have the prison destroyed. We'll build another farther north, although I hate running anything so close to the Red Coast during hurricane season. How soon until we send the stormcloth west?"

The Red Coast formed the northern crown to the desert. While the waters were sometimes blue, more often the strange minerals of the sand turned the entire coast a deep crimson color, inspiring deadly algae to bloom. Storm's then spread the algae, leaving the coast devoid of life until the bloom died down.

"There's been gryphon trouble along the southern roads." Silver shot Mally a look that let him know the *gryphon trouble* was his fault. "The main forces are securing it on their way to us. I'm just waiting on word that it's safe again."

Mally finally cracked open the hard nut. The inside squirmed with grubs and bugs. Silver, an opinicus who had never crossed the line between *going hungry* and *starving,* looked away as he picked up a grub with his talons and tossed it in his beak.

Two of the argent hawks approached Silver to ask for their orders. She told them to stay here; she'd fly back on her own.

"We saw Iony over the glassworks," she explained. "Rybalt won't be far behind. You may find yourself in need of messengers."

"It would take someone audacious to attack the palace," Hi-kun said, "but I suppose Rybalt is that."

Before she left, Hi-kun did a check on her harness. He helped untie the metal talons from her bracers and put them in a pouch. "You know the rules. Nothing shiny in the desert."

Silver looked unhappy to lose quick access to her weaponry, but she hadn't seen what had happened to the last goliath bird caravan. They'd had to bring Mally in to try to identify the bits of the bodies that were left. As best anyone could tell, some white-tailed kite on his first trip through the desert had hung glass and metal trinkets from the birds as a good luck charm.

It had not brought good luck. Hence Hi-kun's current unarmored nakedness.

"Well, if that's settled, I'm going back to sleep." Mally crawled towards the covered wagon. "Wake me when the sun goes down so I can find something more substantial to eat."

8

THE KING AND THE COBRA

Piprik and Lei didn't locate Mia at New Eyrie. Instead, they found another opinicus holding down the fort while the new ranger lord guarded the leaders at Sailfin Point. While the ranger lord would normally handle patrols and military maneuvers, with most of the military at the Crackling Sea for the gathering of pride leaders, *holding down the fort* meant sitting in Reeve's Nest and shouting orders at other opinici.

"She's not here," Foultner explained. "You can leave anything important with me and Henders."

"Oh, we met at the ranch!" Henders was sewing Ashen Weald colors onto an old Reeve's Guard harness. "I can heat up some eels. Are you two hungry?"

"They're not staying, Hends. This is a military fortress, not a butchery." Foultner's comments were directed as much at Piprik and Lei as they were at Henders.

"Food would be nice," Lei said. "I'm getting kinda sick of cold fish and egg fruit."

"It would be nice to have some supplies to take north," Piprik confirmed.

Henders nodded his approval. "Toss me your harnesses, and I'll pack them full."

With help from the Ashen Weald, particularly its Crackling Sea members, New Eyrie had been fixed up. It had lost its military look, though a low barrier still existed to keep the sailfins out of the fishing village. The new wall was made up of sections of the old wall that hadn't burned, but its spikes had been removed. Climbing sections and tunnels had been added to allow wingtorn in and out of the city easily.

There were still watchtower roosts along the circular wall, but each was now decorated with the glyphs and colors of a different member of the Ashen Weald or their allies. Bringing together everyone to fix New Eyrie had been Satra's idea, and there were even taiga and Sandpiper's Dune glyphs along the walls.

The refugee tents that used to extend north of the city walls had been replaced by more permanent nests—raised off the ground to keep the sailfins out, though it turned out baby sailfins were excellent climbers, not to mention how little the precautions did to stop snakes.

New Eyrie's old inhabitants, the ones who hadn't run north to the Seraph King, had left and joined the Crackling Sea Pride. New Eyrie now housed the Ashen Weald rangers, on watch for any sign of attack.

While ex-Reeve's Guard Captain Henders disappeared towards the supply house, Piprik filled Foultner in on what they'd seen in the bog.

She was quiet for a long time. "I'm glad Erlock's alive. I'll see about having some of the wingtorn drop off a few crates of pumpkins near the waterfall. The last thing we need is all of the starlings to end up infected and come spilling over the mountains. You said the crone stays south of the Jade-beak River?"

Piprik nodded. "I don't know that you want to push your luck. If you put them at the base of the falls, you should be fine. But make sure you're not spotted by any starlings. Green wing altruism is a strong impulse."

Foultner kept looking from Lei to Piprik as though trying to work out why two salt traders had been put in charge of so important a task. "And this salt they want, this special salt they think will cure the red-beak sickness. You can find it?"

Lei grinned, a habit he'd picked up from Zeph. "We're salt traders. It's what we do."

"I don't understand fisherfolk," Foultner said at last. "Okay, I empower you to make this trade on behalf of... if not the Ashen Weald, let's just call you Erlock's helpers. You've got a long tail. That's like, what, three fifths of a fantail? Good enough for me."

Lei shifted so his hindquarters and tailfeathers were less visible.

Foultner didn't notice, instead pulling Henders's captain badge off of his harness. On one side of it was his name. On the other side was the tree emblem of the old Redwood Valley Eyrie.

She tossed it to Piprik. "There you go. Everyone knows who Henders is. Just give it to whomever and let them know you're official if you need Ashen help."

"Thank you." Piprik handed the badge to Lei. "And you'll get word to Satra? Or at least Blinky?"

"Definitely," Foultner said. "I mean, Henders will. While everyone is at the Crackling Sea Eyrie, I'm going to try to nap in every nest in the barracks. But Hends will definitely get word to Blinky, isn't that right?"

Henders came back holding two harnesses with overflowing pockets. "Mm-hmm. Will do. Here you two go. Have a fun trip!"

Piprik and Lei turned to leave.

"Wait, hold up!" Foultner shouted after them. "If you see —look, I know this is a long shot—but if you see a bunch of goliath birds from the Clover Ranch, can you bring them back? We had trouble with someone renting them months ago. Just, y'know, on the off chance you head north."

Lei looked at Piprik and shrugged. "Sure, we'll keep an eye out."

"Thanks," Foultner said. "It would make Henders very happy to return them."

PIPRIK AND LEI made their journey north along the western bank of the Crackling Sea. The way Piprik saw it, anyone coming from the south would look suspicious, but if they could find a way past the Seraph King's outposts and then circle back around from the direction of Reevesport, a white-tailed kite and peacock opinicus would look just like any of the king's subjects.

First, though, they needed to meet up with Zeph, Kia, and Cherine. It took most of the day for them to reach the abandoned raftworks building that was their meeting place. Flying higher was easier but made them visible to scouts. Instead, they flew in the sweet spot where they were just out of reach of any leaping sailfins.

"He didn't recognize me," Lei said three-fourths of the way to the raftworks.

Piprik was only half paying attention. "Who didn't?"

"Captain Henders," Lei explained. "I used to chirp hello

to him when we visited the Redwood Valley Botanical Gardens with my mom. Then he watched me every day at New Eyrie. We used to play hide and seek outside the Reeve's Nest. But he didn't recognize me at all—not here, not at the Clover Ranch in the spring."

"He knew you as a chick and as a sick fledgling. Do you want him to know you now?" Piprik knew better than to add *in your fisherfolk disguise*. Reeve Brevin's youngest daughter was now Lei, male fisherfolk from Ashfoot Isle, all the time. Piprik could see Lei's discomfort when they'd come across fisherfolk who only knew him as Mi-Lei.

Lei hesitated before answering. "I don't know. It feels dangerous, somehow?"

"You don't need to decide right this moment." Off to Piprik's right, the water churned with clever fish hiding from the Crackling Sea's fishing opinici. It was well known that the reeve's pet preferred this section of the sea, so everyone gave it a wide berth. "War, conflict, and danger are funny. When things are at their most dire, you don't hesitate to trust strangers and acquaintances. When things are safe, trust also becomes easier. It's just everywhere else on the spectrum, the places where there's a lot to lose and a high chance of losing it, that it's hard to trust."

Lei remained quiet for the rest of their flight, only speaking again when they reached the raftworks.

UNLIKE THE FANCY raftworks along the mangrove swamp or the functional raftworks the Crackling Sea Eyrie used along the southern sea coast, Piprik's meeting place had been abandoned for years.

The docks had collapsed into the water. Where the

pillars still stood, ibis and egrets sunned themselves in the last of the light. Where pieces of the dock lay forgotten in the salt marsh, sailfins lazed atop them.

The raft construction hangar was missing two walls and most of its roof. They found rainwater barrels and a large shed that was still standing and decided to wait the night there.

Piprik went through his medicine opinicus bag and pulled out two new harnesses—the white and gold of the Seraph King and the deep violet and green of Reevesport.

He tossed the Reevesport harness to Lei. "Go clean up and switch harnesses. We don't want to be caught as fisherfolk this far north."

Even though Piprik had prepared Lei for this, the young peafowl balked. "I don't want to. They don't have fisherfolk up north?"

"Not like us, they don't. We'll blend in better without the flippers and shark teeth and..." Piprik gestured at the splash of red on Lei's chest, "fish war paint."

Every coast had some kind of fisherfolk village, though how well they were tolerated by the local eyries varied. Alwren's fisherfolk villages even allowed their gryphon members to become citizens of the kingdom, so long as they were married to an opinicus.

"I don't know how to be a Reevesport opinicus," Lei protested. "I know how to be a fisherfolk."

Piprik filled a bowl with water from the rain barrel and started wiping off the paint. Even Lei's blue plumage was a weak feather paint. He'd molted out of Naya's dye from the spring. "You know Reevesport, you just haven't realized it yet. That's where your family came from, generations upon generations ago."

Lei didn't speak, but he relaxed the way he did during lessons.

"Reevesport started out as a small city, the legend goes, but one day a merchant boat washed up on shore." Piprik wrung out the rag and continued trying to remove Lei's red and green paint. "All of the sailors had been killed, but the cargo survived: four thousand apples."

"That's a lot of apples," Lei said.

Piprik nodded. "That it is. It's considered bad luck to eat the fruit of a shipwreck, but they didn't want the apples to go to waste, either. So they planted them."

"All four thousand?"

"All four thousand," Piprik confirmed. "Soon, Reevesport became known for its orchards. Good apples are notoriously hard to grow as the fruit doesn't always grow into the same tree as the apple that created it. You need to use clippings. But legend says that the Blue Delicious came from those first plantings. It's a Reevesport staple now."

"A blue apple?" Lei took over removing his own makeup.

"It's more of a dark reddish-purple," Piprik said. "Closer to starberry than bog blossom blue. Thing is, with the orchard came bees. With bees came honey. And with honey came the honey-thief ground parrot, a favorite snack of the king cobra."

"Oooh." Lei rinsed out the rag.

"Fortunately for the locals, the forests were full of peacocks. They set up roost in the apple trees and screamed whenever a snake was spotted in the groves. Cobra will try to eat peafowl eggs and chicks, but peafowl are known for teaming up to kill snakes.

"When the king came to visit the orchard with his consort, he was warned to stay near the peacocks, but he didn't listen. He went off into the woods to spend time alone with his mate, but they were attacked by a cobra the size of a weald boa. The royal consort was bitten, and the snake turned its cold gaze onto the king.

"A peacock was flying overhead and let out a cry. The owner of the orchard, with the help of his apple pickers, rushed to the king's aid. The cobra was killed, and the consort's life was saved, though she never recovered enough strength to fly again."

Lei was wide-eyed. Apparently they didn't teach this version of the tale in the Redwood Valley.

Piprik continued. "His mate's inability to fly weighed upon him heavily. It's said he couldn't stand to be near snakes, apples, or peafowl. Yet while the king could never face the site of his folly ever again, he knew things could have been worse. He ordered a new eyrie built in a valley of redwood trees as far from the Alabaster Eyrie as possible and made the owner of the orchard into a reeve."

"So all of the peafowl opinici came from Reevesport?" Lei asked. "They're sort of my distant cousins."

"They are," he confirmed. "And the reason the weapons your mother used were called peacock talons is because they were designed for use against giant snakes after seeing how peacocks kill cobras. You think of them—and that fighting style—as having come from reeves and nobility, but really, it came from apple farmers defending their crops."

Lei laughed.

The sun had gone down during Piprik's story, but their friends had yet to arrive. "Kia and Cherine may have found something at the glassworks that required them to turn back and warn Satra. Or perhaps it's still working just fine and they couldn't sneak around it. Either way, we'll leave a message and head out tomorrow morning."

They gathered enough reeds to make two nests, mindful

of the sailfins, and stored their old harnesses and goods behind an empty barrel.

9

WHITEBEAK

The sky above Whitebeak was full of alabaster opinici looking east, so Piprik and Lei slipped into the forest to the west and made their way by foot around the outpost. The Seraph King's fort showed a surprising awareness of its southern neighbors; a small spiked wall served as token resistance for any wingtorn who might make an attempt at a raid. Whether that meant they were expecting to be at war with the wingtorn soon or not, Piprik didn't know.

By the height of the fence, around six feet, it was clear the *awareness* was as far as their intelligence went. Obviously, the Seraph King's forces had never seen wingtorn in action. Rorin still told tales of having been pulled out of the air by Jun the Kjarr from nearly twenty feet above him.

The forested area around Whitebeak was strange to Lei, and he commented on it as they went. "The trees are so small! And there's no moss. What are they?"

Piprik climbed one to look at the red flowers. "This one is blooming late, but it looks like maple. Maybe some pine, fir, and spruce, too."

"I miss redwoods and rimu," Lei said. "We're missing the mast right now."

Several times throughout the summer, the rimu trees would fill with their bright red, olive-like fruit. It was an important time for the Redwood Valley because it gave an idea of how plentiful ground parrots would be next year.

Lei sniffed the air. "Is that rimu? No, it's not salty. It's more sweet. What am I smelling?"

"Apples." Piprik's nares were open. He started climbing back down when he heard the sound of a large creature running through the underbrush in their direction.

"Up here—quickly!" he called to Lei. His assistant flew up, landing on the branch next to him, and looked down with curiosity.

Attracted by the smell of fruit in the sun, a trio of giant millipedes shuffled through the underbrush. Each of them was the size of three gryphons standing in a line. Piprik remembered them from his days in the Emerald Jungle.

"Oh!" Lei said. "My foster family said they had those where they grew up! They call them megapedes."

Piprik laughed. He'd heard a lot of names for the large bugs, but megapedes was one of the more descriptive. The blackwing military's term wasn't one you would use in polite company.

"Hmm," he mused. "If we can flip one over and use your fishing spear, we might be able to kill it."

"Why would we want to do that?" Lei asked.

"To eat," Piprik replied.

"To eat!?" Lei exclaimed. "I'm not eating a bug!"

Piprik shook his head. With everything that had happened to Lei, it was easy to forget he'd been born to a reeve. Piprik doubted the underbough opinici were picky about what they ate.

"You eat shrimp," he said. "They're water bugs."

Lei's expression suggested that, with this new information in mind, he would not be eating shrimp in the future. "Wait! Why don't we grab the apples?"

As much as Piprik thought it would be a good idea for Lei to learn to hunt and kill things that weren't fish, he was willing to admit it required a very particular set of spices to make megapede meat palatable.

"Okay," he conceded. "We'll find the apples first."

They followed the trail through the underbrush and left the safety of the maple trees behind. The trail led through tall grass that gave way to sand and scrub. Off to the east, the desert's heat warped the light.

A small, packed dirt path led through the tall grasses. Alongside it, three apple carts lay on their side, their contents cooking in the sun.

A half-dozen megapedes of all sizes nibbled the fruit. Other than blood, there was no sign of the goliath birds who'd pulled the cart nor their opinicus masters. Piprik had the beginnings of an idea.

Lei's hackle feathers were up. "Are we safe?"

"No." Piprik wasn't about to pass up an opportunity like this, however. "Do you remember the call Henders had for the birds at the Clover Ranch?"

When his assistant nodded, he asked Lei to make the sound now.

"Awooo!" Lei shouted, his voice cracking a little.

"Mronk!" came the call back from the forest.

Piprik started picking the overheated fruit off the top of one cart and threw them into the field. When the megapedes didn't respond, he bounced an apple off one of their heads. The bug made an angry chittering sound and crawled after the fruit.

Lei continued calling out to the goliath birds. Most of them refused to leave the safety of the maple trees, but he lured three back to help right the cart.

"How would you like to be an apple merchant?" Piprik asked.

Lei tossed more rotten fruit after the megapedes. "I hear that's what my ancestors did. Besides, these here are Blue Delicious. They practically sell themselves."

He took a bite and spit it out. "Ew! Sour!"

"That's a cider apple." Piprik laughed. "All it needs is enough sugar to ferment and opinici are happy. Here, try one from this cart, I believe this is an actual Blue Delicious."

Lei still had tears in his eyes as he carefully nibbled at the dark-skinned fruit. "Oh, this is pretty good. How do you tell the difference?"

"Mostly, you don't," Piprik said. "That's why they're so great. I used to play that trick on my son all the time, and he never stopped falling for it."

Lei finished harnessing the goliath birds. "I remember you saying you didn't have a daughter, but I didn't know about your son. How old is he? Is your mate still alive?"

"A little older than you." Piprik had tried to be open with Lei since his assistant had found out the truth of his identity as Piprik. Still, he didn't care to talk about his family. "I'm sure they're fine. She's probably found someone new by now. Here, take off those trinkets, we don't want to attract more attention than we need."

Lei pulled off some metallic trinkets from the sides of the cart and stuffed them under the blankets. "I don't think your family is safe. Mally remembered you, didn't he? He could go after them."

The same thing had been worrying Piprik, though he hadn't wanted to say anything. "I'm sure they're fine. Mally has bigger things to worry about, and as long as the black-wings keep the Seraph King's forces from crossing the desert, I can't see Mally wasting time trying to sneak assassins in."

"Don't you want to talk to them, though?" Lei pressed.

"The same way we're invisible here among the Seraph King's forces, we'd stick out among the blackwings," Piprik said. "If we can put a stop to Mally and there's still salt left to change my plumage, I'll see about checking in on them. For now, I'm going to assume they're okay until I hear otherwise."

Lei shook his head but didn't respond. The path moved away from the desert and back into the maple forest. While they traveled, Piprik had Lei practice their cover story.

DESPITE PIPRIK'S CONCERNS, the military forces at White-beak were too excited by the Blue Delicious to ask any questions. They were assigned quarters by the Redwood Valley refugee tents, given metal beads for their goods, and told if they were willing to stick around for a few days, they'd be paid to carry supplies back up to Reevesport.

Everything was going better than Piprik had expected until one of the silver hawks saw the fruit and landed.

"Reevesport?" she directed her question to Lei. Thankfully, Piprik's assistant was smart enough to recognize the reeve badge on the silver hawk's harness.

"Yes, Reeve," Lei said.

The argent reeve turned to Piprik. "You look familiar. Are you military? What's your rank?"

"I'm long retired, Reeve Silver," Piprik lied. He was surprised she'd survived her ordeal in the bog but grateful she didn't recognize them from the fight at the seraph. "I was with one of the old Emerald Jungle expeditions. We came through your eyrie several times. I'm sorry for the loss of your predecessor. Terrible way to die."

In the distance, someone was calling for Silver, but she kept her eyes on Piprik. "Yes, it was. How did you come to travel by apple cart?"

"My sister married a peacock," he lied. "This is my nephew's first run. There was another group of carts that went on ahead of us, but we didn't run into them."

Two more argent hawks landed behind Silver but were smart enough not to interrupt.

"Did you take the grasslands route? Did you go by the old prison?" she asked.

Piprik shook his head. "No, there was some kind of megapede to-do going on. We had to head into the maples and take an old tracker's trail to get by. Thankfully, that's much easier with two carts than a dozen."

"Take the same route back. There's been word of black-wing bandits in the area." Silver seemed satisfied. She let her soldiers lead her away to deal with another matter.

"Thank you, Reeve," Lei said.

Piprik didn't know what that was about, but he had an idea of where they'd be investigating tomorrow. They set off to stable their birds and see if the New Eyrie refugees were here. If he was lucky, Lei's opinici would be healthy, happy, and safe. Then they could get back to searching for Mally.

If Piprik wasn't lucky, the refugees would be in a bad spot and Lei would insist on trying to rescue them. They'd discussed a plan for that, but it was risky and required them assuming their alter-egos. With the way Lei had been acting since the incident with Rybalt in the swamp, Piprik was no longer certain his peafowl assistant would be willing to follow that plan.

I guess we'll find out when we locate the refugees.

As they explored the camp a little, however, he caught sight of a makeshift cage on the side of a workshop. At least, he assumed it was a workshop by the way it had been built into the ground. That usually implied medicines and supplies that needed to be kept cold. For Mally, it would also cut down on the light.

Inside the cage were a familiar parrot opinicus and a copper hawk gryphon pair. Silver was in the middle of interrogating Zeph and Kia.

Piprik and Lei wandered the camp under the pretense of looking for the privy. Outside the workshop, he saw several opinici preparing a body for cremation. Their feathers were a pale color with hints of dark red along the tips. Their beaks and talons were starting to turn, too.

Piprik shivered. Assistants who lacked Mally's iron disorder would be more willing to consider ethics when searching for a cure. Those who faced the Nighthaunt's death sentence would be more forgiving of his sinister research techniques.

Back by the Redwood Valley refugees, nests were out in the open with only a basic roof to keep the rain out. They looked miserable but seemed free to go wherever they wanted. Whether that was the actual state of affairs or not, Piprik didn't know. Lei would insist they investigate further.

They unpacked their things, then looked for a way to get close to the prisoners by the workshop.

10

STICKY PRISONERS

Considering how Zeph had expected being captured to go, this was alright. They kept him in the shade, they were feeding him lots of salty food, and he even got to try some apples that had been in the sun for too long.

"I'm being civil because it's just me here," Silver continued, "but don't misunderstand my kindness. You'll want to have answered all of my questions before Mally or Hi-kun return."

"We were curious who owned the glassworks," Kia said. "It's my job to make sure food gets distributed in a way that keeps everyone fed. I thought if we could talk to someone in charge of Crestfall, we could re-open those supply routes."

"Okay, makes sense," Silver said. "But who do you work for? Who are you aligned with?"

Zeph looked up from eating bruised apples. "Hatzel's pride."

"I have no idea who that is," Silver said. "Are they a member of the Ashen Weald? Is that one of the prides who allied with the blackwings? How many of you are there?"

"We were thirty, but I think there are more now since we

started letting opinici join," Zeph explained. "Hatzel was the last saberbeak. She leads a free pride, so we're not really part of the Ashen Weald, though we're friendly with them at the moment."

"So you were born with these saberbeaks," Silver said, "and you wanted to trade with Crestfall, and that's why you were at the glassworks?"

"Oh, no, I was born in the taiga, but when my plumage came in copper hawk brown..." Zeph began, but by then, Silver had decided that none of this was worth her time and assigned one of her argent hawks to write down everything he said.

While he went on about sugar frogs and Younce's tail and parrots, Kia slipped to the side of their cage and whispered something to an apple merchant. Zeph hadn't been surprised when Kia offered to help out Lei and Piprik. Where Lei worried about his obligation to eyrie he'd grown up in, Kia was specifically worried about her parents and brother.

Which wasn't to say that she wasn't sympathetic to Piprik's hunt for the Nighthaunt. She and Cherine were very keen on locating the scholars who had joined forces with the Seraph King or Blackwing Eyrie. Bario the Phoenix and Impir the Mad were dangerous in their own ways, as Lei's siblings had discovered. Impir had killed off Ivess and led the starlings to New Eyrie, while Bario had killed the rest of Lei's siblings in his escape from the Crackling Sea's prison.

Zeph thought checking on the refugees was a good idea and stopping scholars with a darker nature was worth doing. Really, though, he was here to keep watch over his friends.

By the time Kia had finished plotting, Zeph was hanging upside-down from the cage to show off his dewclaws to the applause of the silver hawks who lacked that evolutionary advantage.

The argent opinici left to go run their patrols, giving Zeph and Kia time to talk.

"I like them," Zeph said. "I think the one on the left likes me, too."

"You think *everyone* likes you," Kia scolded. "You're welcome to stay and see if she wants to play gryphon for a season, but I'm getting out of here."

"Was that Pip and Lei?" he asked. "Where'd they find all of those apples, and can they get me more?"

"They're going to investigate the prison north of here and see if they can find a key," she said. "Sounds like maybe the blackwings hit the place. I'm not really sure. But we're on our own until then."

Zeph groomed apple juice out of his fur. "That's not a problem. Just so long as we're out of here before Mally returns. I think we lucked out that it was Silver. She definitely has a crush on me."

Kia rolled her eyes. "Piprik wants us to keep watch tonight to see how the guard rotations work. Do you want now or later?"

"Definitely later." Zeph curled up with his paws over his beak and fell asleep, leaving Kia to take first watch.

WHILE ZEPH SNORED softly in the corner, Kia was able to keep track of the camp. What she found most interesting was that, once a day, a group of refugees was rounded up and brought to the workshop for testing.

Having grown up in the Redwood Valley, she'd seen victims of the iron disorder before. She'd even studied some of the cadavers in one of her classes. Thing was, the liver and kidneys usually gave out fairly quickly. The pale feathers, the red on the talons—victims didn't usually live long enough for those traits to be so pronounced. Yet every opinicus at the workshop running the tests had lost all of their pigment and had Mally's iconic blood beak and talons.

She wanted to ask questions, but she didn't want to risk having more guards assigned to them ahead of Piprik and Lei's rescue attempt. She lucked out when one of the refugees tested positive and was led past them and into Mally's workshop.

"What's going on?" the opinicus asked. Several guards walked with him, though none of Silver's hawks.

"You were treated for redbeak as an egg," one of the assistants explained. "You still test positive for it, but you don't suffer any of the side effects. We're hoping you'll let us do a few more tests and use your blood for a cure."

"I'm not sure." The Redwood Valley opinicus's hesitancy was understandable.

One of the guards tried to look friendly. "We're still finding land and nice nests for all of the refugees up north. If you'll help us out with a few quick tests, we can see to it your family are relocated ahead of schedule."

The red opinicus looked back at the tents, then willingly walked into the workshop, leaving Kia to wonder if he'd ever see the light of day again.

She thought back to her time at the university. Headmaster Neider had always been tight-beaked about the treatments given to eggs. She'd assumed later that his hesitancy came from borrowing Impir the Mad's research for his own uses. Perhaps he'd actually been trying to lure Mally back to the Redwood Valley with the promise of a cure.

When the assistants walked back by her cage to

continue testing, she gave them a good look, and something caught her eye. Accounting for the disease, accounting for the lack of pigment, the assistants were all fairly young. She'd always been told—perhaps incorrectly—that egg treatments had spread from the Redwood Valley to the rest of the world. But if that were true, all of the victims should be older.

She shook her head. She needed more information to make sense of this, information she wouldn't get unless she found a way into the workshop. Sometimes, complicated problems had simple solutions that were only apparent after you could study them for longer. Perhaps the Alabaster Eyrie's religious beliefs precluded them from using blood or treating eggs, and Mally's only option had been to treat them once they were hatched.

Or perhaps something more sinister was going on.

HOPPY AND SPONGE

SAND GRYPHONS

11

PADFEET

Cherine awoke to the feeling of someone trying to pull the metal bit off the end of his beak. He swatted with his talons, and a small creature leapt back. His entire body felt burned, especially his back paw. He blinked sleepily and looked around.

He was in a cave of some sort. No, not a cave, a room made of stone? This wasn't the cave he'd been looking for. He could see the rest of the canyon out of the open balcony.

Layers of red and orange rippled in the canyon walls, hinting at past geological activity. Small doors and balconies revealed where dens had built into the canyon walls. Brightly colored strips of cloth, mostly turquoise blue, drifted in the breeze. Despite the abundance of homes, wind and desert bugs were the only sounds coming from outside.

He tried to stand but winced when he put weight on his back paw. In the darkness around him, he saw bits of metal and turquoise. Tiny eyes peered out of the shadows. They were attached to beaks and ears, so he ventured a greeting.

"Hello!" he called out. "My name is Cherine. Who are you?"

Chirping and cooing, then one of the small creatures stepped forward. His guess had been correct; it was a gryphon—the smallest gryphon he'd ever met. If Zeph stood around three feet at the shoulder, these gryphons were a head smaller than a copper hawk. Only the scars, sun-bleached fur, and lack of feather down convinced him he was surrounded by small gryphons and not a nest of gryphlets.

The one who stepped forward was a sandy, cream color. He had black stripes on his legs and even more on his wings. His crest, orange and tipped with black and white spots, went up and down like a hoopoe bird.

His long, thin beak finally spoke. "Hello, metal beak! I am Hoppy Padfoot, leader of the Padfoot Pride. You are our prisoner."

Cherine looked around. None of the gryphons stood over two feet tall. "How?"

"What?" Hoppy replied.

"How am I your prisoner?" Cherine asked again. "I'm three times your size. How are you planning to keep me here against my will?"

More chirping among the gryphons. Next to Hoppy was another gryphon who lacked his crest and long beak. There was a bit of a sandgrouse look to her. She spoke only in coos.

Hoppy laughed at something she said. "Sponge makes good point. She say: you welcome to fly out into the desert on your own at night, but then we have to run after you and rob you when dead. Much more convenient for *both* of us if you're our prisoner."

Cherine's head ached and his beak was dry. Also, his beak ached and his entire body felt dry. "What if I was your guest instead of your prisoner?"

More cooing from Sponge, then a translation from Hoppy: "We found you at guest cave, that true. Then we bring you here. But there is a problem."

"Oh?" Cherine started going through his pockets, finding most of them empty.

"We do not rob guests, and I have stolen your beak!" Hoppy exclaimed. He pretended to be clutching something in his paws.

Cherine emptied sand from a pocket. "You've taken my pens and everything else I have, but I'm pretty sure my beak is still on my face."

Hoppy re-enacted his dramatic *hide-the-beak-in-his-paws* motion, but this time he said, "We have not taken your pens, but we have stolen your beak!"

"What about everything else in my pockets?" Cherine challenged. "Did you steal those?"

Sponge laughed, or at least made cooing sounds that sounded like laughter.

Hoppy looked upset that Cherine hadn't acknowledged his beak comment, so the opinicus checked his beak with his talons. All of it, organic and metal, was still there.

"How do you figure?" he finally asked.

"I stole you from the guest cave," Hoppy said. "So I stole your beak. It is part of you!"

Cherine blinked. "That makes a kind of sense."

"Excellent," Hoppy said. "If we are in agreement, we may trade."

"I see. Where I come from, you must offer someone water before you trade." Cherine's words weren't untrue. It was common to offer someone something to drink in opinicus culture, but it was more of a courtesy. He just happened to be thirsty.

Hoppy and Sponge cooed back and forth, then Hoppy pushed her forward. "You may drink her."

"What." Cherine had no idea what to say.

Sponge waddled towards him. When her feathers pushed against his foreleg, he realized they were wet. She looked up at him and cooed.

"Oh, she say you're not desert bird. I forget," Hoppy said. "She fly out to oasis, get water this morning. Her feathers hold water for pride. You drink them. Not weird at all."

It was weird. It was very weird. But Cherine was dehydrated. He picked up the appropriately-named Sponge, squeezed a section of her plumage, and drank the water. More and more, he wished he'd listened to Ninox and stayed hidden in his grove with his books.

The water was stale and tasted of feather dust, but he still coughed out a, "Thank you."

Sponge cooed at him and waddled back into the shadows.

"Okay, so what's your offer?" Cherine asked the padfoot.

Hoppy kept his paws closed as though he were holding Cherine's actual metal-tipped beak. "Trade you back your beak in exchange for doing opinicus things."

Sponge cooed.

"Oh yes," Hoppy said. "You may keep beak on your face while you work it off. I did not make that clear."

Cherine considered the offer. "What does *opinicus things* mean? What would I be doing?"

Hoppy and Sponge cooed back and forth. All around the room were more sand gryphons, usually climbing on top of each other to get a better look at their opinicus prisoner. They stacked surprisingly well, Cherine thought.

"Working off the cost of your beak. Doing things gryphons cannot do." Hoppy pointed out the window. "Do you see?"

Cherine crawled to the edge of the domicile. All around the room were the metal flechettes dropped on the glass-works, probably dug out of the sand. A dozen small sand gryphons followed along behind him. The sun had started going down, but he could still feel the heat radiating off the rocks. Across from him, above the canyon, was a huge statue of a blue vulture. Its wingspan must have been at least thirty feet wide. The sand gryphons looked out at it in awe.

"The statue? Does it need repairs or something?" he asked.

"Not statue," Hoppy said.

Cherine watched closer. The statue folded its wings.

He leapt back. "It's alive!"

The sand gryphons chattered happily at his response.

"Yes! For now!" Hoppy said. "Thunder bird is very alive. That is problem. We can get its attention. Need your help."

"What can I do?" He looked at the tiny sand gryphons, then out at the vulture that would dwarf even a Hatzel or Rorin. "Oh, I get it. You live in this canyon. From here, it probably looks like a god. I assume you want me to help you make an offering or something like that?"

The sand gryphons chirped amongst themselves. Sponge cooed. Then Hoppy spoke.

"Silly opinicus!" he said. "Don't want to worship it. Want to *eat* it."

Cherine looked at the setting sun, the monstrous bird, and the pride of tiny gryphons, and made his choice. He'd never make it across the desert without their help, so Zeph and Kia would have to wait. "Okay, deal. But first, I need something to eat. Where I come from, all deals end with food."

12

THE RUINS OF CRESTFALL

The next morning, Cherine was allowed to leave the small room where the sand gryphons huddled together for warmth. He went out with the first light, before things warmed up, and took stock of his situation.

What he'd taken to be a set of canyons carved out of red stone were, in fact, the remains of Crestfall Eyrie. Small caves had been cut into the canyon walls. They were still marked with brightly colored strips of cloth and a few glass wind chimes. Sand filled most of the dens. The bottom of the canyon was similarly sandy.

I guess no opinici have been around to clear out the sand.

He wandered, looking for any signs of life, but all he found were more sand gryphons. Sponge cooed a greeting as she flew off east somewhere, and Hoppy explained that they were going to refill.

"Where's everyone who lived here?" Cherine asked.

"Sand gryphons live here," Hoppy countered. "Is our home."

"What happened to the opinici?" Cherine asked. "To the reeve?"

"Flamingos!" Hoppy pretended to spit. "No good. I rule here now. Reeve Hoppy Padfoot. Not opinicus home any longer. Is now Padfoot Pride nesting grounds."

Cherine smiled in spite of himself. "I thought a padfoot meant a gryphon with no pride, a criminal. I was accused of being a padfoot once."

Hoppy shook his head, fanning Cherine with his crest. "Not true. Prideless padfeet take name in my honor. The name padfeet comes from me. I first padfoot."

"How old are you?" Cherine asked.

"Five floods," Hoppy replied.

Assuming the desert flooded once a year, that put Hoppy at five years old. Cherine had seen the term padfoot going back to pre-Connixation times. Common courtesy dictated he not correct his host.

As they walked around, the sand gryphons moved all of their things out of last night's cave and set up a new camp in a different opinicus den.

"Why do you change dens?" Cherine asked. "Why not stay in the same cave?"

Hoppy chirped encouragement to his pridemates. "White opinici come here searching. Blackwings, too. Always searching, never finding."

"What're they looking for?" Cherine asked.

Hoppy lifted up a piece of dark grey stone and tapped Cherine's metal beak tip with it. "Metal! Armory is full of it."

"Oh! Weapons." Cherine supposed that made sense. Everyone had come to steal Reeve Brevin's treasury after her passing. With a war on, certainly both sides would come searching Crestfall for weapons, too. "They haven't found it yet?"

Hoppy offered an open-beaked grin, complete with spread crest. "No! Sandstorm hit. Then I hide it."

"You hid an entire armory?" Cherine was skeptical. "Where'd you hide it?"

Hoppy tapped Cherine's beak again. "Exactly where it was."

Cherine laughed, and they continued their walk. He felt there was an even chance he was hallucinating all of this. The canyon was sweltering, but the stone encouraged a strong wind to cut through the lower sections. It was a strange feeling, wandering through an abandoned city.

When they reached the southern exit, Hoppy pointed out towards the cave where Cherine had passed out.

"Guest cave," the gryphon said. "Where we find you. And steal your things and beak. No pens, though."

Cherine wasn't sure why anyone would lie about stealing his quill pens, but he supposed he should be grateful the Padfoot Pride had gotten to him before the colossal vulture had. "Why's it called the guest cave?"

"It for guests." Hoppy looked at him like he was stupid. "Come, will show you first home."

Hoppy led Cherine through the canyons, picking up a dozen sand gryphon followers along the way. He was careful to check the sky for 'thunder birds' before they flitted towards a cluster of rocks to the west. It took some digging to get Cherine inside, but this looked like the sand gryphons' original nesting grounds. He wondered if the entire desert was full of small prides of sand gryphons hiding away in caves like this from the sun.

"Opinicus fire." Hoppy pointed at Cherine's talons.

Cherine reached into his pockets, rediscovering how empty they were. "You stole them, remember?"

Hoppy laughed. "Yes!"

Cherine reconsidered. "In exchange for my flint and tinder fungus, I'll light a portable brazier for you."

"Good deal!" Hoppy chirped and one of the sand gryphons came forward and returned the items. More chirping and a small opinicus brazier appeared, too.

Cherine lit it and the room brightened, revealing glyphs scratched into the stone. "Ooh, what are these?"

"Wait!" Hoppy didn't tell him what to wait for, but Sponge and the sandgrouse members of the Padfoot Pride squeezed into the old cave. Sponge cuddled up next to Cherine, soaking his harness.

"Impolite not to drink," Hoppy said. "No drink water, die. Even more impolite."

"Oh, I see." Cherine took a sip.

Sponge cooed up at him and blinked slowly, making it even weirder than his drink the night before.

"Okay, begin." Hoppy pointed at Cherine. "You dumb, but we fix that now. See chart?"

Sponge pointed her head towards the glyphs until Cherine also looked. He saw crude sketches of sandgrouse and a bird that resembled Hoppy.

Several sand gryphons ran over and covered up parts of the drawings, leaving just the birds.

"Good," Hoppy continued. "Before Padfoot Pride, the desert full of hoopoe bird and sandy grouse. Then gryphons arrive."

The sand gryphons shifted, revealing more of the drawings. This time, they were gryphons like any others. Their beaks were open like they were hungry.

"We eat hoopoe birds, became hoopoe gryphons," Hoppy said. "Ate sponge birds, become sponge gryphons. Now birds gone. No longer exist."

"They're extinct?" Cherine said.

"Yes, extinct," Hoppy confirmed.

"But I saw a sandgrouse on my flight over," Cherine said. "So they're not extinct."

"Extinct here." Hoppy's crest went down. Sponge looked up at Cherine like he was a monster.

"Er, yes. Extinct here. I see," Cherine said. "You're absolutely correct."

The sand gryphons against the wall shifted, covering up the birds and plain gryphons while revealing the hoopoe and sandgrouse gryphons.

Hoppy stood up on his back paws to point at the sketches. "That part one."

Cherine found himself intrigued. "What's part two?"

Sponge cooed.

"Yes, yes," Hoppy said. "He got that. Gryphon eat bird, gryphon's eggs hatched as bird. He dumb opinicus, not extra dumb opinicus. Not flamingo."

Sponge nuzzled Cherine with encouragement that he didn't feel. It was strange hearing gryphons echo Impir and Mally's basic theory on how they evolved. Their reasoning was different, but the core idea was there.

"Part two!" Hoppy shouted, and the sand gryphons pulled the brazier next to another wall, then covered up parts of it with their bodies and wings. All that was left was a drawing of a giant vulture like the one from the previous night.

"Thunder bird," Hoppy whispered. "You see?"

"Yes?" Cherine said. The sand gryphons chirped their encouragement, then began to shift very quickly.

"Thunder bird. We catch, you kill," Hoppy said. The sand gryphons were moving around to reveal different pictures of thunder birds and sand gryphons, ending with a dead-looking bird at the end. "Then Sponge eat it!"

Sponge purred loudly. The sand gryphons shifted to show Sponge trying to eat the giant vulture.

"Then... Sponge eggs hatch as *thunder sponges!*" Hoppy shouted.

The sand gryphons shifted one last time, revealing what appeared to be a drawing of Sponge next to a detailed sketch of Crestfall Eyrie. She towered over it like Hatzel over a squirrel. Water was falling off of her like she was raining. The drawing of the eyrie was surprisingly accurate in terms of the layout he'd walked through earlier.

"Easy," Hoppy said.

Sponge cooed her agreement.

Every sand gryphon turned and looked at him.

"So get thunder bird on ground. Then kill it," Hoppy said. "See? Give you beak back."

Hoppy held up his paws as though he was hiding the metal tip of Cherine's beak again.

The opinicus thought over what he'd seen in the canyons. "You're sure you can get it on the ground?"

Hoppy nodded.

"Okay. If you can get it on the ground here," Cherine pointed to a section of the canyon near where they'd slept with narrow stone sides, "I can kill it."

The sand gryphons cheered. When Sponge cheered, water went flying in every direction. He hoped Kia and Zeph had made it to the raftworks okay and weren't worried about him. It seemed he was going to be here for a few days.

13

ABANDONED PRISON

With daybreak, Piprik and Lei slipped away from Whitebeak and back into the maple forest to search for the prison. Silver's warning had doubled as directions, and they'd followed the road north past where they'd discovered the apple carts to locate an abandoned building surrounded by maple trees.

At Piprik's insistence, they watched the structure for the better part of an hour. Bodies littered the outer yard, but nothing moved.

"I don't like this," Lei said. "It's too quiet. There's no one here. What happened?"

"I'm going to take a look at one of the guards. Keep watch from the ridge." Piprik crawled down. The first opinicus he found had been bitten several times and succumbed to her wounds. The next two bodies were similar. The other traders at Whitebeak had all seemed concerned about gryphon attacks along the roads, and he was starting to think it had just been gryphons until he went inside.

The bodies here had silver eyes.

He thought about leaving, but Zeph and Kia were still locked up. He needed to find a key. It would be safer if Piprik and Lei went in together, so he called up to his assistant, who flew down.

Lei pulled out his mother's metal talons. There were times Piprik wished Rybalt had taken those along with the other markings of Brevin's station as reeve, but it was hard to find a good pair of metal talons these days.

"Was it starlings?" Lei asked. "Maybe they took one prisoner?"

Piprik looked around. There didn't seem to be any medical staff. Nobody would bring a sick opinicus here unless they were a prisoner.

The common area was covered in more bodies. Piprik checked to make sure he and Lei had both bog blossom paste, courtesy of Soft Paws, and vials of pumpkin extract, courtesy of Biski. They were going to need to dose themselves when they got out and check each other's eyes twice a day just to be certain it wasn't the resistant strain. While common theories said it took a bite to spread the disease, Tresh's stories of bugs and mummies in the bog raised several unanswered questions.

They investigated the bodies in each room for survivors. Common area, dead. Barracks, dead. Goliath bird stables, dead. They made their way into the prisoner area, but the open door suggested that anyone who could escape already had.

"Is that one of ours?" Lei pointed a talon to a slate grey shape in an unopened cell at the back.

It did resemble a Crackling Sea opinicus. Lei started to run towards it, but Piprik grabbed his shoulder and pulled him back. "No, use the fishing spear."

Lei unattached the spear and used the dull end to poke the opinicus.

In a flash, she shoved her head through the bars and nearly impaled Lei with her beak.

He fell back with a cry.

Piprik sprang into action. He forced the spear cross-wise into the ranger's mouth, then used a strap of leather to secure her beak open.

Lei recovered and grabbed the back of the ranger's head so Piprik could get two vials of pumpkin down her throat.

"It's okay," Lei said. "We've got you. We're going to fix you and get you back home, okay? Just hold on."

It took some wrangling, but they managed to get both of her foretalons tied to the bars before removing the spear from her beak. They backtracked to the common area and found some food, then brought it back and took turns tossing it to her like she was an animal.

He sent Lei to find some clean water and did his best to inspect the ranger from a safe distance. When he'd grabbed her by the head, his white feathers had come back with blue stains. Inspecting them further, they looked to be bog blossom blue. They smelled like the paste used by the bog witches, too, which raised several questions.

"Who are you?" he asked the silver eyes. "How did you end up here? They didn't bring you back from the bog, did they?"

It took more wrangling to get water safely into the ranger's mouth. The parasite caused a violent, hungry reaction in its victims. It was hard to get her to drink while she had targets of her hunger so close.

Most of the day slipped away while they watched their patient. They had no way of transporting her in this state.

Hours after they dosed her with pumpkin, she suddenly

collapsed and lost consciousness. They didn't risk getting within range of her beak, instead continuing to hope for the best.

Her back half had taiga rosettes, which was unusual for a ranger. One of her forelegs had a fancy bracer on it. If there'd been metal talons attached to the bracer, they'd been cut away before she was tossed into the cage. Her harness, however, remained.

Bits of netting, a pouch, a fancy neck protector, and a badge—it didn't add up. The badge didn't have a pink fish on it. Instead, it had a crackling jelly. As far as he knew, only one type of opinicus had a badge like that.

While she slept, Piprik used the spear to cut the badge off of her harness and pull it over. Parts of the jellyfish had been worn away, revealing a blackwing eyrie badge underneath. Now it made sense.

He cursed.

"What is it?" Lei asked.

"I know who this is," Piprik responded.

"Ellore," came the hoarse whisper from the ranger. "Ranger Lord Ellore of the Crackling Sea Eyrie."

Lei Froze.

"Did you bring the parasite here?" Piprik asked.

Ellore tried to stand, but her forelegs were still tied to the cage. "Not deliberately."

"But it *was* deliberate when you brought it to Sandpiper's Dune." Lei's voice rose. "And the taiga."

Ellore shook her head a little, wiping the goo off on her chest feathers. "Yes."

"Come on, Lei. We're getting out of here." Piprik gathered his things and began to leave.

"Pip, wait!" Lei came after him. "We can't abandon her."

Piprik looked at his apprentice like Lei had gone mad.

"She's a traitor. She's one of Impir's pawns. Think of the damage the parasite has done. She was one of three opinici responsible for using it in the south. Let the Seraph King do whatever he wants with her."

"Think of Mia and Bruen," Lei said. "They'd never forgive us if we let her die. She's their friend."

More coughs from the back of the prison, then, "Mia and Bruen survived?"

Piprik frowned.

"They did. They're doing great," Lei said. "And they remember you fondly. All of the rangers you helped save did. Bruen had to be talked out of coming out to search the Jadebeak Dam for your body a hundred times."

Against Piprik's protests, Lei undid Ellore's bindings.

She drank more of the water. "What word of Quess?"

Piprik sighed and grabbed another vial of pumpkin. "Eat something and take another dose. Your old rangers are fine. Vitra's dead, and most of your opinici made it out. Pride Leader Grenkin gave your rangers back pay and let them rejoin the Ashen Weald ranger corps if they wanted. Bruen opted to stay at the shore with Quess."

"Pride Leader Grenkin?" Ellore managed. "Who's the new ranger lord?"

"Mia," Piprik said.

Ellore laughed and then coughed.

"Oh!" Lei said. "Ranger Lord Grenkin, I guess that's Pride Leader Grenkin now, came to the shore to forgive them, and he said you're forgiven, too."

Ellore looked at the peafowl like he was crazy.

"You can come back with us," Lei said. "Your friends are worried. They miss you."

"I can't do that," she said. "I'm glad they're okay, but I *am* a traitor. I don't want any place in the new Crackling Sea *pride.*"

"Sounds like we'll be parting ways here, then," Piprik said. "We have some spare food and supplies we'll leave with you."

He turned to go, but when Ellore started to stand, her strength gave out.

"We have to help her, Pip," Lei said. "Can we take you to Crestfall or the glassworks? Where were you headed?"

"The glassworks is where they caught me. I was supposed to meet Impir there, but the blackwing camp was all dead," Ellore coughed. "What phase is the moon in?"

Piprik told her.

"There's a smuggler northeast of here, by the rock shaped like a whale," she said. "He has a standing agreement with the blackwings. He'll get me across the desert safely."

"Pip..." Lei began, but Piprik cut him off.

"Fine," he said. "We need to grab the keys, but we'll take Ellore to where we stored our stuff in the woods. With Kia and Zeph's help, we can probably get her to the desert border."

Ellore looked like she didn't trust either of them, but Piprik didn't see that she had much choice in the matter.

Once Lei searched the building and located a set of keys, Piprik led the treacherous ranger lord into the forest. They hadn't made it far when a cry sounded. A dozen Argent Reaches opinici flew overhead, dropping jars of flaming oil on the abandoned prison. They returned to burn the bodies on the ground.

14

ZEPH AND KIA RESCUE!

Kia sidled up to the edge of their cage while Zeph chased his tail to distract the guards. When Lei walked by, she was surprised to be passed not only the keys but also a vial of Crackling Sea jelly toxin. The fisherfolk had also managed to steal Kia's glassworking boots, which had been left outside the cage.

Zeph and Kia bid their time, enduring several changes of guard. Silver came to visit them when the sun went down and brought dinner—megapede steak and maple tart. She mused aloud about what to do with the two of them.

"You could let us go," Zeph said. "That would be simplest. You're not at war with the weald."

"Release the Bane of the Red Reeve?" Silver seemed amused. "I'm not sure I've ever held such an important political prisoner before. Though the Duckbill Murder Hen did spend an evening in the Argent Eyrie's cells."

Kia wandered over, careful to keep her harness pocket closed. They'd rifled through her belongings before locking her up but hadn't done so since. "You could trade us to the Ashen Weald. I'm sure they'd give you something."

"I thought you two weren't members?" Silver pressed.

"We're not, but we have a lot of friends," Zeph said. "Everyone in the south had to work together not to starve after the fires and outbreak."

Silver nodded. "I see."

"You said it yourself," Kia continued, "if you don't make a decision about us, Mally will do so instead. You've seen what goes on in his workshop."

It was a long shot, but Silver didn't rise to the bait. "I have, yes. Have *you*? I didn't think so."

"Why do you stay here?" Kia asked. "You don't seem like the rest of the Seraph King's advisors. Not like a true believer."

Silver finished up her meal. "Trying to convert me to the cause? Satra the Kjarr doesn't have the weapons to hold the south, let alone protect the Argent Heights. The moment I join sides with your Ashen Weald, they'll raze my eyrie to the ground. And even if the king doesn't, the blackwings won't waste any time. The last time we were neutral, they sent assassin after assassin against us. I'd prefer to fight battles I can win, thank you."

Reeve Silver left to talk to the night guards, giving Kia and Zeph several minutes of privacy.

"I think you're starting to get to her," Zeph said.

Kia laughed. "I'm not so sure. She's right. She has a small eyrie on the border she can't defend on her own."

"That means she can't defend it from the Ashen Weald, either, though," Zeph said. "Couldn't they sneak in and grab it fast?"

"And hold it with what weapons?" Kia shook her head. "The Ashen Weald has a large army of gryphons and opinici, but no metal for the metalworks. Just look at the fancy opinici the Seraph King has here at Whitebeak. I think Satra's better off waiting to see who we end up fighting. Ten beads to a parrot, the moment she shifts her forces west, the blackwings show up again."

Zeph considered this. "Well, this is all information we need to get back home. When do we make our move?"

"Not for a while yet." Kia looked up at the moon. "When it gets near dawn, lure the guards close to the cage."

Zeph's ears perked up. "How?"

"Just hang upside down." Kia went back to eating her megapede steak. "They seem to really like that."

KIA PREENED her feathers and got ready for action. Just before the sun came up, Zeph chirped quietly for the guards to come over from his hanging perch. Kia had a piece of parchment open on the ground next to the edge of the cage and held pens in each talon. They'd drawn a crude map and asked if the guards, both silver hawks, could show them where the Argent Heights were located.

When the hawks put their talons through the bars to point, Kia used the pens to scratch the guards. The Crackling Sea jelly toxin did its magic, and soon both were unconscious.

Kia unlocked the gate, then she and Zeph slipped out of the cage towards the refugee camp, stopping only to close the door behind them and pose the silver hawks so it looked like they were sleeping. Piprik and Lei met them by the first nest and handed over a well-worn Redwood Valley harness for Zeph to put on.

They also had the boots Zeph and Kia had been wearing from the glassworks. Lei had sewn the tips of the talon protectors onto a pair of back paw protectors and gave them to Zeph. While it would be strange to see anyone wearing footwear, it did make him look like an opinicus, except for one small problem.

"Here, put this on." Piprik held out a cloth hat. It had feathers sticking out of the top of it, bright blue plumage facing backwards.

Zeph turned his beak up at it. "I'm not wearing that."

"It's for your ears." Piprik and Lei put it over the copper hawk's head. His ears were hidden underneath it, and with the feathers pointing backwards, their shape was obscured.

He looked to Kia for help, and it took all of her willpower to hold in her laugh.

"It looks very fetching," she said. "You should wear it around the weald this mating season."

Lei shrugged. "They're all the rage in Duckbill. The merchant who sold us the hat said so."

"So where do we go from here?" Kia asked, changing the subject before Zeph took the hat off.

Piprik pointed to the nests. "The best place to hide a Redwood Valley opinicus is with other Redwood Valley natives. We're going back to our quarters. Come meet us later. Once they're sure you've already escaped back south, we'll take you to hide with our other guest."

The sun's first rays reached across the desert. As the world brightened, Kia started by looking for any empty nest to claim. But the more she searched, the more she realized her eyes weren't seeking vacant beds, they were looking for Olan and her parents. She ran through the nests until she saw the familiar blue crest of her father and the red feathers of her mother.

They blinked up sleepily at Kia, not realizing it was her until she started crying.

"Kia?" her father said. "Is that you?"

"We thought you were dead, dear," her mother said. "Is Mia with you? Is she okay?"

Kia filled her family in on what had happened since the night of the fire while Zeph looked as out of place and awkward as his hat. She spared no detail, going so far as to talk about her fights with Cherine at Hatzel's nesting grounds, her time at the shore, almost everything.

"I'm sorry," Kia said. "I was just so worried about you. You have to come back south with me. Where's Olan?"

"He's already gone north," her mother said. "He's getting an orchard ready for us. The king gave it to him in exchange for helping with a cure for the redbeak sickness."

"Kia, we're proud of you," her father added, "but we don't want to go back. We like it here. There's running water, food, and medicine. And soon we'll have our own little farm. Why not come with us? Our reeve's dead, and the Seraph King is going to take over the south sooner or later. Come to Reevesport, sit out the war. Be with your family. Be happy for once. You were always so worried about your grades. I'll bet your brother could get you into the university at the capital."

Kia's heart sank. "Is that how all of the refugees feel?"

Her parents looked at each other, then her mother spoke. "It is. It's why we came up here. New Eyrie was a terrible time in our lives. No one wants to go back. Brevin is dead, our homes burned down. There's nothing there."

Mia and I aren't nothing, Kia thought, but she didn't say it aloud. Instead, she said the one thing she was certain she shouldn't have. "Mom, Reeve Brevin's daughter is waiting near here, and she needs to speak to you."

She ignored the look Zeph gave her.

15

EMERALD RUINS

Erlock flew over the canopy of the Emerald Jungle, careful not to pull too far ahead of her escort. Her long tail streamed below her; her brown and green plumage soaked up the sun's rays. While the expanse of trees looked uniform green, they hid a myriad of creeks and streams guiding water from the summer storms towards the ocean.

Most of the fantail's time in the jungle had been spent waiting to molt and then currying the favor of the various starling prides. Only once they were certain she wasn't a threat did they let her speak directly to the pridelord.

The experience wasn't one Erlock would forget.

She'd met reeves and Kjarrs, pride leaders and fisherfolk elders. Sometimes, they were massive in size and stood out from their peers—the Hatzels, Merins, and Rorins of the world. Sometimes, they wore necklaces, crowns, and talons to show their station. That was more of a reeve habit. Opinici enjoyed wearing jewelry or harnesses.

Even the lowest of gryphon pride leaders did something to mark their appearance. The Parrotface Pride's elder used starberry juice to stain her fur. Erlock had heard rumors the taiga pride leader was sometimes pink.

The starling prides, when their green wing altruism wasn't sending them into a frenzy, were similar to the weald prides. They wore stolen opinicus jewelry sometimes. They stained their fur with berry juice. They did all of the usual gryphon appearance modifications, which was why meeting their pridelord was so strange.

He was just a starling. Small, perhaps the size of Tresh. If an opinicus painted the scene of the starlings Erlock met that day, she'd never have been able to pinpoint who was in charge. To know that, she had to see the way the starlings moved.

When the pridelord looked in a direction, every starling looked with him. When the pridelord walked, the starlings flowed around him. Not like he was a fish in water, but more like they were his shadow, creating designs in the spaces he left behind.

Or like a long, feathery tail.

Where a gryphon wore feather paint or an opinicus put on jewelry, the trappings of the station of pridelord were living, breathing starlings.

It had taken weeks to negotiate the deal that Piprik and Lei were now working on fulfilling. Most of Erlock's difficulty came from a lack of trust. A hook-beaked gryphon had come through years ago, made deals of trade, and then disappeared without fulfilling his half of the bargain.

Merin's eldest.

With help, she'd gone searching for signs of the lost weald gryphons. The starlings were indifferent to their plight. What made it most difficult was that, as best she could tell, Merin's son had visited every part of the jungle at some point or another.

How did he bypass the altruism?

So Erlock had searched the Emerald Jungle, everywhere except the southern coast, without luck. The starling prides down there were especially wary of outsiders—not because of their altruism; they were just stubborn. It would take another pride leader's intervention to let her search Stormtail.

Time was running out, but before Wendl and Nighteyes would take Erlock to continue her search for Merin's lost child, they insisted upon a small detour along the edge of the jungle.

Really, Wendl insisted, and Nighteyes made it happen. Erlock wasn't sure what they needed to the north that couldn't wait until later.

"We're just about there," Wendl said. "Mind the pride glyphs."

It wasn't hollow advice. Erlock had stepped near unseen borders several times only to have Nighteyes hiss at her. The starlings took their territory markers seriously. The fantail couldn't even get close enough to see whose glyphs formed the northwest and northeastern borders.

Nighteyes flew overhead, perching on an emerald spiketrunk with a practice Erlock didn't think she'd be able to replicate without impaling her posterior.

"Let's see, where would it be." Wendl picked through the forest floor detritus. The remains of several tents were now broken poles. A wooden building had collapsed. Everything was buried under leaves, and her search disturbed a family of escaped capybaras, one of whom wore a Clover Ranch collar.

"You're a long way from home," Erlock mused at the frightened rodent. "Anything I can help you find, Wendl?"

"Not unless you can lift up the building over there," the starling scholar said.

Erlock couldn't lift a building, but with a little help from Nighteyes, they managed to break through several walls to get Wendl where she wanted to go.

They tiptoed past broken glass. Every so often, blood-stains marked the sites of fighting, though the bodies had long been taken by animals.

From outside, the building appeared to disappear into leaves and fallen branches. Thus, Erlock had incorrectly believed the broken complex to be a quarter of the length it really was. The sense of crawling into a small building that didn't end raised her hackles.

"Almost there," Wendl singsonged. "These are my old quarters. We slept where we worked there at the end."

The walls of the room had been painted with a mural featuring mostly blackwings, a strange brown-and-grey opinicus type Erlock had never seen before, and a pale Redwood Valley scholar—presumably the Nigthaunt before his transformation.

On the fantail's entrance, squirrels scattered into holes too small for gryphons to follow. Unlike the brown weald squirrels, the jungle variety lacked gliding membranes and were a mix of purple and yellow.

"We should capture one, name it Nighteyes," she quipped.

Her violet starling companion was unamused.

Past the scientists' nests, they found what Wendl was looking for. There was a hole in the side of the complex, now filled by vegetation, where presumably Wendl and Piprik had escaped through ages ago. Purple-stained vats littered the room, clashing with the rust-colored brown of dried blood on the floor.

A pile of harnesses—rotten, chewed, and turned into a nest for more squirrels—filled a corner. Nighteyes made a noise of disgust, but Wendl dug into them.

"Hmm, I hope a magpie or squirrel didn't steal it," she said. "Oh, I think this is a new type of grub, will you save it for me for later?"

"No." Nighteyes stared at her.

Wendl, unfazed, sifted through the remains for several moments before letting out a squeal of happiness. "Got it!"

Erlock craned her neck to look over Nighteyes's shoulder. Wendl was cleaning off a badge. One side had the black wings and swirled orange emblem of the Blackwing Eyrie. The other side read *Khalim*.

"That's it? A piece of metal?" Nighteyes turned up her beak.

Erlock didn't share the Nightsky pride leader's disdain. An opinicus badge had set her off on this adventure. "Are we good? I need to finish my inquiries before Piprik returns with your salt."

Wendl led them back out, ignoring several closed doors. Whatever experiments happened there, she clearly didn't want Nighteyes seeing them.

"Where to next?" the violet starling asked.

"Stormtail," Wendl said. "It's time to help Erlock with her investigation."

16

LITTLE LIGHTNING BOLT

L ei used his cut of metal beads from the apple delivery to pick up food and supplies for Ellore—salted meat, two flasks of water, and some ointment for where her fur and feathers had rubbed against the cage bars.

We may need more than two if she's going to sneak across the desert, Lei thought. Well, that could wait for later. First things first, he needed to make sure Ellore hadn't run off.

He chirped a greeting to the guards, saying he was going to check out the maple trees. As luck would have it, maples didn't grow near Reevesport, so the guards thought it charming that an apple merchant wanted to go look at trees.

"Keep an eye out," a white-tailed kite warned. "Two of the Ashen Weald's cronies escaped earlier today. They probably went south, but who knows? Gryphons do crazy stuff all the time."

"Aye," the other gate guard said. This one was a silver hawk. "I hear the copper hawk has a spike on his foot, and it's full of venom. Knocked two of our lot out cold."

"What?" the first guard said. "No, you're thinking of the fisherfolk near Alwren, the duck-billed lot."

"Well, I'll definitely watch the feet of anyone I meet," Lei said before he was pulled further into the conversation. He worried for Zeph if the guards were looking at feet. Lei might need to modify Zeph's boots.

"Stay out of the dark," the argent hawk called after him. The phrasing wasn't lost on Lei even if the meaning was.

I wonder if the gryphons that have the guards on edge are owls?

On his flight to where they'd hidden Ellore, he couldn't help but notice that most of the megapedes foraging near the opinicus outpost and roads were much smaller. If they wanted to try to hunt the larger megapedes, it might be worth holding onto the apples that had gone bad. The bigger bugs had sniffed out the scent of apples in the sun from an impressive distance. He wasn't sure his fishing spear would be strong enough to get through their chitinous exoskeleton, though.

He arrived at the hiding spot and found it empty. He was about to head back and tell Piprik that their prisoner had flown the coop when a soft heron call sounded from above.

Ellore glided down. The silver was gone from her eyes, though it still stained her cheeks. "Sorry. I didn't want to stay out in the open."

"You seem to be recovering quickly." Lei handed over the water and food. From his time at New Eyrie, he knew Ellore was fond of the usual Crackling Sea fishing spices. He hadn't found them premixed, but he'd gathered the individual ones he knew and got to work trying to combine them in the right ratios while she drank.

She put down the flask and watched him closely. "Thank you, little lightning bolt."

He froze, realizing his mistake. Levin knew Ellore and Crackling Sea spices, but Lei wouldn't—nor would Lei know what a Crackling Sea ranger liked in the proper ratios.

"I didn't recognize you in the prison," Ellore continued.

He felt naked without his fisherfolk paint and apparel.

She went back to eating. "I didn't mean to make you uncomfortable."

"Please don't call me lightning bolt out here." Lei said. "It's dangerous."

"That it is." Ellore used a liberal amount of fish spice on the megapede steaks. "Go on, I see the question in your eyes. While we're both alone and away from our respective armies, ask it."

Lei settled down to eat his own lunch. "You used to try to teach me to fly at New Eyrie. You stopped in a half-dozen times over nearly two months. Were you a spy that whole time?"

"Yes." Her voice held no remorse. "Headmaster Neider recruited me when he saw Ranger Lord Grenkin had sent all of the opinici with kjarr or taiga blood to guard the nesting grounds. He promised me that if I helped the black-wings, I'd someday get to live in the Crackling Sea Eyrie again."

Lei poked the white meat, dyed orange by spices, with a talon.

Ellore drank more, a common reaction for the newly-cured.

"Did you know what Impir was going to do to my sisters?" Lei asked.

"Not until just before it happened," she replied. "I found out moments before I left for the bog."

Lei's body felt like it was overheating. He remembered Ivess holding court, the Reeve's Guard taking a break for lunch, then collapsing as the poisoned carrots did their work. Ivess cried out for help and Impir was there, black-steel talons already secured, and killed her in one slash.

Lei—Levin—had frozen. He'd been found hiding by Askel later, but in that moment, he couldn't move.

"Not you, little lightning bolt," Impir said with his uneasy grin. "Someone wants you alive."

Lei recalled his sister's last moments to Ellore, who stopped eating. "He said *lightning bolt*. I thought he meant the blackwings wanted me for something. But he meant you, didn't he?"

"I asked him not to kill you," Ellore said. "I suspect the blackwings wanted you dead, but they didn't realize you were too weak to fly out to the island where Bario's explosives killed the rest of your family."

Lei was quiet for a long time, then he asked his final question. "What happened to my dad?"

"How would I know?" Ellore played coy. "He was a Reeve's Guard, right?"

"Nobody will tell me," Lei said, "but I feel like they know something I don't. You were a spy. Aren't those kinds of things your business?"

"Nobody paid much mind to your mother's trysts." Ellore finished eating and started grooming her feathers back to flightworthiness. "She didn't like them to be part of her children's lives. Your father was persistent. I just assumed she had him killed."

Lei's heart warred with his attempt to stay calm. "Maybe. But how? Where's his body?"

"Tell me your name again, fisherfolk," Ellore said.

"Lei of Ashfoot Isle, fisherfolk of the southern shore." Lei spoke with conviction.

She looked into his eyes. "Reeve's Guard Captain Larren was assigned to lead the wingtorn against Swan's Rest. Your guess is as good as mine as to what happened, but if he never came back from the shore, you have your answer."

Lei was quiet. He already struggled to accept Zeph and Kia. Most of the time, he really liked them—loved them, even, like they were his aunt and uncle. But he also knew they'd killed his mother. He thought back to the stories of Rorin raining spears upon the *wingtorn and their opinicus jailors*. Had his father been one of those jailors left to rot on the end of a fishing spear? There were tales of Tresh erupting from the water below an unsuspecting Reeve's Guard and pulling him under like a shark. Had that guard been Lei's father?

Many of the same gryphons and opinici who had killed Lei's family had then raised him.

"There's a clarity to choosing a side." Ellore packed her harness.

Lei noticed that the Crackling Sea jellyfish badge, the badge of a ranger lord, had been sanded away to reveal the swirled black and orange Blackwing Eyrie logo underneath.

"Come with me to the north," Ellore said. "We'll leave now, before your friends arrive. The smuggler can bring two across the desert as easily as one, especially when one of those two is Levin, heiress of the Redwood Valley Eyrie, named after the bolt of lightning that struck Reeve's Nest the same time her egg cracked open."

He hated hearing the word *heiress* on her beak. He'd felt a euphoria at getting to become Lei, and having it stripped away by someone trying to appeal to his past life raised his hackles.

He liked that when he was among friends or away from the shore, no one pressured him to be someone he wasn't: specifically, Mi-Lei or Levin. He thought of them as different opinici, which was true in Mi-Lei's case. The real Mi-Lei had drowned off the coast of Crane's Nest.

With Levin, however, he was starting to wonder if she'd ever existed. The more time that passed, the less real his time at the eyrie seemed. He felt like he'd hatched at sea, washed up on an island as Lei.

He shook his head to clear his thoughts. What Ellore offered wasn't something he took lightly. It was the life of a reeve, a life of real power, and there was a lot to consider about his current predicament and friends.

Zeph and Kia had murdered his mother. Rorin and Tresh might have hidden their role in the death of Lei's father from him. But Reeve Brevin had ordered the gryphons burned alive to make room for more farmlands, and Reeve's Guard Captain Larren had forced an army of wingtorn to destroy the eggs at the fisherfolk villages. Even Ivess had ordered five hundred wingtorn declawed.

Family was never easy. But it wasn't the Reeve's Banes or Rorin or even Tresh that helped make up Lei's mind. It was Piprik, who'd seen Lei cry at night and told him stories of the world to make him feel better. It was the peacock family at Ashfoot Isle who had taken him in when their daughter was killed. It was flight lessons with Quess and Bruen, makeup with Naya, learning to fish with Carru and Gressle.

"My name is Lei of Ashfoot Isle," he said. "We'll be back after dark to help you escape."

He turned and flew south, back to Whitebeak.

17

POISON AND FROST

While the Padfoot Pride searched for a long list of items Cherine needed to kill the thunder bird, he wandered through the abandoned eyrie, imagining the lives of its previous inhabitants.

There was no Reeve's Nest building, which was unusual. Brevin's gilded cage once sat atop the spires of the Redwood Valley, and the Crackling Sea reeve had a library, throne room, and large balcony that served the same role. But none of the housing here was fit for a reeve. Small homes were carved into the stone with just enough bedding and storage for one or two opinici to live together. It was more like the underbough than the northern quarter.

He didn't find a university, either. He asked Hoppy where to find paper and was directed to an office overlooking a stone goliath stables on the southern edge of the city. There, he discovered a few trade routes, but only three areas marked with the pink and black Crestfall glyph: the glass-works, the eyrie, and something called the Palace of Fire and Ice. The palace appeared to be a mountain to the north, beyond his ability to see. Based on how many goliath birds died making the run north, it seemed to be the most dangerous location in the entire desert.

Which, counterintuitively, would make it the safest place for Crestfall's residents to hide. Though if Hoppy were to be believed, they'd gone north and forgotten their weapons.

How did he put it? He hid the armory exactly where it was?

Cherine borrowed a map from the stables and searched, but the numbering was wrong. It was like someone had gone through and reordered the shingle outside of every home. Considering the sand gryphons' sense of humor, it had probably been them. Right now, several of the Padfoot Pride were running through the sand around the eyrie with grey rocks in their mouths, stopping only to shuffle their beaks from side to side in the sand every so often.

"What're you doing?" Cherine asked Hoppy.

The sand gryphon blinked. "Magic rock. Finds other rocks, metal rocks."

He tapped it against Cherine's beak.

"Oh," the opinicus said. "You wanted to see if my beak was metal, so you... where did you find those magnets?"

"Glassworks," Hoppy said with his beak full of magnets. "Good magic rock. Help find metal to trade. White eyrie drop metal, we find and return for goods! Unless price bad. Then give to the blackwings. Win either way!"

Cherine wondered what sorts of goods the sand gryphons got in exchange for retrieving the flechettes. *Maybe the Ashen Weald can match their price.*

Hoppy saw him looking pensive and tapped the magnet against Cherine's beak. "Sorry metal beak fake."

"Oh, it's not fake," Cherine tried to explain. "It's just that not all metals react to magnets..."

Sponge let out a squawk from the western side of the

eyrie and Hoppy ran off with his magnet. A few moments later, they pulled some shiny objects out of the sand.

Cherine shook his head. He'd come here looking for the top glassmakers in the continent. Instead, he'd discovered a gryphon 'reeve' the size of an overfed squirrel.

Without thinking, he cooed at a sandgrouse gryphon who was walking by, and when she cooed back, he lifted her up and squeezed the water out of her feathers for a drink, setting her back down gently.

Well, he had a thunder bird to kill, and that was going to require sticks or small wooden planks. He'd seen some broken carts just south of the city, near the 'guest cave,' so he went off in that direction. He was outside the canyon when he heard Sponge's squawk of warning and looked back at the eyrie.

From the east, gryphons and opinici appeared in the sky. He recognized the familiar shapes of Rybalt Reevesbane and Iony.

CHERINE DUCKED into the guest cave before they could see him, peeking out to watch the flight descend upon the eyrie ruins. The sand gryphons had mostly fled west to the burrow where they'd held their cave painting story time, leaving the city to the opinici. A few slipped into holes and cracks in the red stone.

So much for Crestfall belonging to the gryphons now.

Behind him, the blackness stretched deep into the earth. From the desert, the darkness was like a wall. As his eyes adjusted, he still couldn't tell how far back the caves went. His hackles rose, but he concentrated on a more immediate threat than the nebulous depths.

While the blackwings and glacier gryphons searched the homes for something—or someone—three of them sat atop the entrance of the city and talked. Cherine's hearing wasn't owl-quality, but he learned a lot from seeing the way they moved. Rybalt, still wearing his torn leather bindings, splashed Iony with water. The glacier gryphon's coat had been shaved down to let him survive the desert.

While those two were interesting enough, what really caught Cherine's eye was who they were arguing with. Iridescent blue in the desert sun, Impir the Mad's head swayed back and forth like a snake's as he argued with Rybalt.

What brought you out of hiding, I wonder? Cherine thought. Was there something of medical significance out here? Perhaps they were after the Nighthaunt and thought his old apprentice might make good bait?

Impir the Mad had been locked up in a Redwood Valley cell in the northern quarter since before Cherine started his apprenticeship. The mad peafowl continued writing monographs on egg and chick treatments that saw publication even from his incarceration, and there were rumors that Brevin's children were a result of his alchemy.

When the city burned, Impir had escaped west with Ivess, who some said was his daughter. Cherine didn't know if there was any truth to those claims, but Impir had ultimately betrayed New Eyrie, luring the starlings in to finish it off after having poisoned and murdered Ivess for his blackwing masters.

Iony, Rybalt, and Impir leapt off the eyrie gates and flew south, towards Cherine's hiding spot. He slinked farther into the cave, looking for a spot out of sight. The sun glinted off of several circular black orbs in the walls. He wondered idly if they were hematite, but he found an outcropping and pushed himself against the stone, which was softer and warmer than he expected, perhaps some previously undiscovered type of feathermoss.

Outside, Rybalt and Impir continued their discussion, this time within hearing distance.

"Goldfeather said we'd find Mally here, caw-ha," Impir squawked. "Perhaps he lied to you."

"I find that unlikely," Iony said. "Rybalt is very persuasive when he needs to be. Goldfeather is a glorified mouthpiece. He told us where Mally is located because he honestly believed we'd find him here."

Rybalt had his back to Cherine's hiding spot, looking north at the eyrie. "I have a hard time imagining any serious scholar hanging around ruins and caves, but I can think of one more place to search. How far away is the palace?"

"Too far, ha-caw." Impir swayed in the heat. "We'd never make it there and back without a place to rest, and the high desert is not kind."

"What happened to the Blackwing reeve's last emissary?" Rybalt asked. "I never heard from my cell."

Iony shook sand off of his paws. "They sent back his bones, bleached white and picked clean by vultures."

"Charming." Rybalt looked towards the city, where one of the glacier pride held a sand gryphon in his mouth.

The sand gryphon had gone limp. The glacier pride brought it over to the trio and dropped it at their feet.

"More vermin," Impir said.

Rybalt motioned to Iony to wake the sand gryphon, reminding Cherine that a single touch was all it took for the Reeve's Bane to poison his foes.

A sense of unease came over Cherine, but it didn't come from the assassins outside. Instead, he had the strangest feeling that something deeper in the cave was watching him.

He chalked it up to paranoia, but there was a tickling at his ear holes, the faintest of clicks.

Iony poked the sand gryphon, who just cooed back angrily and hissed.

The glacier pride leader laughed. "I don't think they speak common. What do you want me to do with her?"

"No sense antagonizing them," Rybalt shrugged. "Toss the little sand fish back where you caught her. It's time for us to leave. If the Nighthaunt were here, we'd have found evidence by now. Let's head back to Blacktalon."

It took another twenty minutes for the blackwing allies to clear out, by which time Cherine quickly vacated his hiding place. The faint clicking had grown louder, as though deep in the earth something was making its way up towards him. As much as he'd love to believe it was just bats—well, when was the last time someone had actually *seen* a bat?

18

THE METALWORKS

Cherine watched as Hoppy lived up to his name. Apparently, in the sand gryphon's mind, there was some sort of agreement that while the blackwings or white opinici could search the ruins, they weren't allowed to pick up any of the Padfoot Pride.

Sponge cooed at Hoppy to calm him down without success. The feathers on her neck ruff were still bent from being scruffed by the glacier gryphon.

Finally, the Padfoot Pride leader came to a conclusion that the best way to get back at the blackwings was by trading.

"Fetch metal bits," he commanded his pridemates. "We trade with white opinici."

Cherine moved out of the way as a dozen sand gryphons ran past him to the eyrie. A moment later they returned, surprising him with the amount of metal they brought back. He'd slept in the same stone nests as them, watched them search the eyrie for flechettes, and hadn't seen that number.

More chirping and cooing before Sponge pointed at him and Hoppy translated.

"Sorry," the sand gryphon said. "I forget you dumb. You speak one language? Yes? Sponge speak thirteen."

Cherine was skeptical but didn't question his host. "You're going to trade with the white opinici, you said? May I come along?"

Hoppy made cooing noises at Sponge, but she cooed back angrily and swatted him with a wet wing.

"Sorry, sorry!" Hoppy said. "You secret weapon. We no tell Metalworks we have own metal opinicus."

More cooing from Sponge.

"Hmph, fine," he said. "We bring you, but you hide, yes? We dig a hole and you peek out. No talk to white opinici."

Cherine agreed that this was fine. Then, under his agreement to do *opinicus things*, he tied the metal spikes around the Padfoot gryphons headed north and filled his empty pockets with more flechettes.

Sponge started to leave, but when Cherine tried to follow, Hoppy stopped him. The other sand gryphons were laughing at the opinicus.

"No, you stay," Hoppy said. "Sponge stealthy. Sneak up to their camp, tell them to meet us at secret place. You go, they see you, then they steal the metal. Sponge go, they no see her when she sneak away. Yes?"

"Yes?" Cherine wasn't sure how a flying orange raincloud could be stealthy, but obviously the sand gryphons had survived out here for a long time without his intervention. They must have some sort of system.

After Sponge had been gone for two hours, Hoppy led the other sand gryphons into the desert. They passed by dozens of different pride glyphs, hinting at a large network of sand gryphons hidden in the desert other than the Padfoot Pride. Whenever they stopped by a watering hole with a new glyph marking it, they left a bead behind to say thank you.

In between the watering holes, one of the wet drinking gryphons stayed next to Cherine. They stopped a couple of times in the shade. Usually, it was next to hidden barrels of stolen water, an oasis that was invisible from above, or just to get out of the sun.

Several times, however, it was because of a massive shadow from above, reminding Cherine that before he could leave, he'd need to kill one of the giant birds.

ON HIS FLIGHT NORTH, from the sky, Cherine had seen only sand and rock. Traveling with the sand gryphons, watching what they inspected, he began to realize that the small den next to Crestfall Eyrie had been one of perhaps a hundred hidden across the desert.

They found shade, rest, and water in the strangest of places. They gave the desert scorpions names like *deathstalker,* the snakes names like *deathbiter,* but held no fear for either. They snacked upon them like they were kabobs or salted fish bars that moved. Where the Seraph King and Blackwing Eyrie reeve saw an impassable desert, the sand gryphons saw the largest hunting territory of any set of prides.

Belatedly, he realized if the Padfoot Pride left him out here, he would certainly die. They'd gone northwest as best he could tell, passing over the dry river bed. They were approaching a red rock plateau in the center of the desert.

A plateau with a waterfall. He started moving towards it, but Hoppy bit his tail.

"No, bad," the pride leader said. "Flamingos up there. Bad opinici. Bad water. No drink."

Cherine shook his head. He knew better than to question, but he was thirsty and curious where the water went. It seemed to pool into a massive lake, but he couldn't tell how deep it was. He didn't see a river flowing out of it.

They stopped at a large rock nearby, and the gryphons began digging in the sand until it revealed a small cave entrance. They pushed him inside, then got to work removing the flechettes from his harness.

I need to warn the Ashen Weald about the rain of metal, he thought. It was an interesting way to take a small amount of metal and turn it deadly. The wingtorn, unable to fly higher than their assailants, would be in a lot of trouble if caught off guard.

As the sand gryphons warmed up to him, several had allowed him to trade things to get his belongings back, whether those were scritches or just lighting a brazier at night for warmth. None of them had returned his quill pens, claiming he didn't have any when they found him.

He tried to take out a small travel inkwell and dip a talon in it, but one of the sand gryphons accidentally kicked it to the back of their hiding place, splashing the wall with his favorite shade of Crackling Jade.

He sighed. Notes would have to wait for another time.

Next to the teal waterfall was a gazebo with a barrel of drinking water. Sponge waited atop it. Hoppy flew out to meet her, and while they waited, Hoppy used his long beak to peck at the barrel until they broke through, soaking Sponge.

By the time the Seraph King's envoy had come out to meet them, they'd stuffed a rock in the hole to create a tenuous stop-gap. None of the white opinici commented on the puddle Sponge stood in.

The envoy was someone Cherine had heard described secondhand: an opinicus wearing so much metal armor as to be impractical as anything other than a show of wealth and power. The sand gryphons' nickname for him, *The Metalworks,* was appropriate. He looked down at the small gryphons with disdain.

The negotiations went in parts. The Metalworks would hand over beads, fruit, or trinkets, and Hoppy would let out his *hoo-poi!* cry, summoning several sand gryphons to grab the goods and run, at which point Hoppy would point to an object in the desert where he'd hidden the flechettes.

The Metalworks would then issue an order, sending out an opinicus to go fetch the metal weapons. This gave Cherine his first look at Crestfall's original masters.

The opinicus who came into the desert had a long neck, down-turned beak, and bright pink plumage. When she opened her wings, black markings along the primaries provided a striking contrast.

Where a Redwood Valley harness was designed to be practical, with leather straps and pockets, the Crestfall harness was made of thin braids with no pouches. Instead, the cloth served as a latticework to hang small glass baubles from. The Crestfall opinicus jingled as she flew.

Whatever Hoppy was saying to The Metalworks, he must have said something wrong, because Sponge smacked him upside the head with a wing. The fact that he cast a glance towards where Cherine was hiding worried the opinicus.

It took two more hours, but finally, the small trades were done. Their hideaway stank of spilled ink. Cherine kept sipping on the gryphon next to him. The feather dust taste was easy to overlook when he was thirsty. He wondered what the sand gryphons would think of the bog gryphons' flavored water. Maybe he could try rubbing one of the sand-grouse gryphons down with goldmint or pumpkin leaf later.

They stayed in hiding a while longer to be certain it was safe, then Hoppy let out a sound and one group of sand gryphons flew back into the desert, finding a new hiding spot. Hoppy let out a new sound, and Cherine's companions pushed him out of the rock. He got to fly near the waterfall on the way to his next hiding spot and the smell of salt and chemicals hit his nares hard. The Padfoot Pride was right, this water wasn't safe to drink from.

Past the waterfall were pools of every color—verdant greens fed into toxic blue and crimson red streams. Where some of the pools were open to the sky, beyond them shone the Palace of Fire and Ice. It was as magnificent as the paintings of it that used to hang in the headmaster's study.

Stained glass of a spectrum matching the pools below depicted larger-than-life opinici in royal garb. Like a prism, it sent spears of rainbow light across the nearby dunes. It looked like someone had shattered a rainbow and then fused its shards into a temple.

When Cherine's little brother was a chick, he feared the darkness. The only thing that let him sleep was a tapestry with little pieces of colored glass woven into it. Cherine would hang the tapestry in front of a brazier and let the rainbows of light play across their single bedroom home until his little brother fell asleep.

Cherine's chest ached. His brother had never been able to see the palace for himself. He'd never even been able to attend the university and see the painting of it in the head-master's study.

The sand gryphons had to herd Cherine away from the

sight of the colored glass. There was something magical about opulence, even for an underbough opinicus like himself. His only consolation was that he truly believed that until an eyrie could feed its citizens, it didn't deserve to construct wonders like the palace or the Snowfeather Dam.

It took the rest of the day to take the goods back to Crestfall Eyrie, but once they returned, he had a look at them: mostly strange things to eat. While the sand gryphons celebrated, he picked out some slightly off goliath meat and started cooking it. There was no sense in anyone getting sick.

The sand gryphons looked on with curiosity and hungry, open beaks. It took him a while to cook it through, during which time he sent gryphons searching the ruins to find spices and salt for him. By the time he was done cooking, he'd become every sand gryphon's favorite opinicus.

"This good," Hoppy said. "You dumb, but make food taste good. Good combination. Should stay, be padfoot gryphon."

Sponge made a cooing noise.

"Sponge say you stay the winter, be her mate," he translated. "You no thunder bird, but you pretty tall. Maybe help eggs."

"Oh, no, I need to get back to my friends." Cherine wasn't sure he wanted to be in a relationship with someone who didn't speak common, even if she understood it fine. "No offense, obviously. Sponge is great."

Sponge puffed up and cooed something.

"It okay, can say you afraid." Hoppy touched his magnet to Cherine's beak. "Sponge say many afraid of her. She not so scary. Also, she full of water."

Sponge shook her feathers, drenching everyone nearby.

"I have a mate," Cherine said.

Hoppy's ears perked up. "A gryphon?"

"A gryphon," Cherine confirmed.

Sponge cooed.

"Easy!" Hoppy laughed. "Sponge fight for you. Other gryphon lose. No problem. Other gryphon forget water, die of dehydration. Not Sponge. Sponge best of us."

The other sand gryphons all chirped their assessment of Sponge.

"I'll, er, take it into consideration when mating season arrives." Cherine felt very uncomfortable with the way Sponge was looking at him. "So tomorrow, we'll catch the thunder bird, and you'll give me my beak back, right?"

Hoppy nodded. "Yes. Sponge eat thunder bird. You get beak. Though..."

"Though?" Cherine asked.

"You die of thirst if you try fly away," Hoppy said. "Need us to trade you water first. Perhaps you tie string around more magic rocks to find metal with so Padfeet can wear them?"

"Sure! Bring me some magnets and string." Cherine was reminded of Kia's advice. She always said that the best kind of trade negotiation ended when both sides were happy. Tying a couple of knots in exchange for water felt like that kind of deal.

He kept his eye open when the gryphons ran off to get the hidden magnets. They disappeared behind a corner as they made their way down, but they were on foot. He read the glyphs they passed in their descent before they moved out of view. Six, Five, Four. The nest the Padfoot Pride would be sleeping in tonight was marked Three. Below them was the mark for Two, then the ground.

"Say, Hoppy," Cherine began. "While I tie these, tell me about the day you took over as leader of Crestfall Eyrie."

"Sure!" Hoppy said. "Blackwings and white wings both come. Not good for flamingos. Lots of fighting. Everyone nearly died, but then, the sandstorm came. Everything fill with sand. Flamingos fly north to big rainbow poison water rock. Then eyrie fill with sand. Then fill with sand *gryphons!*"

Hoppy's story went on as more and more magnets appeared at Cherine's feet. He tied a string around each and placed them atop a new sand gryphon's head. He'd expected a pawful of magnets, but the supply seemed endless.

"How many magnets do you have?" he finally asked.

"Oh, you not tie string to all of them," Hoppy said. "Hide *big* magnets in armory. Have wall of them. Once walk by in shiny reeve outfit, get stuck, need Sponge strength to pull me down. Not enough string for all those. Maybe when you and Sponge's gryphlets grow big."

By the time Cherine was done, his talons ached, but he'd given every padfoot their very own magic rock trinket.

The eyrie filled up with sand, he thought as he curled up to sleep. It had taken him a couple of days, but he now knew where the armory was hiding—exactly where the flamingos left it.

19

WORKSHOP INFILTRATION

Piprik sighed at his apprentice's tardiness. Every day they spent at Whitebeak was another opportunity for someone to see through their ruse. "What happened with Ellore?"

"Nothing." Lei's raised plumage said otherwise. "I just stayed to eat. She's doing fine. The silver is gone from her eyes. She'll be good to go tonight. Why? What's going on here?"

A lot was going on here, Piprik thought, and he caught his apprentice up on what had happened. Most of the army had gone south to search for Zeph and Kia. Silver had sent her argent hawks to check in every direction. Even Mally's assistants had been dispatched to the burned outpost to dispose of the bodies and make sure no one was hiding inside the smoldering husk.

The sum of these events was something Piprik hadn't expected: his old master's workshop was now empty and completely undefended.

"It's time to take a look inside." Piprik grabbed a small

bag of apples so they could claim they were delivering it if they were caught.

"And steal some salt for Wendl," Lei added.

The back of the workshop butted up against the soldiers' rest area, so they walked right in the front. Since not everyone shared Mally's love of the dark, there were several small braziers and a host of rushlights left lit and forgotten when his assistants departed to go check the burned prison. What appeared to be a small building was actually built into the earth.

Piprik's nares recognized the familiar scent of salt and blood coming from the right passage. There were several warning signs about chemicals that could not be brought past that point. "That's where they treat opinici. His work area will be the other way."

The passage down was lined with cases full of notebooks.

"What's in the books?" Lei asked.

Piprik opened one to a random page. "He's testing something new. Looks like it's a treatment that slows down the effects of the iron disorder. The blood comes from opinici who have the affliction but aren't succumbing to it. I wonder where they found such large quantities?"

They continued their descent. Mally used old journals like decorations. Even their Emerald Jungle outpost had been full of them. The important findings, however, he always kept in his personal quarters. That's also where Piprik felt certain they'd find the salt.

A few more turns revealed why it had been necessary to build the workshop into the ground. Lei shivered as they passed by a cold room. Blood deteriorated if left in the heat. By the ocean smell, the ice had been harvested from icebergs.

Down the next hallway, they passed empty vats hung up to dry and crates of common ingredients before coming to another split. There were more signs along this section of the corridor warning against bringing sulfur, blackwater extract, or blastwort past this point. Piprik recalled seeing barrels of blackwater outside the workshop. They were the Seraph King's counterpart to the flaming oil Bario used to spread the weald fire, currently in use burning down the infected prison.

To the left, Piprik smelled opinici. *Perhaps the assistants' quarters?* Rather than risk anyone having remained behind to take a nap, they went right.

Mally's quarters were dark, but there was a single brazier, which Lei lit for them. On the ground next to a cushion was a book labeled *Mal Grimoire*. Setting atop it was a seal he could only describe as decadent.

It wasn't just any elegant seal, it was *the* royal seal of the Seraph King, for use only by his top officials. Piprik started to move it out of the way before he realized how useful it could be. He stamped several blank pieces of parchment and carefully folded them into his harness before running out of wax and setting the royal seal aside and grabbing the tome. He opened the book up and flipped through the pages.

"Oh, is it a book on gryphons?" Lei asked. The first few pages had sketches of starlings. "Oh, a taiga gryphon! She's so pretty."

Piprik didn't comment. The shape of the taiga gryphon's eyes, the ruff of feathers around her neck, the notch in an ear—even before he looked at the handwriting on the page to confirm it was his own, he remembered this gryphon from Mally's lab. It was a poor salve to his soul that he'd given her a proper burial after they were done studying her.

Next came the bulk of their research in the Emerald Jungle. He made mental notes of which subjects had been resistant to the iron disorder. Twenty starling studies passed by before the pages started to reflect a new type of gryphon.

"There's no pride name," Lei said. "But the location is the Abyssal Naze. What's a naze?"

"A fancy name for a hole in the ground." Piprik looked at the drawings. The gryphons had brown fur and feathers, long whiskers, and black eyes. The dark orbs looked very familiar.

The book acquired scratch marks and bloodstains for a few pages, then the drawings stopped for a while. Mally's writing changed here, and part of a sentence had been torn away, but *they hold a grudge, but I can see them now, hiding in the dark places* was still legible.

The Nighthaunt's writing changed one more time, right after a sketch of a decayed seraph. Neither Lei nor Piprik spoke. Its shape generally matched the mummy in the swamp. According to the notation, the body had been used in a failed treatment—the subject again being Mally himself —and the seraph's bones now hung in the Halls of the Seraph King.

There was a ribbon marking a page farther along in the book, and he sent Lei to open the crates marked Crestfall to search for salts. Unlike the normal flamingo emblem, these were marked with a mixture of paint, wax, and real glass— the seal of the Palace of Fire and Ice.

While his assistant was preoccupied, Piprik opened the book to Mally's most recent experiments. As he feared, the blood for the latest experiments was locally sourced. He closed it and started to put it back before curiosity got the better of him.

When he looked at Mally's findings and hypotheses,

Piprik was horrified but fascinated. Not only could Mally change a gryphon's bird-like front half, but if he treated them without adding in blood, they seemed to revert to other birds. It explained why sometimes a gryphon hatched with strange markings—Biski's bright blues and oranges.

By treating them over and over and documenting the types of birds they resembled, he'd tracked the spread of the gryphon prides across the continent. Hidden in the subtext where no respectable reader could take offense at it was the implication that opinici had spread the same way. In fact, what Mally had really sought and failed to find was the essence of a seraph.

Even more fascinating to Piprik: before the subjects died, they had begun to resemble birds that no one could identify. Had they gone extinct? Were they even native here? Piprik's mind was racing at the possibilities when Lei interrupted him.

"Greyfeather Pip?" Lei's voice was heavy with concern.

Piprik blinked at his surroundings. He'd forgotten why they were here for a moment.

"I found the salts?" Lei prompted.

There weren't many vials, but it should be enough to make Wendl and the starlings happy. Mally must be out collecting more at this very moment. Piprik got to work wrapping the glass containers to put into his harness.

"Check the roster, would you?" he asked Lei. "I want to know the ages of Mally's assistants."

"A few are older." Lei pawed through the papers. "Most are younger, like me. Shouldn't the egg treatment have kept them from being sick?"

"Yes." Piprik didn't elaborate. Lei was smart; he'd figure it out soon enough. Either Mally had deliberately made sure the egg medicine hadn't gone out so he'd have more opinici with his disease to experiment on, or—well, the problem the starlings now faced proved he had no qualms about using his knowledge to cause the disease in others. It was difficult to get patronage to cure a disease only a handful of opinici had. It was much easier if the chicks of the nobility and tradesopinici also suffered from it.

"One more stop," Piprik said. "Then we're getting out of here."

Lei preened, a nervous habit in peacocks. Piprik considered telling his apprentice to stay back, but Lei had wanted to see the world. What lay down the other path would help inform his choice whether or not he wanted to be a leader.

Beyond the other path lay his subjects.

PIPRIK LED Lei into the holding pens. Some of the opinici here looked too sick to flee, but the fact that they'd all been chained to the wall as a precaution suggested they were stronger than they appeared. The patients didn't acknowledge Piprik and Lei's arrival. With Piprik's plumage, they probably assumed him one of the Seraph King's soldiers.

He examined the charts and glyphs outside the pens, but they only confirmed what he already knew: these were the Redwood Valley refugees who had been 'cured' of the iron disorder by Headmaster Neider years ago while still in the egg, now grown up. Some looked healthy, if weak from giving blood. In other cases, the Nighthaunt's meddling seemed to have turned the disease back on.

In the pen next to Piprik, a parrot opinicus sat pale with red beak and talons. The name on his chart was Olan.

The holding pen was just large enough to fit three opinici. Piprik pulled Lei in.

"Are you strong enough to fly?" he asked the parrot.

Olan's eyes were blank. "Fly? Where to?"

"There's talk of moving you all to a new outpost to the south." Piprik didn't give Lei a chance to speak. "You've given a lot, and it's time to rest and recover. The Seraph King doesn't approve of what Mally's done here. We'll find another way to create a cure."

A small glimmer in Olan's eyes. "I think so. Something Mally gives us after we give blood keeps us healthier than we look."

"Excellent," Piprik said. "We'll be back later to have you moved. Mally doesn't know yet, so please don't tell his assistants."

Olan blinked a few times, trying to see his liberator in the dim light. "Who are you?"

"Piprik, Eyes of the Seraph King." He held out the badge Erlock had returned to him. "Your sisters are both alive and well. I thought you'd want to know."

Piprik shoved Lei out of the pen, and they hurried upstairs. He could hear the sound of someone crying below them. With the Seraph King's armies south looking for Zeph and Kia, Piprik couldn't smuggle anyone out yet. But before they left, he'd find a way to get the prisoners out of the pens the same way he'd set the starlings free in the Emerald Jungle.

He also had one more surprise for his old master. He reached into his harness pocket, dipped his talon into ink, and scribbled down three things: sulfur, blackwater extract, and blastwort.

Do not bring past this point, indeed.

20

STORMTAIL

With their first errand out of the way, Erlock Fantail continued her search through the Emerald Jungle escorted by Wendl and Nighteyes.

When she'd first arrived here, the fantail gryphon had thought the jungle was all the same. Its emerald broadleaf trees covered the landscape from mountain to coast. The more time she spent here, the more she began to recognize the peculiarities of the different sections of the jungle.

The starlings used pride glyphs along their borders with outsiders but not within them. Instead, she'd learn to distinguish different plants that indicated she was entering a new pride's territory. The Nightsky hunting grounds, for example, had parasitic vines that grew out of the broadleafs. When they bloomed, the dark canopy lit up with bright white flowers, resembling stars in the night sky.

The Jadebeak Pride controlled the center of the jungle. Anywhere that wasn't clearly claimed by another pride was theirs. Their landscape rose and fell in predictable ways, and it wasn't until she'd been permitted into one of their nests that she realized there were stone structures buried under the vegetation. Above-ground catacombs, once home to opinicus remains, now housed gryphon nests. She could even spot some of the spires and cities of a long-abandoned eyrie, now verdant with life and starlings, rising up from their core.

The Jadebeak and Nightsky Pride territories were impressive, but the Stormtail territory was the easiest to find.

Erlock looked out upon it now—an area of the jungle where the rapids met the ocean. The sky above the Stormtail nesting grounds was experiencing a thunder storm—the exact same storm that had been there yesterday and the day before. In fact, the storm had started four months ago and still raged today.

Wendl said the thunderstorm faded only for the winter. It was something to do with air currents and river currents and ocean currents all hitting at just the right location. Something to do with the rainshadow effect and mountain air currents and weather terms Erlock was unfamiliar with. The Stormtail Pride seemed happy enough there, but she personally thought it was a good place to catch beak rot.

Unfortunately, it was also the last place anyone had seen Merin's eldest son. Erlock and her escort flew low and braced for the cold rains. Lightning crackled nearby, striking one of several spires.

"The spires are relatively new," Wendl chirped. "The other scholars and I constructed the lightning rods to stop the nesting grounds from getting hit. Careful not to get too close."

When Nighteyes fell behind, Erlock asked Wendl if the other starlings knew who she really was.

"I mean, we told them," the opinicus said. "They just don't believe us. They think we were born when some opinici mated with some starlings, and then we came home after being born with starry plumage."

"How does that work with the green wing altruism?" Erlock asked.

"They're not really aware that they have it, exactly." Wendl looked back to make sure Nighteyes couldn't hear them. Her tone said to tread carefully. "It was hard to convince our friend back there to drink the elixir. They think it's ceremonial and not medicinal, more like a kind of ritual to drink the elixir before visiting other prides."

Erlock shook her head. She'd spent so much time here just trying to figure it out. The starlings had some strange blind spots.

They landed outside the Stormtail nesting grounds and walked the rest of the way in. They were covered in mud by the time they reached the nests, prompting Erlock to ask why Wendl hadn't added a boardwalk the same time she put in the spires.

Wendl shrugged. "Wood rots."

"That didn't stop the Crackling Sea opinici from building with it in the bog," Erlock countered.

"Maybe they have a special way of treating it? It's a lot dryer up north," the opinicus replied. "We didn't really have those problems."

These were the moments where Erlock was reminded that she wasn't talking to a starling, she was talking to a blackwing opinicus. Or at least an opinicus who was allied with the blackwings.

"What's the Blackwing Eyrie like?" Erlock prompted.

"I don't know!" Wendl's ear twitched. "I grew up along the farm belt, but I met Khalim outside the Mothfeather Eyrie. I'm sure you've heard of it."

Erlock shook her head.

"The sleeping city?" Wendl prompted, but Erlock still had no clue. "Well, I suppose that's fair. Still, it's so nice to be awake, isn't it?"

The fantail pride leader let Wendl chatter went back to her walking quiet. She was learning to cut through the noise with Wendl. There were important things to remember, but the opinicus scholar tended to focus on what universities were best or the cultures of the eyries who'd allied themselves with the blackwing reeve.

While they finished walking to the nesting grounds, Erlock let her companion ramble to Nighteyes while she concentrated on trying to figure out where Merin's eldest had gone. They had to wade through chest-high water and let the current take them to the nesting grounds.

The inhabitants of Stormtail wouldn't speak to any of them. There was currently some sort of disagreement with the stormtails and jadebeaks, so their borders were closed off.

Only the Nightsky Pride leader's introduction granted them access. Unfortunately, Nighteyes was surly at having been dragged out here. "Stormtail, meet Fantail. She has questions for you."

While the white spots or 'stars' were common plumage decorations for all of the starling prides Erlock had met so far, they weren't all dark green. The Nightsky Pride looked purple under direct sunlight, and the stormtails were an intense blue with white stripes on their feathers. Like Erlock's own Fantail Pride, the Stormtail Pride had long, feathery tails instead of the usual gryphonic fare.

Unlike her own pride, the starlings' tails were thick and muscular, with the feathers going out in a pattern resembling a dolphin or a shark's tail, depending on the individual. Their bodies were similarly thick and long. She couldn't quite place it, but their gryphonic half, as an opinicus might say, looked off to her, though she couldn't get a good look at their paws with all the mud and water about.

"I'm busy," the Stormtail Pride's leader said. "Come back tomorrow."

The thought of wading up the current, slipping between lightning spires, and finding a place to rest—*just to return tomorrow*—did not make Erlock happy. They also needed to get back to the Jadebeak River to wait for Piprik and his assistant.

Thankfully, she didn't have to ask the rude questions.

"Will you be busy tomorrow?" Nighteyes asked. The thick canopy overhead directed the rainwater into spouts. Where they landed and formed small rivers, the nests had been cleared away. Still, a few drops slipped through. One of them landed on Wendl's head, and she shook her ears.

Stormtail's thick tail swished back and forth with annoyance. "Probably."

"Then it sounds like now's as good a time as any," Nighteyes said. "Erlock? Ask quickly."

Past the storm, mountains of green foliage drifted in the ocean. Kelp, perhaps? Seaweed? Erlock didn't know. It looked heavy like a broadleaf.

"I'm looking for a weald gryphon from Merin's pride," she said. "He had a long beak that turned down at the end like an icicle. He was large, bigger than I am. I heard from the other prides that he came south. Did he stay here? Where did he go next?"

The Stormtail leader looked Erlock over. "He left years ago. He was like you."

"How's that?" Erlock couldn't think of any way she resembled Merin. "A weald gryphon, you mean?"

"No, part starling." The leader seemed unaffected by the

weather. The water rolled off her oily feathers like she was a fisherfolk.

"Sorry, but he wasn't." Erlock had met Merin's eldest. He didn't have the star markings that existed in her faded fur. "He was a harpy eagle with hints of feathermane. He didn't have the stars."

"He smelled like you," was all the reply she got.

"I assumed it was sight. Is it smell that triggers the starling's response?" Wendl reached for her harness pocket but reconsidered taking out paper in a wet jungle. "Did he drink anything?"

The Stormtail Pride leader trilled and some of her pridemates came over with a snack of shellfish. "Your friends rubbed something into their fur and feathers. I was young then, but I remember them doing it all the time. They came as the rains ended."

Erlock would have to remember to ask back home if any of the medicine gryphons knew what that might be. Having an ointment that allowed someone to approach the starlings would make communication between the two factions much easier. Until now, the Emerald Jungle had been an impassable green wall that no gryphon dared approach.

Of course, it would be easier for her if she could just ask Merin's son for the recipe directly. "Where did he go from here?"

The Stormtail pride leader chewed on an oversized crayfish. "Southwest."

"What's southwest of here?" she asked.

"King's Reach and the winter jungle," the pride leader said.

Getting information out of starlings felt like plucking feathers to Erlock. "Okay, so great! We'll go there. King's Reach, then the 'winter jungle.'"

The starlings looked at her like she was insane.

Wendl was kind enough to explain. "While you're a guest here, you represent the starlings. You can't go into King's Reach. It's not in their territory."

"Fine," Erlock sighed. "Then we'll check the winter forest."

The Nightsky pride leader laughed.

"What's so funny?" Erlock bristled.

"Winter jungle," the Stormtail leader said. "*Winter* jungle. It's summer now. The jungle isn't there."

Erlock was having trouble processing this information.

Wendl pointed out to the ocean. "That's it. See?"

"No." Erlock didn't see. She watched as the clumps of green seaweed floated in the water.

"*That's* the winter jungle," Nighteyes explained. "You're staring at the tops of trees."

Erlock stared blankly. They were right. She wasn't seeing seaweed, she was seeing an entire section of the jungle poking out of the top of the water.

She may not be able to reach King's Reach now, but she knew a few gryphons and opinici with rafts who might be able to check in with them later. "Who owns King's Reach? Do they trade with fisherfolk?"

"The white opinici," Wendl said. "And yes, I've seen ships come from the north. But please be careful. The winter jungle is Stormtail territory. They will attack any ships that pass over it."

The Stormtail leader nodded.

This was a strange place for Erlock's journey to end. She had two leads, one of which wouldn't reappear until winter and one of which required a very long raft ride that would be perilous in the summer and fall where the outline of the Stormtail's territory wasn't obvious.

She shook herself dry, too tired to worry about offending the Stormtail starlings. "Okay, let's head back. With any luck, Piprik will return soon with your medicine."

Wendl and Nighteyes seemed just as keen to put formalities to the side and fly out from the nesting grounds themselves. They preened dry, then all three flew back northeast, towards the Jadebeak Mountains.

With any luck, Erlock would see herself home before the summer ended. She only hoped her pride had fared well in her absence. With Zrim and Merin gone, the Ashen Weald would be lacking in strong leadership. She'd need to fix that.

21

THUNDER BIRD HUNT

Asingle sand gryphon working alone wasn't particularly strong. Twenty of them, however, with the right leverage, tools, and guidance were able to move some very large rocks into position along the top of the canyon without too many incidents.

Which wasn't to say there weren't any. Cherine had been standing down in the canyon when the first boulder fell and nearly crushed him. After that, he'd ordered everyone topside until the rocks were in place. With some help, he'd managed to get a dozen ready to go, rigged with small sticks and strips of leather so the Padfoot Pride could send the rocks falling into the canyon below.

Sponge cooed her encouragement.

"You're sure you can get a thunder bird to land here?" Cherine asked.

"You no worry!" Hoppy touched his magnet to Cherine's beak. "Will have your beak back in no time. Then we give water and you go back to mate."

Sponge cooed.

"Or stay here," Hoppy amended. "Be padfoot. Sponge like you."

More cooing.

Hoppy nodded. "She say it fine to bring old mate along. How much water she hold?"

Before he could stop himself, Cherine's brain started running the calculations on how much water owl micro-feathers could hold. He settled on, "Not nearly as much as Sponge, but still enough. She leads her own owl pride, though."

Sponge made a determined sound.

"What?" Hoppy looked at Sponge. "No, you don't! I pride leader. You... Sponge."

Cherine recognized the angry tone of Sponge's cooing and decided to intervene before his beak-return ceremony was delayed any longer. "I think what Hoppy is trying to say is that you're Sponge, Champion of the Padfoot Pride. You're the one all the other sand gryphons look up to. Hoppy is in charge, but you're the muscle. And water."

Hoppy nodded, and when Sponge made happier sounds, translated. "Sponge say she accept both you and owl as mates."

"That's not going to happen." Cherine looked up at the sun. "When do we start?"

"Oh!" Hoppy chirped orders to some nearby sand gryphons, and they ran to fetch bits of metal. With Cherine's help, they modified a ragged Crestfall harness intended for a chick to fit on Hoppy. Then Cherine secured the shiniest pieces of metal to the harness.

"I don't think this is going to protect you from a thunder bird's beak," he warned.

Sponge looked at Cherine like he was an idiot.

"No worry, I help make him less dumb." Hoppy turned from Sponge to Cherine. "Thunder birds attracted to shiny things. Opinici dumb, not realize this, so thunder birds eat their goliaths, chase them away. Then Padfoot Pride steal their stuff."

Sponge made a sound halfway between a laugh and a coo.

"Ha!" Hoppy agreed. "Is good game. Take metal, stick it on caravans while opinici not looking. Then thunder birds find them. All sand gryphon prides play."

Sponge fluttered into the air then stomped down like a thunder bird crashing upon an unsuspecting caravan. Water splashed everywhere on the landing.

Cherine blinked. It hadn't occurred to him that this small bunch of fluffy, wet sand gryphons were actually flyway robbers. They lived up to their padfoot title.

He finished adding a few reflective pieces of glass to the mix. "You're ready."

Hoppy chirped, and the Padfoot Pride scattered. They all had hiding places up top so the thunder bird wouldn't see them. Sponge and Cherine waited in the canyon to give the sign to start the rocks falling.

"Okay, Hoppy," Cherine said, "go find us a thunder bird!"

HOPPY PADFOOT DASHED out of Crestfall Eyrie and into the desert. He jingled when he flew, which was fine. He wasn't trying to catch anything. He was the prey.

His least favorite thunder bird made its roost on a hill that had once served as a guard tower, now abandoned by the flamingos. It considered Crestfall Eyrie within its territory, and that was a problem for Hoppy's pride. Killing it was a matter of public safety, and it'd keep Sponge happy.

Keeping Sponge happy was a large part of being a pride leader.

The small sand gryphon fluttered between the cactus shaped like a crab and a shade rock. There was a scorpion hiding under the rock, which two claws and a beak quickly disarmed and then ate.

He looked up at the sky. No thunder bird.

He fluttered out to the next marker, which had water, and drank. He marked the rocks nearby with his scent so any gryphons who came by would know that this was part of his territory. He didn't mind if others used his shade rocks or water so long as they knew those things belonged to the Padfoot Pride.

He liked guests. Why else have a guest cave if not to have guests?

He searched the sky again. Still no thunder bird.

He didn't get dressed up all shiny just to not have any thunder birds show up, so he fluttered in the direction of the bird's nest, letting out his *hoop-poi, hoop-poi* call as he went.

In the distance, a small vulture shape grew larger.

The chase was on.

Hoppy resisted the urge to dive under a small rock or burrow. For one, the rocks wouldn't be big enough. A bird with a wingspan like that could flip over most objects he'd hide under. For two, he needed to get the bird to land and go into the small canyon where their Metalbeak had set the trap.

Sponge had been skeptical about his plan to have the opinicus do things. She thought opinici were dumb, especially ones who had lots of ink and no pens.

Hoppy had shown Sponge that with some patience and teaching, he could make an opinicus seem smart. Especially one who was partially metal.

Even if the beak was fake.

The shadow of the thunder bird passed over Hoppy just as he reached the start of the canyon. He dove into the shady sand, hiding behind a cracked clay pot. The thunder bird went past, not landing, then circled back around.

Normally, a thunder bird wouldn't chase a gryphon this far. They were too small to make for a good snack.

But a *shiny* gryphon was something else. It could use the shinies to decorate its nest. That was worth pursuing—or so Hoppy's reasoning for the bird went.

He dashed out into the sun so the vulture could see him when it came back around, then went into the canyon. He didn't have long to wait before the massive vulture landed at the entrance.

Thanks to Metalbeak, they'd lined up a few reflective pieces of glass and metal to shine spotlights into the canyon.

Hoppy took a deep breath, stretched his legs, then dashed out from behind a rock and through the first spotlight.

The moment he lit up, the bird began running after him. Thunder birds were made to soar, not to run, but it had long legs, and he was starting to worry.

At the end of the canyon, Sponge was shouting at Cherine to drop the rocks.

Sponge often forgot that Metalbeak couldn't speak sand gryphon. Thankfully, when she bit the opinicus's tailfeathers, he squawked, and the Padfoot Pride took that as the sign.

Rocks began falling into the canyon, some landing very close to Hoppy.

"No, it's too soon!" Cherine shouted at Sponge as she cooed angrily towards him. "You don't want the rocks to fall on Hoppy!"

He let out a squawk when the sandgrouse bit his tail, and the gryphons pulled the leather straps holding the rocks in place, sending them hurtling towards Hoppy.

For a moment, Cherine thought the giant vulture would get lucky. Then a rock caught it right on the back and it went down.

It was probably dead on impact, but Sponge flung herself at the giant bird, pecking its unmoving head and declaring victory with a coo.

"You okay there, buddy?" Cherine asked the Padfoot pride leader.

Hoppy panted. "Good. Sponge killed bird?"

"Sure." Cherine went to unhook the shiny harness from Hoppy, but the sand gryphon swatted his talons away.

"Is good victory armor," he said. "No good when thunder birds overhead, but took care of that."

"Anything else I can do for you?" Cherine asked.

"Thirsty," Hoppy panted.

Cherine reached up and caught a wet sandgrouse gryphon out of the air and gently set her down next to Hoppy so he could drink. While the pride leader refreshed himself, Cherine wandered over to Sponge, who stood atop the giant bird making cooing noises.

One of the nearby hoopoe gryphons translated. "Cook it!"

Several more took up the chant, and soon the entire canyon was full of gryphons begging Cherine to cook the largest bird he'd ever seen. He sent some of them in search of wood, fire, and spices. Sponge was already chewing on the thunder bird. With some cooing, they organized which parts would be eaten raw and which were for roasting.

Hoppy was still panting on the ground in the shade, so Cherine caught another grouse gryphon out of the air and squeezed some water on top of him.

"Want me to carry you over to thunder bird to eat something?" he asked. "Or would you rather wait for the cooked meat?"

"Killed for Sponge," Hoppy panted. "She eat first. I eat later. Armor is hot. No know how Metalworks do it."

Despite Hoppy's protests, Cherine lifted him up and took off the Crestfall harness. He could feel the sand gryphon's heat radiating out from Hoppy's paws and ears.

"I guess you need to be naked to regulate your body temperature," Cherine commented. Hoppy was already feeling better and ran up to drink Sponge.

Cherine shook his head and got to work creating several fire pits. The nice thing about being surrounded by small gryphons was that they shouldn't eat much. Or so he hoped.

22

CELEBRATION

Cherine was drenched in sweat. In hindsight, lighting a bonfire in the desert in summer was one of his least intelligent moments. Sponge had already led the sand-grouse gryphons to and from the oasis several times to keep everyone hydrated—and to provide moisture for the sauce he was cooking.

The Padfoot gryphlets were brought out from their hidden burrows and had to be dragged away from the fires several times. They were currently in the shade of a ground level home's balcony chewing on Hoppy's harness and trying to get the bits of metal off it.

For the most part, only Sponge wanted the thunder bird raw. Everyone else was willing to wait and nibble as different sections finished cooking. They were less tolerant of salt, which made sense for desert-dwellers, but they didn't seem to mind a little bit. He'd have to look at drying or smoking the extra to preserve it if they were salt-intolerant.

Four sand gryphons pulled over some rocks for Hoppy to stand on so he was eye level with Cherine while they chatted.

"What type opinicus are you?" the sand gryphon asked. Behind him, several of his pridemates flew meat and turquoise beads to the guest cave.

Cherine had been around enough gryphons to know they weren't asking if he was a Redwood Valley opinicus or even about his golden eagle markings. He also knew the proper way to explain his profession so they'd understand: "I'm a food scholar."

A sandgrouse cooed at him, and Hoppy translated. "She want know how become food scholar."

"You start out by cooking a lot of food like this and learning to do it well." He skipped over the part where a meatborne pathogen killed his little brother and inspired him to work at the butchery. "Then you go to the university and learn about the types of food—capybaras, goliath birds, starberries, craneberries, egg fruit, honey. You learn how to acquire, prepare, and mix them to feed the most opinici possible."

He also failed to mention that the only reason he'd been allowed to join the university was that Headmaster Neider had intervened with a scholarship. Thinking about the terrible things that had happened due to Redwood Valley scholars tore out Cherine's heart.

Even here, in the heat, he remembered one cool evening on the shores of Crater Lake where the headmaster introduced him to another apprentice, Kia, who was interested in flora and fauna—though not for eating purposes. They'd become fast friends and then lovers, though that fell apart just before he finished his apprenticeship.

He missed Kia's friendship. He missed Ninox's fierce, caring curiosity. He missed Orlea's conversation, the kind that challenged him to think through the implications of what he did. He even missed Hatzel and Zeph.

A lot of gryphons and opinici had worked very hard to liberate him from the Ashen Weald's prison. Once he was free, however, he'd found himself without a home, without friends to spend time with. It wasn't safe to lounge on the shores of Crater Lake. Not that it was much of a lake after Kia and Zeph blew up the dam.

"Why look sad?" Hoppy asked. "Go home tomorrow. Back to home pride. Eat food there."

"I don't really have a home pride anymore," Cherine said. "I was staying with the owls, but I'm not sure they want me as a member. They're also peculiar."

Sponge cooed and Hoppy translated. "She say she know lots of peculiar gryphons. That what guest cave for. Also say she know real reason you sad."

"Oh?" Cherine asked.

Hoppy nodded. "You say earlier you padfoot and have no pride. Well, we say, you be padfoot and join Padfoot Pride."

Cherine grinned.

"No need to stay here if you no want. You be our... what word?" Hoppy asked. Sponge cooed to him. "Oh, ambassador. No trade with south. You fix that. Bring gryphons north who want metal. We give metal. They give food. Cooked food."

The opinicus scholar considered their offer. "Okay. I may need to rejoin the Redwood Valley Eyrie or the pride my children are in some day, but until then, I would be honored to be a sand gryphon."

"No sand gryphon, just Padfoot Pride," Hoppy said, but Sponge hit him upside the head, her wing traveling in an arc that sprayed everyone nearby with water. "Okay, okay! Sponge say you sand gryphon. Tall sand gryphon. Not... what type of opinici you?"

"Red," Cherine said. "We get called *red opinici* a lot."

Hoppy and Sponge both stared blankly at him. Sponge pointed at the cherry-colored sauce nearby and cooed. Then she pointed at the red rocks of the canyon around them and cooed again.

Hoppy translated. "Red mean something different in opinicus? Not that color?"

"Nope, it means the same thing," Cherine said.

Both sand gryphons were looking right at his shiny metal beak and golden plumage. "Sponge right. Opinici dumb."

Cherine stood and started to put away the cooked meat, packing it so his new pridemates could run it back to their nests and burrows to hide it away for later. "Well, it's a good thing I'm a sand gryphon, then!"

Sponge shook her head and cooed.

Hoppy was too busy chewing on a piece of thunder bird to translate for her.

In fact, all three were so busy they didn't notice the Seraph King's forces until they were already over Crestfall Eyrie.

CHERINE DUCKED behind a pillar right as The Metalworks landed on the dead thunder bird. He had on a stripped-down version of the armor he'd worn at the palace. None of the other white-tailed kites or argent hawks had come with him. Instead, a hundred flamingo landed atop the canyon. On their foretalons they wore glass ornaments set into metal.

Well, that doesn't seem particularly useful in a fight, Cherine thought until he saw their paws. They wore deadly-looking metal claws on their back legs, allowing them to swoop down and lacerate their opponents from the sky.

"By edict of the Seraph King, I demand you turn over the stolen flechettes, armor, and talon weapons," The Metalworks said. "In addition, via order of the Crestfall reeve, you're to vacate *his* eyrie."

"Not his eyrie!" Hoppy shouted from the stables. "Padfoot Pride nesting grounds now. Tell flamingo to go stick his long neck—"

Wherever Hoppy wanted the Crestfall Reeve to stick his long neck was lost in the scuffle that followed. Some of the sand gryphons fought, some ran. Most hid.

Sponge flew nearby and herded Cherine into an abandoned home with a divider between the sleeping nest and the living area. Before she pulled the curtains closed, he could see her wet footprints leading here.

That's not optimal.

By the flamingo profanity and shouting outside, the gryphons were mostly escaping. Unfortunately, one of them had taken offense to the flamingo invasion and was antagonizing the opinici.

"Go away!" Hoppy shouted. "Not your eyrie. My eyrie!"

Either by luck or Sponge's wet footprints, Hoppy led The Metalworks and several flamingos into the same domicile where Sponge and Cherine were hiding, which only had one way in and a small window.

From a tear in the curtains, Cherine could see Hoppy backing up towards their hiding spot.

"You think you special," Hoppy shouted at the Seraph King's commander. "You not. We have our own metal opinicus!"

Cherine only belatedly realized Hoppy was talking

about him when Sponge shoved his back side, forcing just the tip of his beak through the curtains.

"You go now!" Hoppy shouted. "Our metal opinicus kill thunder birds. Not like you. You fly around in armor, wonder why you get hot. Dumb opinicus. Dumber than flamingos. The dumbest!"

Through the slight break in the curtains, Cherine could just make out Hoppy's opponents. They had paused, calculating the chances that Hoppy really had his own version of The Metalworks hidden behind a curtain.

When they stepped forward, Hoppy shouted, "Attack!" and pulled back the curtains with his long beak to reveal Cherine.

The opinicus scholar blinked.

The flamingos and white-tailed kite opinici attacked.

Cherine surrendered quickly, remembering how things had gone with Merin when he'd tried to fight. For what it was worth, his verbose surrender monologue confused the opinici long enough for his friends to escape out the window, though Sponge became stuck and Hoppy had to pull her through, leaving behind a surprisingly large puddle.

"Who are you? What're you doing here?" a flamingo asked Cherine.

He considered the question. "My name is Cherine Metalbeak. I'm a sand gryphon in the Padfoot Pride."

The flamingos looked at him like he was mad. It was a nice step up from the sand gryphons, who looked at him like he was stupid.

The Metalworks poked the badge on Cherine's harness and pointed to the ink stains. "A Redwood Valley scholar. Probably one of Impir's spies who got lost."

More shouting came from down below. "The armor and weapons aren't here! It's empty."

Several flamingo opinici stood on the sand and pointed at the first floor. "They must have hidden it in the desert or traded it to the blackwings."

The Metalworks's lightly-armored tailfeathers twitched back and forth. Cherine could see the calculations going on inside the soldier's mind, but he didn't reach the conclusion Cherine had.

"Let's go," The Metalworks said. "We caught a spy. Mally will know what to do with him. If we see any of the caravan goods around Blacktalon, we'll come back and show these sand squirrels what flechettes are good for."

With a rope secured around his neck, Cherine was led back north towards the Palace of Fire and Ice. Having chased Mally from his tattered grimoire in the weald to his workshops in the mountains to the desert, it was a strange feeling knowing that he'd finally get to meet the Nighthaunt in person.

23

HOPPY AND SPONGE

Hoppy was mad. He'd traded in good faith with the white opinici and flamingos, then they came back and tried to steal his metal.

Thankfully, no one had been seriously injured. The gryphlets had been carried back to the den. There were some scrapes and bruises, a couple of sprained legs from slipping through cracks in the eyrie walls or through windows, and Sponge had lost half of her water weight trying to get out of the window with Hoppy.

But they'd taken Hoppy's opinicus. *Sand gryphon,* he corrected himself when he saw Sponge's expression. He could tell how angry a sandgrouse was by how dry they were. Considering the way she wasn't dripping at all, she was even madder than he was.

She cooed out a plan.

"Can't do," Hoppy said. "Too many flamingos."

More cooing.

He shook his head. "Glass hard to steal. Breaks, scratches, then no one buy."

While the other sand gryphons came back and hid as

much of the remaining thunder bird meat as they could find, Sponge ordered several of them to take bits of metal, hide near the oasis, and put them on the Seraph King's caravans so the thunder birds would attack them.

Hoppy paced. He wanted to get back at the flamingos and white opinici. He could trade some of the metal to the blackwings, but he was still mad at them. They didn't deserve his treasures.

He could fetch Metalbeak's old friends and bring them here. Except Hoppy had never gone south of the glassworks and had no idea what lay beyond its salty shores.

Sponge nuzzled him. No wet spot was left in her wake.

"Okay, I know," he said. "We trade. But no trade metal! We trade what blackwing really want."

Sponge cooed a question.

"Yes!" He nodded with excitement, his crest going up and down. "Trade water and shade rock locations."

More cooing.

"No, no, not all!" he said. "Just few. From Blacktalon to palace. Exchange for Metalbeak."

Sponge puffed up and made a few suggestions to improve his plan.

Hoppy nodded along. "Oh, yes, you right. In exchange for Metalbeak *and* food. I no forget."

Before they left, he checked in on the armory. He was torn between bringing his favorite magic rock with him for luck or grabbing another one that wasn't as good at finding metal. In the end, he decided he needed the good fortune. He wandered through the hidden room, looking at his reflection in the shiny pieces of armor, the rows of glass trinkets, and his special collection.

When he first rearranged his armory, he'd made the mistake of putting the shiny pieces next to his special collection. That had not worked, because Hoppy's special collection was made up entirely of every magic rock they'd been able to steal from the glassworks, eyrie, opinicus outposts, and even some particularly strong magic rocks taken from daring palace raids.

So now the glass section stood between the metal and the magic rocks. And the magic rocks had all been tied down or secured against the wall and ceiling.

Hoppy was, he believed, the richest gryphon on the entire continent. Failing that, the richest gryphon in the desert. In fact, he was probably richer than the opinici, since he now had more magic rocks than they did.

He nuzzled several bars of blacksteel, the metal the blackwings used to make their swirled metal claws with. Perhaps he should try to find a metalworker to make Metalbeak a new beak. A real metal beak, not fake. One that reacted to magic rocks.

If he rubbed some metals on the magic rocks, they became magic for a while. Metalbeak could do that, then stuff his face in the sand to find metal pieces. That would make him very happy, Hoppy thought.

Sponge stuck her head down through a crack in the ceiling and cooed that they were all re-hydrated and ready to go. Several drops of water fell on Hoppy's head as she spoke.

It was time to strike a deal.

REEVE RYBALT REEVESBANE shuffled sea shells across a wooden game board against his favorite opponent, Iony. Rybalt had thought himself miserable in the heat, but his discomfort paled before the pure unmitigated hatred his glacier gryphon friend held for sand.

The heavy desert winds threatened to blow away their small outpost. Where Blacktalon kept watch on the northern section of their border with the desert, a handful of tents and a single tower watched the southern dunes and canyons.

Halfway through their game, Iony stood up, shook himself wildly, and sent a cloud of sand blowing towards the east. "Enough! I've had enough of this. It gets in my ears. It gets in my fur. It gets in my eyes. I even have sand in my—"

"Reeve Rybalt!" a voice shouted from the west.

Rybalt hadn't remembered telling anyone to stand watch against the desert, but it seemed like something he'd do while grumpy—and he was nothing if not grumpy in the desert.

"Yes?" he called out. "Report."

The scout landed. "An army of gryphons is approaching from the south!"

While several of his blackwings strapped on their claws and hardened leather armor, the pitohui tossed off the sheets they'd been wearing to keep from poisoning their allies.

Iony beat Rybalt into the air but called down an all-clear. It took the pitohui a moment to realize how you could have an army of enemy gryphons on your border and get an all-clear. His glacier friend shouted down the identity of the invaders.

"Sand gryphons?" the Reeve's Bane asked the scout. "You interrupted my game for vermin?"

Iony flew out to see what they wanted, then called back. "They're asking to speak to the opinicus in charge. This is

Reeve Hoppy Padfoot, and he won't speak to anyone who isn't of comparable rank."

"Tell him you're a pride leader," Rybalt shouted. He was already pulling over the light, opaque cloth that kept his poison off the scouts and the sun off his back.

The corners of the blanket were frayed, and it seemed mad to Rybalt that he'd managed to successfully steal most of an eyrie's worth of treasure and was still forced to endure ratty blankets in the desert.

Of course, the bulk of the metal beads had gone on ships to every port controlled by the Blackwing Alliance. It was true that some of the wealth was headed back to the Pitohui Eyrie to line his own coffers, but most of it would travel the eastern world being used to buy goods, weapons, and raw materials. Those materials would then find their way to his homeland.

There was always the risk that someone would figure out what he'd done. That's why he'd hidden his wealth well. In every box of live scarabs shipped as food to a pitohui district was a lining of paper-wrapped beads.

There was a tone of amusement in Iony's voice when he coughed to get Rybalt's attention. "He says he won't talk to me after I scruffed one of his pridemates."

"Of course he won't," Rybalt grumbled. He pulled his wings out of the blanket and flew towards the sand gryphons. There were meetings that required full ceremonial pitohui garb, meetings that required his usual outfit, and meetings where anything would do.

From their tent, Impir and Bario looked out at the proceedings. Unlike Rybalt and Iony, they weren't permanently stationed here. They were just on a stopover on their way to Blacktalon with a shipment from the Mothfeather Eyrie. The flameworks wasn't up and running yet, but a saltpeter mine had been opened east of the Sleeping City, and the front lines demanded black powder.

Blacktalon and Whitebeak faced an interesting challenge. There was no safe path across the desert, so they simply amassed arms and soldiers along the edge. In theory, either could go up to the coast and follow it. While there wasn't much freshwater there, the beaches had coconuts and fruits that contained non-saline moisture. An enterprising captain, blackwing or white, could even send a ship along that path.

The issue was the water. The trees were coated in blood lichen. The water was full of blooming crimson algae. It covered boats and crippled opinici and gryphons. One small storm, one wrong wave, and that was it for the crew.

Not that the white opinici had stopped trying. They created boats that were waterproof. Hence the need for Blacktalon to have saltpeter to blow them up with.

The Reeve's Bane landed next to the sand 'reeve.' Iony was in deep conversation with what could have been a wet puffball and not a gryphon. The sandgrouse was attempting to speak owl to Iony, but the glacier gryphon was out of practice.

"How may I help you... Hoppy, I believe you said your name is?" Rybalt asked the head sand gryphon.

"You reeve?" Hoppy asked. He only continued after Rybalt confirmed his rank and that he ruled the Pitohui Eyrie off the coast. "Good. We trade. You give food, salt, firewood."

Rybalt had seen the sand gryphons stealing flechettes and goods from the glassworks and assumed he knew what was coming next, but he went through the motions. There were crates marked for his allies at Blacktalon that contained everything on Hoppy's list. "And what are you offering in return?"

"Water and shade." Hoppy's tone was serious.

"I have both of those things nearby." Rybalt's camp was set up in the closest watering hole to the desert. Though it appeared that without he and Iony to hold down his tent, it was now blowing away.

He sighed.

"No, dumb opinicus," Hoppy said. "Palace, yes?"

Rybalt didn't know if he should be offended. A couple of days ago, he'd been fairly certain sand gryphons couldn't speak common. "The Palace of Fire and Ice? Yes, I know it. The pink reeve is on my list."

The gryphon didn't ask which list that was. "We take you to palace. Through desert. Know shade rocks, water."

Rybalt considered. "How many soldiers could you get to the flamingo's roost?"

"Twenty," Hoppy said. "Water holes fill slowly. No more. Not able to get back if drink all water going there."

Twenty opinici was enough to assassinate a reeve. Or a one way trip with forty, though after all of the blackwings mysteriously failed to survive their expedition into the bog, their reeve had been less interested in assigning more of his subjects to Rybalt's care. Still, without control of the glass-works or his eyrie, the pink reeve was a low priority target. There was no sense in killing a leader who would turn plume the moment another faction owned both sides of the desert.

"Why should we want to go to the palace?" he asked at last. They had their scouts, but the desert wasn't a kind place. It was hard to get anyone across it. Only the sand gryphons knew its true secrets—and a handful of smugglers who refused to divulge their methods.

Hoppy motioned for Rybalt to lean down. The Reeve's Bane did so carefully, saying, "Be careful. My feathers are...oily."

The hoopoe gryphon whispered several magical words into the opinicus's ear hole.

Rybalt looked to Iony. His friend's long ears had picked up everything. "Oh, is *that* what they're hiding out there?"

It was easy to forget there was a war on. Sure, he'd go assassinate someone important. Then the white opinici would throw a fit and send a small force after some low priority target. It was a kind of birdsong and mating dance they played while they waited.

It seemed the Seraph King had grown tired of the Black-wing reeve's courtship ritual and decided to amass enough supplies to finally cross the desert. Rybalt had his own plans that required the war to stay cold awhile longer, but this wasn't something he or Iony could ignore. The glacier pride leader flew to fetch Bario without requiring instructions. They'd need all of the phoenix's black powder for this.

"We'll provide you with the goods, and you provide us with the path tonight. Do we have a deal?" Rybalt asked.

Hoppy started to say yes, but the wet gryphon cooed at him, and he changed his mind. "Also, need you to rescue someone while there. Part of deal. No negotiating!"

Rybalt's left eyecrest went up. "A sand gryphon?"

"No," Hoppy said. More cooing. "Yes, fine, sand gryphon. Sand gryphon in shape of golden opinicus. You rescue, bring home safe. Promise?"

"You have my word." Rybalt didn't have to think. If what the Seraph King was hiding at the palace was true, if the white opinici really had enough food and water to help an army cross the desert, Rybalt needed to get there tonight and take care of it.

In the distance, Bario was out of his tent preparing the explosives. Iony hooted orders to his pride and the pitohui.

"Where would you like your goods?" Rybalt asked. "Food and gryphon, if you want them delivered to different locations."

As Hoppy gave directions on where the sand gryphons would meet them, Rybalt reached into his harness and pulled out a small notebook that smelled of mint. Upon returning to Poisonmaw before heading home after the incident, he'd gone searching for the headmaster. He'd only found this journal written out to Neider's apprentices hiding in a cave and bloodstains in the grove outside. The last time he'd seen Cherine, he was dying of pitohui venom, so it seemed unlikely the journal would return to its intended recipient.

He tore a page out and began to write down the directions.

THE PINK REEVE

CRESTFALL OPINICUS

24

THE PALACE OF FIRE AND ICE

Cherine had never been in a palace before. The Crestfall opinici led him through a side entrance, away from the pools and waterfall he'd only gotten a glimpse of up top. A large wooden structure had been constructed along the western base of the mountain that housed the palace. They brought him through there. Inside was bed and crate after bed and crate. It looked like there should be an army housed here, but instead, they were all empty save four, two of which housed sleeping argent hawks. When he passed by an open crate on his way into the mountain, he saw food and water. Near the indoor goliath stables was a barrel marked blackwater.

There was enough food and water here to house an army overnight. *How long has the Seraph King been sending supplies? Is he hoping to cross the desert?*

Partway through, Hi-kun ordered the Crestfall jailors to take Cherine down a different path. "Let's see if the Nighthaunt recognizes him."

By the heat and humidity, he'd have guessed he was going to a hot springs. The eye-watering smell of chlorine dissuaded him of that notion. Glass tubes went in all directions with different colored liquids flowing through each. He was pushed into a large open cavern where several pools of different shades of purple boiled.

A long opinicus with primaries on his legs and a split tail looked up. He blinked black eyes without pupils at Cherine, taking in the badge, harness, and ink stains. "Redwood Valley University?"

Cherine jumped at the sound. He was expecting a voice. Instead, it was more like a click or a growl that echoed across the cavern. He was grateful to see that the flamingo guards also winced.

"Scholar Cherine," Cherine said. "I was in charge of raising capybaras and running numbers on farm production before the night of the fire."

The black eyes considered him. "What was your thesis on? Who awarded you scholar status?"

"Preservation and preparation as factors in foodborne pathogen prevention." Cherine hadn't expected to be quizzed on his dissertation. He wished he'd had time to prepare notes. "While we eventually found a cure for the monitor plague, I believed there were ways to prevent new meatborne illnesses from killing our children. Headmaster Neider and Felicio were my sponsors."

The Nighthaunt had turned his back and was tending to the pools of purple. With the addition of fire or strainers, several were producing a concentrated salt mixture.

"If I may ask," Cherine began, "what was your dissertation on? All of your old files were sealed except for the nachlass."

"Bats," the creature said. "Squirrels and capybaras, too. I predicted that the storm that brought the red water to our valley was fatal to a relatively new type of creature, of which gryphons are a subspecies, and that it caused the decline in the bat population."

The Nighthaunt continued his work, not looking back. There was a low clicking sound that he sometimes emitted in addition to what passed for speech. "Why did you become a scholar?"

"I wanted to help opinici." Cherine would have liked to amend *gryphons* to his statement, but that was a relatively new development. When he first set out on his journey, he'd never spent two minutes considering that what he did might help them, too—or harm them. The fire and trial had helped strengthen his resolve to make the world better for both opinici *and* gryphons.

"Don't we all?" The sound Mally made was a little like a laugh. There was even a hint of Redwood Valley trill to it. "I believe the pink reeve will want you killed. He's cranky these days. If not, I could use a new apprentice. I imagine you're feeling quite lost since the headmaster's death."

This was the first Cherine had heard of Neider's death, but as he asked his questions, Mally made a sound and the flamingos pulled Cherine upstairs towards the palace proper, where Hi-kun was waiting.

SECTIONS of the mountain had been hollowed out to allow for more passages. Cherine walked past few lit braziers, but the ones he did go near illuminated streams of vibrant liquids flowing alongside him. Belatedly, he realized that most of the chemicals he could identify by scent were potentially toxic. Suddenly, it made sense why you couldn't house a full garrison here for any length of time. In addition to the lack of fresh water and food in the desert, except for what they'd now stockpiled here, prolonged exposure to the steam coming off the pools would be fatal.

And, in fact, Cherine could see the effect it was having on The Metalworks. Hi-kun did not look well. With his heavy armor, he was breathing in more of the fumes than Cherine and had developed a cough.

"You really shouldn't stay here," Cherine told the white opinicus. "None of this is healthy. You can develop some very severe conditions if you keep breathing in all of this. Honestly, none of you should be here! Who thought colored sulfur water would make a nice decoration?"

The Crestfall opinici laughed at him, and it occurred to Cherine that they must have been living out here for years or at least long enough to have built a palace. Perhaps the flamingos had a natural immunity. If they did, Hi-kun didn't share it.

"We'll be done here before long," Hi-kun said. "I hope to never return to this abyssal place again."

"Soon, the eyrie will be ours again," one of the guards said. "It'll be nice to return home."

Cherine thought back to the long, red rock canyons in the desert and the thousands of homes he'd seen there. The plateau that housed the strange salt pools and palace wasn't large enough to have relocated everyone.

He thought about asking but decided he'd better not. The Seraph King and Blackwing reeve's war had raged up north long before it reached the Crackling Sea and Redwood Valley Eyries. As much as he loved his new sand gryphon pridemates, they didn't need an entire canyon's worth of opinicus homes.

The passage gave way into a room the size of the largest university auditorium. The northern wall was all pink glass. The southern opened up into several toxic pools that flowed over the ledge, creating the waterfall he'd seen when the sand gryphons had come to trade. The ceiling of the palace was obscured by a thousand hanging chimes. There was more water than dry land up here, and he carefully followed the path between pools of different colors.

By his estimate, perhaps four hundred opinici filled the top of the plateau. Their plumage ranged from an off-color grey for the servants up to the most vibrant shade of pink for Crestfall's reeve.

"Why are those ones grey?" he asked The Metalworks while they waited for the reeve to acknowledge them.

Hi-kun pointed to the small bowls of food. "The shrimp."

The reeve's advisor motioned to Hi-kun, and the guards escorted Cherine across the center of the court. In front of the throne was a large pool fed from a hot springs underground. It had a thick glass covering, which Cherine now stood on. Despite the toxic smell, the water beneath his paws was full of shrimp and other small creatures.

"My lord reeve," The Metalworks began, "we present you with a spy we found in your eyrie. He claims to be a sand gryphon."

The honking sound of flamingo laughter filled the court.

Crestfall's reeve was the most vibrant shade of pink Cherine had seen. He was almost painful to look at. The reeve's harness was dyed the same color as his feathers and fur and was practically invisible. Glass trinkets and baubles seemed to be suspended directly from the opinicus himself. Glass bracelets adorned each of his limbs. Swirled glass was wrapped around the base of his neck, prompting Cherine to wonder how he got it on and off.

The base of his throne had waves of glass coming off of it. The glass alternated red and blue, creating a sense of both fire and waves. The backing of the throne reached into the sky like a tree of quartz. Chimes and trinkets hung from the branches. According to the old texts, each represented a past reeve to rule over the palace.

From his throne, the pink reeve inspected Cherine. "A scholar with a sense of humor? How rare. Okay, *sand gryphon,* who are you?"

"My name is Cherine, and I was a scholar at the Redwood Valley University." Several long-necked heads turned to look at Cherine when he said that.

"How is my dear Brevin?" the pink reeve asked. "How many daughters is she up to? Twelve?"

"Nine, Lord Reeve," Hi-kun said. "And the red reeve has seen better days."

Crestfall's reeve shot Hi-kun a look that silenced him. "Have you traveled to the valley? No? Then I'll hear it from one of the reds himself."

"Reeve Brevin is dead," Cherine said. "Her daughters were later killed by the blackwings. Her eyrie lies in ruin."

"Then why hasn't your *king* taken those lands, Commander?" the pink reeve hissed at Hi-kun.

"Reeves and eyries aren't what they used to be." The Metalworks didn't back down. "We control the blue reeve. A king built the Redwood Valley Eyrie. A king can rebuild it."

The flamingo extended his neck towards the foreigners. "Not the same king."

"Excuse me," Cherine interrupted. "The Crackling Sea has no reeve. It hasn't for years now. How can you control its reeve when it hasn't one?"

"We have the crown, talons, and heir," Hi-kun said. "With the blessing of the king, that's all it takes to make a reeve."

"What good is a reeve without an eyrie?" Crestfall's leader rolled his eyes.

Hi-kun made a show of looking around the palace. "Indeed."

The white opinicus held the pink reeve's gaze. The flamingo's talons dug into the cushion, but he didn't order his guest killed. At least, not that guest.

"I tire of your Redwood diversion," Crestfall's reeve said at last. "Chain him to the far pools and let him freeze to death. We'll feed his body to the shrimp in the morning."

"As you wish, Lord Reeve." The Metalworks motioned to the guards, who began to take Cherine towards the southern edge of the pools.

The food scholar tried to be strong—this wasn't his first time facing death—but his legs went weak once he was out of the court and the flamingo guards had to carry him the rest of the way to the edge.

25

THE RED REEVE

Piprik chirped a greeting to Zeph and Kia when they met up later in the day. But when Kia explained what she needed of Brevin's child, Lei threw a fit.

"That's not me," he protested. "I won't do it."

Kia looked to Piprik for help, but he was at a loss. Something had changed in his apprentice ever since taking Ellore her food.

Piprik didn't know what that was, but it went against *their* plans, too. "Lei, aren't you here to help your subjects? Kia's parents are part of those opinici. Why not do a test run? If you can rally the refugees, it'll make it easier to convince them to return home."

Lei was unwavering. He stood adamant that he wouldn't put on the Redwood Valley harness, badge, or his mother's infamous talons. "We'll do it another way."

It took Kia pleading another two hours while Piprik mixed ingredients to convince Lei. And it wasn't really Kia's words so much as Piprik and Lei's secret that ultimately swayed the peacock's heart, as he admitted when Kia went to fetch her parents.

"If it'll help with Olan, I'll do it one last time." The peacock's unhappiness was palpable.

Zeph cast a worried look to Piprik, who shook his head. He'd known his apprentice had become more Lei than Levin, but their plan had always been to use their alter-egos of reeve heiress and Eyes of the Seraph King to save as many refugees as they could. It seemed Lei was no longer on board with that plan. He was still determined to help the Redwood Valley opinici, but he didn't want to do it as Brevin's youngest daughter.

"You said you had a surprise guest for me to meet?" Zeph asked to distract from Lei and Kia's fight.

Piprik motioned towards a nearby maple. Partway up the tree, their ex-prisoner was hiding.

"Oh!" Zeph said. "I didn't see you there. Hello, how are you? My name is Zeph. I hear we're helping you get home?"

"Not home. Just east." Ellore hesitated before spreading her blue heron wings and gliding down. Her eyes were clear, but the silver stains remained. "Nice hat."

Zeph looked at her curiously.

"Her name is—" Piprik began.

"—Ellore," she finished.

Zeph's hackle feathers went up. "You poisoned the taiga. You nearly got Younce killed."

"Yes." Ellore didn't deny it. "He claimed to be Mignet's friend but he let my daughter fall in with a *kjarr* gryphon, and it cost her life. I know who you are, copper hawk, despite your disguise. What kind of friend were *you* to my daughter?"

Zeph hissed. "Mignet's death was an accident."

"What I did wasn't." Ellore walked right past Zeph and speared a piece of jerky with her beak, using her talons to remove it and toss a chunk in her mouth. "Are you Ashen

Weald, little lost taiga gryphon? Do you run behind Satra licking at the same paws that held my daughter's head under the water?"

Zeph's had puffed up to twice his usual small size. He circled around the deposed ranger lord. "Is there anyone you haven't betrayed? Why are you still alive? Why don't we kill you before you do more harm?"

Lei put down the mortar and pestle he was working and started shouting. "Because of me, okay? Ellore was kind to *me* when I was just a frightened little fledgling who couldn't fly. Ellore helped Bruen and Quess, and those are *my* friends. I'm only alive because Impir owed Ellore a favor."

When Zeph opened his beak, Lei shut him down and kept talking. "You killed my mom! All of you kill too much. You and Kia and Rorin and Tresh. You can't just keep killing opinici or gryphons. It's not solving anything.

"I look at Silver and she's not that different from Quess. Everyone on all sides is the same, and there has to be a solution this time that isn't just... killing someone and walking away. That's not working."

Lei turned and started walking into the woods.

"Lei..." Zeph began, but the peafowl waved a talon in the air to stop him.

"I'm going to put my Redwood harness on," Lei said. "I'll be my mom's daughter one last time. We'll see if it works. But that's it. If this fails, we're just leaving the refugees here."

Piprik had nearly finished preparing the ingredients. He wondered if his son had the same character, if there was any way for him to find out. "Ellore, you know what blastwort looks like, yes? Could you fetch a little more for me."

Zeph's fur and feathers slowly smoothed down when the heron opinicus left. "I didn't want to kill Brevin. I didn't even mean to."

Piprik looked up from his makeshift alchemy lab in the forest. "Zeph, you can make the right decision and still have it hurt people. That doesn't mean you shouldn't feel bad or try to do better next time. It's just life sometimes."

The copper hawk gryphon looked helpless. He milled about a little longer, then finally asked, "What are you making?"

Ellore returned with the blastwort. "Will this do?"

"It will." Piprik pulled out two pages. "This here is the formula we used in the Emerald Jungle. I'm sure Mally has improved upon it by now, but it gives us a hint of how the purple salts work."

Ellore and Zeph both nodded along.

"This is what we found in Mally's lab whenever we got near where they actually use or store the salts." Piprik held up the other piece of paper listing the ingredients that couldn't be brought past that point. "I don't know how much elixir he has hidden away. I don't know if he has crates of salt hiding back home, but I don't think he'd be right here next to the desert where the shipments come from if he had a stockpile. And I do think, based on both of these pages, that I have a good idea of what kind of mixture would completely ruin the source of the salts if we tossed it in."

Zeph's eyes got wide.

Ellore laughed. "I hope you don't mind if I tell the black-wings this was part of one of my plans. I may need the good will."

"Lei came back different after he talked to you." Piprik took advantage of Ellore's temporary good mood. "What happened? What changed?"

"I..." Ellore paused to consider both Piprik and Zeph. "I called him Levin. I thought he'd want to go north and be treated like a reeve. He looked so happy when he was Levin, youngest daughter of the reeve. I just have a hard time seeing that sweet little chick as a fisherfolk."

Piprik changed the subject before Lei returned. "Do you think your smuggler would be willing to take two more with him? I'm old and frail. Lei's going to be needed here to keep the reds in line. But I'd like for Zeph and Kia to take this mix to the palace and poison the well. It might create a divide between Mally and the king. If nothing else, it should delay his experiments a while longer."

Left unsaid were his thoughts that he didn't want Kia around when they tried to evacuate Olan from the workshop. It was better if she didn't see how her brother looked. With luck, they might be able to reverse the damage if Piprik could get Olan to New Eyrie.

Ellore shined her Blackwing badge. "Considering what you're going there to do? I'm sure I can persuade him."

There came a rustle from the woods. Zeph and Ellore crouched down like the predators they were. Piprik wondered idly if it the smells had attracted a megapede. Instead, it was Lei who walked through the underbrush.

The metal talons of the Redwood reeve glistened in the light, complimenting his blue and gold harness. Henders's badge was polished to a shine.

There was something else, however, that Piprik only now noticed. Lei had been using bits of feather paint to change the shape of the markings around his eyes. He'd been holding himself differently. With that gone, Piprik could see Levin and Mi-Lei again.

"Where are—" Lei cleared his throat, made a few chirp noises, and then tried again with his old voice. "Where are we meeting Kia?"

PIPRIK GUIDED Lei to a break in the maple trees outside of the argent hawks' patrol route. He was finding he liked the forest here. It was pleasant, and while not altogether familiar, it reminded him a little of the trees where he'd grown up.

Back home on the ranch, a tall tree wasn't one you could perch in as an opinicus. Squirrels and songbirds might hide in its canopy, but they were thin and small. Going to the Emerald Jungle had been a shock. The emerald broadleaf and emerald spiketrunk trees made up the foliage there. Both reached high into the sky, creating shadows that followed you no matter where you went. The redwood forest near Swan's Rest was even more massive, though without the spikes.

It was nice to be around flora that didn't dwarf him. It was nice to be in the north again, even if he was on the wrong side of the desert.

"Greyfeather Pip?" Lei asked.

Piprik shook his head. "Sorry, sorry. My brain was up in the canopy playing with the squirrels. Are you ready? They should be here any moment."

Ellore and Zeph had stayed behind. Ellore, because anyone's first reaction at seeing her would be to assume she was either an Ashen Weald or Blackwing spy. Zeph, because no one could think of a good reason to put the Reeve's Bane on display while trying to earn the trust of Brevin's biggest supporters. Piprik didn't trust his disguise to live up to close scrutiny, either.

"They're going to want my mother, right?" Lei asked. "How did she act around other opinici?"

"I don't know," Piprik admitted. His route from Emerald Jungle to Swan's Rest had deliberately avoided both the

Crackling Sea and Redwood Valley Eyries. "How did she act around you?"

Lei paused. "She used to tuck us in every night. After the Crackling Sea, she was terrified that Rybalt was going to come kill us in our nests while we slept. She'd tell a story about snakes to each of us, then kiss us on the forehead and go back to work at Reeve's Nest."

Piprik wasn't sure how to respond. There was a saying amongst the Mothfeather opinici: even a monitor has a mother.

"But she was a monster, wasn't she?" Lei asked.

"Yes." Piprik put a talon on Lei's shoulder. "You can be the best of your mother without being the worst of her, too. You know that, right?"

Lei nodded.

"Good. Now, here's how the reeves I've met held themselves." Piprik had just finished going over confidence and what questions didn't need responses when Kia arrived.

Her parents were a mixture of reds and blues with a hint of green, leaving Piprik to wonder what color Olan had been before walking into Mally's workshop.

"My name is Reeve Levin, daughter of Reeve Brevin, sister to Grand Reeve of the Twin Eyries Ivess," Lei said.

It was a little wordy, but Piprik's advice had been to remind these opinici of their former loyalties. It also had the intended effect of making both of Kia's parents kneel in the presence of their ruler.

"Where have you been?" Kia's mom asked.

"How did you survive?" Kia's father echoed.

Both were questions Lei had been prepared for. "My sister ordered a captain named Henders to get me out of the city as Impir's poison took hold. I've been raised by advisors and tutors ever since, waiting in secret."

This answer satisfied them, so Lei continued. "I know our home is ash and ruin. If you want to stay among the Seraph King's lands, I won't stop you. But I believe the south has a proud heritage, and it's poorer for losing you. Will you turn back and help rebuild? The northerners' conflict isn't ours. There's a lot of good left to be done, and we can do it together."

"Pardon my hesitation, Reeve Levin," Kia's mother said. "It's been a long year. We're tired of living in tents and eating squirrels. We just want to feel safe."

"I'm tired of brackish water and food," Kia's father said. "I just want to rest. Our son has an orchard up north. We'll be headed up soon to be with him."

Kia looked at Lei and silently pleaded with him. Piprik shook his head to dissuade Lei from doing what he knew his apprentice wanted to do next.

His apprentice sided with Kia.

"Olan isn't up north," Lei said. "He's being held in Mally's workshop. I saw him myself. There are thirty more of my subjects in there, and none of them are healthy."

Kia turned to Piprik in alarm. He nodded the truth of the matter.

"You don't have to stay at New Eyrie," Lei said. "Our home is gone. Our people are scattered. I'm as much the reeve as a ground parrot. But will you help me free the last of our sick? Will you help me carry them to get treatment? Piprik here is the best doctor in the south. If anyone can find a cure, he can."

What happened next was a lot of crying, disbelief, and anger. Partway through it, Lei adopted his masculine voice again out of habit. There was distrust, even between Kia and her parents, but they said they'd talk to the other refugees.

If it was true, if Lei could produce Olan and the other

test subjects, the Redwood Valley refugees would return home. That just left Piprik and Lei to try to convince Kia to go with Zeph and work the elixirs instead of staying behind to go into the workshop.

This proved to be an uphill battle.

26

THE OPINICUS SMUGGLER

I t took Piprik the rest of the afternoon to convince Kia that, as the best flyer among them, she was needed in the desert. It was nearly dark when they reached Ellore's hiding spot to wait for the smuggler. Their strange group stood in a small blind spot formed by the convergence of several boulders on the edge of the desert.

What caught Piprik off guard more than Kia's acceptance was the appearance of an old acquaintance.

When the smuggler showed himself near sunset, he seemed just as surprised to see Piprik. The privateer's dark, parakeet plumage was the same as it had been when they shared a raft off the bog coast. What wasn't as familiar was a strange, new addition—the feathers around the smuggler's eye, the start of his crest, and part of his face were bright green. Upon closer inspection, the green feathers were a different consistency than the dark ones. His eyes, too, no longer matched in color or size.

"Ellore, I have standing orders to take you across." He turned to Piprik and tilted his head to the side, inviting the white opinicus to introduce himself however he liked.

"Greyfeather Pip," he said. The name he'd given the smuggler when they'd met in the Jadebeak Mountains had been neither Piprik nor Khalim. He didn't have to ask how a smuggler came to work for the blackwings. You didn't get markings like that unless someone dipped your face into a boiling vat of purple elixir.

"Zeph," the copper hawk continued, filling the silence. "This is Kia, and that's Lei. Just me and Kia are coming along with you two."

The smuggler nodded. "I need a few words alone with Ellore."

They walked out to another boulder where the smuggler had tied up a ground parrot-sized desert monitor. It licked the air with its tongue and looked east. From the few words that filtered over, there was a disagreement as to whether or not the smuggler could get Zeph and Kia to the palace and what the price would be.

Everyone was confused when he sent Ellore back and asked for Pip to come over.

"Why's he want to talk to you?" Zeph asked.

"As the eldest, he probably wants me to talk some sense into Ellore," Piprik lied. "That's very common for several eyries where parakeet opinici live. I'll see what I can do."

Once he and the parakeet were out of earshot, the smuggler started in on Piprik. "What's going on here? What do you have to do with them? Is this some sort of setup?"

"Have I ever lied to you or set you up?" Piprik asked. "I paid you exactly what you asked for. I never told a soul."

The smuggler's mismatched eyes narrowed as he tried to figure out the angle.

"What happened to your ship?" Piprik prompted. "I thought you ran the trade lanes down south."

"The bleeding starlings happened to my trade lanes. As did the Seraph King *and* the blackwings."

"Yet you work for the blackwings," Piprik said.

"I'm a smuggler," the parakeet replied. "I take any opinicus where they need to go if the price is right."

Piprik pointed at the splotch of green plumage. "I don't know how you got those, but I sure as the depths know who gave them to you. Take Kia and Zeph to the palace. They have a surprise for the Seraph King. It'll be like getting revenge."

"I figured out who you are," the smuggler said.

Piprik tensed.

The parakeet continued. "Rybalt would pay a pretty price to know where the Eyes of the Seraph King is hiding."

"Will you tell him?" Piprik's body was already relaxing. He was less worried about anyone knowing where he was as Piprik so much as someone telling Mally where his family as Khalim was located.

"I will," and the smuggler meant it. "Do you have any idea what the blackwings would do to me if they found out I ran into you and didn't tell them?"

"Will you get Zeph and Kia to the palace before you do?" Piprik asked.

The smuggler grinned. "Aye. I'll do that much for you."

Well, that'll have to do, Piprik thought.

He went back to where the group was hiding. "He says he'll take Zeph and Kia. Once Ellore gets to the other side, he's going to tell Rybalt he saw the Eyes of the Seraph King here."

"Who?" Kia and Zeph asked.

"An opinicus I bear a passing resemblance to," Piprik said. "You three go on ahead. Kia, you know how to handle the elixir. You take care of that. Lei and I will get your brother out and head south. When you're done, don't come back to Whitebeak. Get home however you can."

Zeph and Kia went out to meet the smuggler, keeping their distance from his sand monitor. Lei and Ellore were less ready to part. There were a lot of unspoken words between them, then there were a few spoken.

"I won't tell the blackwings who you are," she said at last. "Who you were. Go on, Lei of Ashfoot Isle. I'm sorry this is how you get to see me, but I'm not sorry I got to see you again."

Lei hesitated, but ultimately gave in and hugged Ellore. He reached into his harness pouch and pulled out the peacock talons. "When no one is watching, tell Rybalt he left these behind in the bog."

Ellore looked confused, but Lei was already flying back to the maples, so she turned to Piprik. "And whose side are you on?"

"Hmm?" He looked up from taking a few notes for later. "Oh, I'm a medicine opinicus from Swan's Rest. If you'll excuse me, I'm needed elsewhere."

27

SAND SWIMMERS

Once the sun had gone down, Zeph shivered in the cool night air. The smuggler had a strange method for traversing the desert. He held a somewhat tame desert monitor beneath him in a special harness pouch while he flew. Every so often, he'd land and let the lizard loose.

"Locals call them sand swimmers," he explained at their first stop. It had its own harness and leash. It would sniff around and do one of two things. If it buried itself in the sand, the smuggler would dig it back up, and they'd fly away. But if it ran off in a direction, there was either a small hideaway or fresh water there.

"How'd you train a lizard to sniff for water?" Kia asked. "And how big do the desert monitors grow?"

"Big as a gryphon, if you believe the tales," the smuggler said. "And it's not water he can smell. Most of the liquid we find out here we have to dig for. His nose ain't that good."

"Then how does he know where the water is?" Kia sketched the lizard in her notebook by the moonlight.

The smuggler pointed towards a rock near the watering hole and told her to smell.

When she did, she pulled back her beak and made a face. "What *is* that?"

Ellore rolled her eyes, refusing to participate in the impromptu lesson.

Zeph sniffed. The scent was acrid. "Oh, a gryphon marked this rock."

The parakeet peered at Zeph's boots and hat. "Didn't realize we had a four-paw with us. I coulda had you smell for them. But yeah, the sand gryphons mark 'em. As long as you leave behind a thank you token, they don't mind."

Despite his words, he didn't seem to mean anything by the paw comment. Zeph supposed the parakeet had to deal with whoever could pay him and wasn't too particular about if it was a gryphon or opinicus who had the beads.

In contrast to the general appearance of his hat, it had kept his head warm, and Kia looked cold. Having already been discovered as a gryphon, he offered it to her.

With a sigh, she put it on. Since she had blue in her plumage, it didn't look nearly as silly as it did on a brown copper hawk.

The smuggler made a show of pulling out a string of cheap imitation turquoise beads and burying them next to the stone. "See? Nothing to it, so long as you know the general area to look. Well, smell."

They ate some jerky, drank the sandy water, and talked a little about how strange the desert was.

"It's time to head out," the parakeet commanded.

"I need to pee before we go," Zeph said, but the smuggler just shook his head.

"That's a no go." He pointed to the marked rock. "You don't want your scent near theirs. There are hundreds, maybe over a thousand sand gryphons out here, and they *will* track you down. They look sweet and cuddly, but their beaks are like fisherfolk spears. I also don't want any thunder birds finding your scent where I might return back to. They've been known to stake out locations opinici have been. Last thing you want is giant vultures guarding all the good watering holes."

"But..." Zeph began.

"Hold it," the parakeet warned. "Fly with your legs crossed if you need to. We'll take a small detour in an hour and everyone can pee then."

Zeph whimpered but obeyed the command. He'd never seen a sand gryphon before and wondered if they were large or small. Maybe they had tiny wings but huge heads. Or huge wings and tiny heads.

He laughed to himself at the image, earning him a look of disdain from Ellore. As they flew, Ellore and Kia had spoken about Mia. It was a few stops later before she asked the question that was on Zeph's mind.

"How do we find any sort of peace with the northern eyries?" Kia asked Ellore.

"How should I know?" This watering hole was shallower than usual, and Ellore had trouble drinking with her long beak. They were under strict commands not to drink all the water, leaving half in case they ran into trouble and needed to backtrack.

When Kia kept looking at Ellore, the ranger gave up and answered. "I didn't choose the blackwings because I thought it would bring peace. I joined because I thought it was the only way to get to stay in my home. And because I thought the Crackling Sea had lost its way."

Kia fished through her bags, locating a piece of paper. She lit a rushlight and wrote out a letter of some sort. While Ellore was busy trying to figure out what Kia was doing, Zeph slipped in beneath her and drank from the water.

"Here you go." Kia folded the letter and handed it to Ellore, who was no less confused. "At some point, one of the eyries north of the Redwood Valley is going to want to open up trade with the south. Famine, sickness, red fern—something will be more tempting than whatever the Blackwing reeve promised. When that happens, have one of the glacier pride take that note to Ninox or Hatzel's pride, and we'll send Bruen or Mia to meet you near Poisonmaw. Just to talk."

Zeph's ears pricked up. Something was making a high-pitched noise southeast of them.

Ellore didn't respond to Kia's entreaty, but she did put the letter away in her harness.

"Do you hear that?" Zeph asked.

Kia lifted up the sides of the hat. "Hear what?"

"This way." The smuggler blew out the rushlight and guided them past several dunes to a boulder. "Watch for scorpions. Don't make a sound until it's gone."

They huddled up together for warmth against the rock. Although the moon was high, Zeph couldn't see anything. Instead, all he could hear was the sound of... something. Bats? Night birds?

The clicking came close, then turned away several times. It went silent right before a large desert monitor let out a squeal of pain.

Not a hundred feet away, they could hear a large animal eating the dead monitor. None of them made a sound.

The smuggler put his talons over the harness pocket where he kept his pet. Ellore looked confused, but Zeph and Kia had some idea of what might hunt in the night after crossing the Nighthaunt in the bog.

When the sounds of eating ended, one last round of clicks came, then silence. In the moonlight, Zeph could just make out a white shape with feathered legs flying towards a crack in the mountain nearby.

"How close are we to the palace?" he asked.

The smuggler pointed a talon towards where the figure had gone. "That's it. We're here. I just figured I'd keep you two close while me 'n Ellore drank."

"Do you know where Mally's workshop is?" Kia asked.

"My job is to bring opinici past the palace unseen, not poke around inside," the smuggler huffed. "You're going to have to find that on your own."

Zeph pointed his beak towards the crack at the plateau's base.

Kia nodded, then turned to the parakeet. "Thank you for your help. If you ever want to work for someone who isn't embroiled in war, find me down south. Pip said you used to run rafts? Ask for me at Swan's Rest."

The smuggler made a noncommittal noise. "When you need to get back, have your gryphon sniff around the places we stopped until he smells the sand gryphon markings. Those'll lead him to the water. Should be safe. We didn't drain any, and they tend to replenish with the morning dew on the rocks."

The smuggler and Ellore left Zeph and Kia to brave the last bit of desert together, disappearing into the darkness on their path to Blacktalon.

ZEPH CREPT TOWARDS THE PLATEAU. The same moonlight that illuminated the shape in the desert seemed to make Kia's feathers glow, so he'd scout a bit, look around, and then chirp for her to come out from hiding and follow.

The palace atop the plateau wasn't visible from this

close. Instead, rocks and sand stretched out in all directions, and a barracks was nestled against the base. Next to the barracks was the crevice the Nighthaunt had fled into. It had no guards, but charms and baubles decorated either side of the entrance.

Zeph stopped to listen as he drew close. The sound of glass chimes filled the night, making it hard to hear the sounds of any guards who could be lurking around the corner. He put a paw inside, seeing two passages, then stopped to sniff. He'd become so accustomed to trying to smell out sand gryphon markings that he was overwhelmed by strong scent of black powder surrounding a small barracks to his right.

"Saltpeter," he whispered to Kia.

Her eyes widened. "Is it a trap? We should hurry. We don't want to be anywhere near here when it goes off."

If it was a trap, it didn't seem to be for them. With Zeph's nares, they managed to follow the scent of monitor blood. Most of the pathways led upwards and reeked of sulfur. Only one way led down. When they heard the sound of guards ahead, they had to stop and reconsider.

"Do you still have the Crackling Sea toxin?" Zeph asked, and Kia nodded. "Okay, then we don't have to kill anyone. We can just knock them unconscious. Put it on your talons, I'll distract the guards, and you claw them until they black out."

"On my talons?" Kia asked. "And knock myself unconscious every time my butt itches? I don't think so."

Zeph had to cover his beak to hide his laughter. Kia had come a long way from scholar to fisherfolk and back again.

"Okay, fine," he said. "Even if I take off the boots, my claws retract, so I can't put it on them. Do we have anything sharp?"

She went through her harness pockets and brought out one of her pens. "This worked on the argent hawks. As long as the guards here aren't armored, we should be good."

Zeph missed the first hints of what a Crestfall opinicus looked like—the tall ceilings. So he was surprised when he rounded the corner and came up to the tops of the knees of the two guards there—whose necks reached even higher—and immediately ran between their legs.

"Was that a sand gryphon?" one asked.

While they stretched their long necks down to look back between their legs at the scampering shape that had run past, Kia pricked each with her toxin-laced quill pen, rendering them unconscious before they figured out what was going on.

Zeph's ruse worked on two more sets of guards before they reached the workshop. They waited outside, listening for the clicking in the desert.

"There's someone in there," Zeph said. "I think it's Mally. He's going to be able to see us in the dark."

Two paths led into the Nighthaunt's chamber. The one they came up was now full of unconscious flamingos.

From the other came Hi-kun. "The salts are packed up in the barracks. I put the blackwater at the other end, where the sun won't light them up come morning. We'll get the goliath birds ready at dawn and head back."

Both Zeph and Kia shivered when Mally spoke. It had been months since the incident at the dig site, but neither would ever forget the sound of his voice.

"When the army arrives, will they raze the palace?" the black-eyed opinicus asked. "No, no, don't tell me. I imagine that's up to the Seraph King's whim. Tell your soldiers that these pools are to be protected at all costs. Anyone who interferes with the king's ascension will be split open and tossed into the sea for the blue reeve's pet."

"My soldiers know their job," Hi-kun said. "Come up with me so we can pay our respects to the pink reeve when he wakes. I don't want to wait in line for hours for the sake of formalities. Not when our own forces will soon reach Whitebeak."

"Indeed. The depths forbid we forsake politeness at this point." It was strange hearing sarcasm from the Nighthaunt's beak. "Certainly not after Crestfall has been so kind to us."

The sound of Mally's strange feet on the stone continued up the passage without the unconscious flamingos, giving Zeph and Kia their opening.

Zeph kept watch on the hallway while Kia searched her harness for Piprik's chemicals and began mixing them and tossing them in pools. They had to light the braziers to tell, but the springs seemed to be changing color. Purple, pink, a lighter pink, and then black. It was like the pools were a living organism that had just been poisoned. The bodies of shrimp and water bugs floated to the surface.

The strange water systems inside the plateau must have been connected because soon pools she hadn't touched were turning black.

"Looks like we did it," Kia said. "Now it's time to get out of here."

Shouting came from a passage. To Zeph's surprise, it wasn't the one with the incapacitated guards. Instead, the commotion was coming from the way Mally and Hi-kun had gone.

The sound of the baubles on Crestfall harnesses jingled as flamingos ran around above them.

"Sounds like the wind chimes outside my old nest at the

university," Kia said. "But wait, they can't be here for us, can they?"

The jingling grew louder.

While her sense of smell was the same as any opinici's, Zeph began to detect the scent of other gryphons—glacier gryphons—and decided he didn't want to stick around to see how they fit into the saltpeter he'd smelled in the barracks.

"Time to go!" He pushed Kia down the safe passage just as several guards rushed into Mally's chamber.

While she struggled to get over the bodies of prone flamingos, Zeph was in his element. He was used to the crowded foliage of the Redwood Valley, so he knew how to manage a little hop-glide with his wings half-closed to get down the path.

The tall ceilings made this even easier. Kia was lagging behind since she was used to the open skies where she could fly circles around him.

"Who's the better flyer now?" he turned to call back to Kia.

A moment later, he was tangled up in some hanging chimes.

She sighed and pulled out her fishing knife, a gift from Rorin for helping Swan's Rest open up trade with the weald, and cut Zeph down. He landed on his feet and returned to searching for the path out—mindful of the hanging chimes this time.

They got outside just in time to hide. As they slipped behind some sand gryphon-marked hiding rocks below the southern plateau face, Zeph caught sight of a very bright red opinicus lighting a fuse with a rushlight, blowing it out, and then flying towards the top of the plateau.

He turned to ask Kia if she'd seen that, but she was sniffing the rocks.

"Does this smell like ink to you?" she asked. "Like expensive ink, Crackling Jade ink?"

He blinked. She was right. It smelled like Redwood Valley ink. A fact he only knew because Cherine's harness stains always had that scent to them.

He followed the smell to the back of the cave. He located the inkwell and dragged it to the hideaway entrance. "Is this Cherine's?"

Kia held it up to the moonlight. "It could be. How did he make it this far from the glassworks on his own?"

28

THE PINK REEVE'S DAUGHTER

Before nightfall, Cherine's feet burned in the pools—both from their temperature and the chemicals. Once the sun went down, the boiling water quickly turned luke-warm, chill, cold, and then into ice, freezing him in place.

The toxic pools spanned the top of the plateau, though most were in the palace itself. The pools feeding into the cerulean blue waterfall were all along the southern edge, where he now sat. The waterfall had gone silent as the water froze. From this height, with nothing better to do, he could see what appeared to be a dry riverbed that stretched to the south. He'd heard some of the sand gryphons brag about catching gryphonflies, some sort of giant flying bug that only came out during the wet season. Perhaps the dry, cracked bed had been a true river back in the spring.

Four guards stood in a circle around him, indifferent to the extreme temperatures. To Cherine's surprise, they only put their avian halves in the water, keeping their furry back paws out. They balanced in such a way that pulled three of their legs up under their feathers and wings while only one leg was in the water.

Cherine asked them all manner of questions about the pools—what were they made of, what lived in them, how long had they been here—but they ignored him. Whether they weren't interested in extreme organism adaptations or just found him annoying, he wasn't sure.

But he knew a way to find out.

"Hey, guards! Why do Crestfall opinici stand on one leg?" he asked.

One of them opened an eye to glare at him.

"So they don't fall down." Cherine grinned.

The guard let out a sigh. "We should have tied his beak shut before we froze."

While Cherine tried not to think about frostbite, exposure, or being food for shrimp, he looked up at the stars. He saw the five stars that made up the Fantail Constellation. He could just see the Northern Cross, the set of stars fisherfolk used for navigation.

He was about to open his beak to talk about how the bog pride actually had a different name for the northern cross—a name that translated to *Leafcutter Swarm*—when he saw the dark plumage of an opinicus staring at him from a nearby ledge.

Cherine shut his beak and tried to wave, forgetting his legs were all frozen into the pool. Instead, he tossed his beak into the air.

The black and orange opinicus seemed to be rubbing his temples as though he had a headache. Along with two more pitohui and a long-eared grey owl gryphon, they crept up on the sleeping guards and killed them where they stood.

Even in death, they remained upright, balanced on one leg.

Rybalt stared at Cherine and seemed to want to say something several times. When he finally spoke, it was with a story. "Do you know the fable of the pink reeve's daughter?"

Cherine shook his head. He always enjoyed hearing the stories of other eyries and prides.

"Generations ago, the reeve of Crestfall had a daughter," Rybalt began. "Her love of all things pink sent her across the continent. Everywhere she went, she found herself in peril from snakes, monitors, starlings, and padfeet. Everywhere she went, a handsome guard captain showed up at just the right time to save her from mortal danger."

"Oh!" Cherine said. "Are you my handsome guard captain?"

Rybalt's headache appeared to have returned. "I'm going to ask you a stupid question, and I'm fully expecting you to give me a stupid answer in return."

Cherine stared blankly, unsure what the question would be.

"Are you the missing sand gryphon?" Rybalt asked.

Cherine grinned.

The Reeve's Bane rubbed his temples.

Iony returned the grin. "A promise is a promise. Break the pink reeve's daughter out of the ice and free him."

Two pitohui had metal talons and attempted to claw their way through the ice while Iony kept watch.

"Don't you have something to give him?" the glacier gryphon asked the Reeve's Bane.

"I suppose there's no harm in it." Rybalt reached into his harness and pulled out a Redwood scholar journal. It was a deep red leather with the seal of the headmaster on it. He wiped his oil off of the book with spare piece of cloth and offered it to Cherine before realizing Cherine's legs were still constrained by ice. He used some of Cherine's harness straps to secure it to the scholar's chest with Neider's emblem pointing out like a shield.

"You'll want to wipe it clean before you open it," Rybalt said. "I removed several pages for obvious tactical reasons, but it's all we found of Neider. He would have wanted you to have it, daft bird that he was."

"Mally said that he's dead. How did it happen?" Cherine asked. After a moment, he added, "Wait, you tried to kill me with a vial of poison last time we met!"

"Keep it down," Iony hissed.

The wind whistled through openings in the palace, and Cherine felt exposed. All that stood between him and hundreds of flamingos was glass. If one of them woke up and went for a walk, their cover would be blown.

"Poison?" Rybalt's voice was dry. "Did I do that?"

"You did," Iony confirmed. "You handed him one of the poisoned vials you gave the blackwings."

Rybalt inclined his head and spread his wings in a bow. "I *am* an assassin. It wasn't personal. Had I known there was so much value in rescuing you over and over again, I'd have let you live. How is Ninox? Does she know you're a sand gryphon?"

The pitohui opinici broke Cherine's talons free, and he rubbed them together for warmth. Before he could answer Rybalt's question, a new face emerged from the western side of the plateau and crept towards them—a face Cherine recognized from the university.

"Oh, hello, Cherine." Bario's red feathers caught the moonlight in a way that made him glow.

"You two know each other?" Rybalt asked.

"Different departments," Bario said. "Cherine used to come by to study with my father sometimes. Not much of a phoenix, he just wanted to know about bats."

"Just about got the back legs free," one of the pitohui said. "Took a few moments because we had to chip out his tailfeathers, too."

Cherine tried to look back over his shoulder. "I appreciate that. I'm not due to molt for months."

"Anytime," the pitohui said with a tone that suggested the opposite.

"Is he one of the ones from Reeve's Nest?" Cherine asked.

"No, but they've all heard about the trouble you and Ninox caused for us in the weald, and they all feel pretty similarly about you," Rybalt said before turning to Bario. "Are the explosives set? I'd like to leave before the sun comes up. Small explosion, yes? Just enough to destroy all the fresh water and food?"

Bario scratched at the back of his head, a habit that reminded Cherine of Felicio. "We're still working out the kinks on the black powder and new fuses. I think it'll be small but thorough. Just enough that they'll probably assume that someone lit a rushlight a little too close to one of Mally's crates."

"You put the saltpeter next to Mally's crates?" Cherine asked. He had another limb free and shook it to get feeling back. One more leg and he'd be out of here, assuming Rybalt wasn't going to betray him.

Bario nodded.

"What were the crates full of?" Rybalt asked, predicting where this conversation was going.

"Nothing too dangerous," Bario said. He listed off several chemicals, ending with "and then there were several boxes of fresh water and blackwater at the other end of the building."

"Blackwater?" Iony asked. "What's that?"

"I don't know. I assumed water." Bario opened a notebook labeled *Alabaster Eyrie Science Terminology*. He let out a sound that was half profanity, half squeak. "We should go."

Iony and Rybalt shared a look before the gryphon asked Bario, "Is this going to be larger than a small fire?"

Bario rubbed his talons together. "It'll be fine. Fine. No one will notice. We should just go. We should be gone."

"Oh! Blackwater!" Cherine finally remembered the term. "That's petrol, isn't it?"

"Got your back leg!" the pitohui called.

Cherine stood and hopped a few times. It didn't feel great, but he could walk off the terrace to get airborne if he needed to.

"Did the fuse go by any of the blackwater crates?" Rybalt asked every word slowly. "Is there any reason to think that the fuse won't give us an hour head start?"

Bario had just begun to say that he was certain the dark stains on the crate weren't blackwater when the explosion flattened all six of them.

Every piece of glass in the palace shattered. Within twenty seconds, every brazier in the main hall was lit.

Cherine turned to flee east with his liberators, but a new shape seemed to coalesce out of mist along the edge of the plateau. Mally's long, pale body and red talons were unmistakable.

"Oh, it's you again," Rybalt stretched his wings and rubbed some of the poison from his oil glands over his chest and talons.

The Metalworks and a hundred angry flamingo guards flew out of the shattered palace.

Iony grabbed Bario the Phoenix by the scruff and pulled him off the ledge.

The sound of a startled copper hawk gryphon and

parrot opinicus echoed up from the desert floor beneath the plateau.

Rybalt hissed and rushed straight towards Mally, but the Nighthaunt's eyes weren't on his opponent. They were on Cherine.

More specifically, they were on Headmaster Neider's journal tied to Cherine's harness.

The pink reeve's daughter leapt off the ledge and headed south, towards the Padfoot Pride's nesting grounds, shouting for whom he hoped were Zeph and Kia below.

29

SHATTERED GLASS

"Cherine? You *are* alive!" Kia shouted to her scholar friend. Together with Zeph, they flew south as fast as they could go. Despite the confusion, half of Crestfall's guards were hot on their tailfeathers.

"We need to go west," Zeph said. "We'll die of dehydration when the sun comes up without water. I can't sniff out the watering holes if we don't know where they are."

Cherine shook ice off of his back legs as he flew. "If you can really sniff them out, I can land us pretty close to the ones south of here."

Zeph and Kia shared a look in which she also happened to see all of the flamingos chasing them. Their strange glass jewelry caught the moonlight. She beat her wings faster, but she knew Zeph was their slowest flyer, and he wouldn't deal well with the heat.

"I don't think we can afford to stop and sniff out much of anything." She stuffed Zeph's hat into a harness pocket. "The moment we do, they're going to catch up to us. This is their home, so I'll bet they handle the heat a lot better than we do."

Cherine began talking crazy. "It's not their home. This land belongs to Hoppy Padfoot. Fly south as fast as you can! Rybalt said they're expecting me. They'll save us."

"Who will?" Zeph asked.

"My pride, the sand gryphons!" Cherine shouted. "I'm a sand gryphon now."

Zeph and Kia shared their second and last look. With the glittering flamingos gaining on them, they really had no choice except to follow Cherine and pray he hadn't gone mad.

The night gave way to morning, and Kia's back paws went from frigid to sweating. Zeph must have felt similarly, because he let his opinicus boots fall, hitting the sand without a sound. She had two flasks of water, and she drank a third of each, then handed them off to her companions.

As the copper hawk drank mid-flight, Kia risked another glance back. She couldn't see the Crestfall opinici because the glass trinkets hanging from their thin rope harnesses caught the light and shone brightly.

The sun continued to heat the desert. The illuminated flamingos had paced themselves, most likely believing that this was a race won by stamina and not speed. From the way Zeph was starting to wobble, they were probably correct.

On the trio's journey, they passed over several goliath birds that had fled when the explosives went off. They flew by several rocks covered with sand swimmer monitors sunning themselves. They even passed by what might have been a bat, though she'd never expect Cherine to admit that.

Hi-kun had fallen behind with his heavy armor, but Crestfall's guards were nearly upon them. Another twenty minutes and they'd catch Zeph. Much longer than that, and Kia didn't think she could fly without more water.

A shadow passed overhead, and Cherine let out a warning. At least, his tone suggested it was a warning. His actual words had been, "Thunder bird!"

When Kia looked up, she saw a vulture larger than any avian she'd ever heard of circling overhead. Despite the warning, the thunder bird didn't seem interested in them. It was fixated on the shiny, glass jewelry worn by the flamingos.

From up high, its dive caught one of the two Crestfall captains chasing them. The sound of a giant bird cashing into a small flamingo was the same sound as a dropped pair of glass chimes hitting a stone floor—the opinicus seemed to shatter mid-air.

The other flamingos scattered, attempting to attack the bird before it fed upon them. There was another screech, and two more of the giant vultures dove down to catch the glistening opinici.

"That was amazing," Zeph panted. "I've never seen a bird so big."

The copper hawk gryphon was losing altitude.

"We have to land and get water," Kia shouted to her fellow scholar. "We're not going to make it."

Cherine had a wild look in his eye. "We don't have to land to drink!"

She didn't have time to argue with him. She was about to grab Zeph and force him to descend by some shade when sandy-and-orange colored gryphons sprang up from the desert itself.

They were small, smaller than Zeph, and came in more than one type. The ones with long beaks and crests chirped greetings to Cherine, calling him Metalbeak.

The round, fluffy ones kept trying to fly into Kia's face. She batted one away and her talons came back wet.

While she fought to keep from being bombarded,

Cherine grabbed one of the sandgrouse gryphons in his foretalons and drank from her feathers. Kia was at a loss for words, but when she turned to Zeph, he'd seen Cherine and was doing the same thing.

Kia put things off until she felt light-headed, then finally caught the sandgrouse the next time he flew next to her face and sipped him.

When she was done, he cooed at her and flew off. She didn't know what to say. Not about Cherine, not about the sand gryphons, not about the giant birds. Mia was never going to believe any of this.

With the thought of her sister, Kia realized that Piprik and Lei should be making their own escape about now. She hoped things went better for them than they had for her.

From behind, she heard an angry honking sound. The flamingos had finally killed the thunder birds and were back in the air pursuing Zeph, Kia, Cherine, and a tiny army of sand gryphons.

30

THE SILVER REEVE

Silver spent her evening going over reports from across the kingdom. She wrote notes in the margins, signed the appropriate papers, and stretched her talons as they ached. Somehow, being taken off the front lines while recovering actually meant she was still on the front lines, she was just the one left in charge of the busy work.

What the documents reflected was anxiety. The Seraph King's subjects didn't trust in their lord to protect them. King's Reach, the southernmost port city, was worried about starlings. Understandable, considering they were nestled south of the Emerald Jungle. Alwren shared their concerns, so Silver wrote down something appropriate about increasing the number of guards and left it at that.

It was nice that the starlings were almost superstitious about glyphs. Really, if the ferocious speckled gryphons decided they would no longer tolerate Alwren and King's Reach along their border, there was little any opinicus could do about it. The Seraph King would let them go. Only Duck-bill and the Argent Heights would be protected, since they were on the path to the Alabaster Eyrie.

She flipped through more correspondences. Reevesport wanted rubber tree sap. Alwren wanted apples. Silver didn't see why they couldn't figure that out amongst themselves and save her signing trade documents. When her talons cramped up, she grabbed the pen in her beak, scribbled something on the last few pages, and went for a walk.

The cool night air felt nice on her legs. The braces were warm, and she'd been scolded more than once by the medicine opinicus for trying to scratch an itch under them using a quill pen.

Her foretalons disliked walking as much as they'd disliked writing, so she decided to get some flying in. She looked around to make sure no one was watching her but realized her mistake. Of course the guards were concerned for her safety. It wasn't that long ago she'd been saved from a painful death by two goliath bird ranchers.

She swallowed her pride and raised herself up on her back two legs, careful to keep her forelegs against her body. She pushed up and beat her wings. The takeoff was slow and awkward, but it got her in the air, where she'd feel good —until it was time to land.

Whitebeak's braziers illuminated it from the sky. To Silver, the pattern of the lights felt like constellations in reverse. From up high, she could see the goliath birds being saddled to the wagons from the swamp. With the incident at the prison camp, she didn't want the stormcloth sitting here any longer than it needed to be. The path by the Abyssal Naze was dangerous since Mally's old workshop had been destroyed, but she'd turn north at the river and follow it to Reevesport, then follow the old trade roads west.

Hi-kun should be back soon. It would be poor form to leave Whitebeak without sufficient leadership when the main army would arrive at any time to begin their desert crossing, but her orders were clear: the stormcloth had priority.

She finished her circuit and was getting ready to land when she caught sight of one of her own falling out of the sky. The argent messenger caught herself, but only just, hitting the ground hard enough to cause damage.

Silver flew after her, taking the time to slow her landing on account of her forelegs. She shouted for the medicine opinicus and grabbed water.

"Crestfall." The messenger got out one word before the cold water sent her vomiting. Her eyes lost focus, and she fell over, unconscious.

The medicine opinicus opened his bag and located a special vial of toxin, but looked to Silver for confirmation that it was okay to use it. The messengers swore an oath, and this type of revival fit within their job description.

Unlike the jelly toxin the Crackling Sea used, this extract was taken from jellies down by the coast near King's Reach. It didn't render its victims incapacitated; it put them into excruciating pain for over an hour—preventing them from falling unconscious again.

The medicine opinicus dipped a small, thin blade into the toxin and made a light incision.

The messenger regained consciousness with a scream. A few moments of heavy breathing, pupils dilated with pain, and she gave the rest of her message. "There was an explosion at Crestfall. The barracks is gone, the palace shattered."

"Espionage?" Silver asked. "Or are the blackwings making a move?"

The messenger shook her head. She didn't know. Silver left her kin in the medicine opinicus's care and went off to think where her profanity wouldn't be heard by her troops. Once that was out of the way, she considered her options.

Crestfall was not a defensible position. She'd send her own argent hawks out to the oasis to wait further orders. A new messenger, or perhaps Hi-kun himself, should arrive soon. In the meantime, if the Blackwing reeve really was attempting to cross the desert, it was time for Silver to safeguard the stormcloth.

She sent most of the troops east, sent a few to check to the north, and nearly forgot to leave a handful behind to watch the Redwood Valley refugees. She walked to the workshop, finding its door barred. She balked at the indignity of a reeve knocking on a door, but she could always order them disciplined later. With her forelegs in pain from the landing, she turned and kicked at the door with a back leg.

It took half a minute of kicking for the door to open. A pale face and red beak looked out at her, one of Mally's cultists.

"Yes, Reeve Silver?" his voice rasped.

She choked down her annoyance. "There's been an explosion at Crestfall. You've all had basic medical training, yes?"

The pale opinicus lowered his head in confirmation.

"I don't think the blackwings will try to hold it," she said, "but I'm sending scouts to find out. I only have so many wagons I can spare to send through the desert, and I want all of you on them. You're to treat every one of the wounded."

The red beak turned, shouted something into the darkness behind him, then looked at Reeve Silver. "What of our master?"

"The first messenger only just arrived," she said. "As soon as I know, you'll know. But until Hi-kun orders you otherwise, you're all assigned to the medicine opinici. You have ten minutes to gather your things before the caravan leaves."

Her next stop was by the stables. She ordered the apple merchants' goliath birds and wagon commandeered, but neither merchant was around to notify of the fact. Well, they'd figure it out sooner or later. There was already a panic spreading through the refugees, and when she ordered some of the clean water and food sent with the medicine opinici to Crestfall, she nearly faced a mutiny.

"The army will be here in a few hours," was the magic phrase Silver used to calm them down. In truth, she thought they'd have been here by now. The army was taking longer than expected to secure the naze roads from gryphon attacks. Mally had really stirred up a hornet's nest there.

Belatedly, she wondered if Crestfall was the work of the gryphons who'd chased him out of his last workshop but scolded herself for thinking such absurd thoughts. Gryphons couldn't make things explode.

She was seconds away from joining the goliath bird caravan west with the stormcloth when she remembered the royal seal. Under no circumstances were they to leave it unattended at Whitebeak. With Hi-kun and Mally at Crestfall and potentially in little pieces, it was her duty to bring the seal with her.

She ordered the caravan to start without her and went back into the workshop. "Hello? Is anyone still here?"

No response, but the passages lined with books had a way of suffocating sound before it traveled too far. She shivered at the scent of old blood. She'd let the assistants know that Alwren limes could remove the smell, something she'd learned after her predecessor's assassination.

She'd retrieved the seal from Mally's chambers and was

on her way out when she ran into the apple merchants outside the Redwood Valley holding pens.

"Ah, Reeve Silver," the white one stuttered. "We have apples to drop off. I'm so sorry, but everyone seems to have gone."

Something was off about them. They weren't wearing Reevesport harnesses anymore. In fact, the white one was wearing the harness used specifically by agents of the king, while the peacock wore some sort of blue and gold harness without an eyrie badge.

That was when it clicked. She'd nearly killed this opinicus in the bog. She'd been in the middle of a dive that would have ended his life when the Reeve's Bane knocked her out of the sky, breaking her legs. But she'd also seen the little one nearly take out Rybalt's eye, so they weren't Blackwing Eyrie allies, either. Most likely, they were somehow related to the Redwood Valley gryphon and opinicus couple that had escaped.

With her injuries, could Silver take them? Probably. Neither seemed military. But not *definitely*, and no one would hear her cries for help from within the bowels of the workshop should they prove capable opponents.

The fact that they'd waited for the guards to leave before entering, combined with the fact that they'd gone straight for Mally's little blood farm, suggested they were doing what she didn't have the bravery to do herself.

Before they could lie to her again, she said, "The key to the opinicus restraints is hidden behind the warning sign," and walked out of the workshop and into the dawn, taking the seal with her and leaving them to it.

31

PIP AND LEI'S ESCAPE

Piprik pushed through the holding pens, freeing Mally's prisoners. While Lei seemed confused by Silver's actions, Piprik wasn't—there were points in war where doing the right thing became more important than your allegiances. He'd seen that for himself living with the fisher-folk. He'd gone from one of the more dedicated blackwings to near indifference over what his old eyrie wanted.

His betrayal in the jungle and time on the shore had changed him. Politics eroded before a desire to do the right thing, which was sometimes different from his old allies wanted. In Silver, he saw a kindred spirit.

Lei helped lead the experiments up the stairs. There were apples and water near the workshop entrance. Only Olan remained behind, insisting on helping Piprik unlock the chains. When it was just the two of them, they made their way up.

Piprik paused in front of the cold room where the blood was kept. This close to the desert, the feel of ice stung his face. He looked around to see if there was anything to destroy the blood with.

"Don't," Olan said. "If he can find a cure with the blood already taken, doesn't that help more opinici?"

"I don't know," and Piprik really didn't. If leaving the blood meant Mally didn't come south again, maybe that was okay. Wendl's plan to test every starling until she found someone who was immune was a long shot. Maybe it was better to leave the blood.

Ultimately, shouting from above made the decision for Piprik. He and Olan ran upstairs. One of the guards had come in to fetch ointment and saw the holding pens.

"What's your name, soldier?" Piprik asked.

The guard's eyes went straight to Piprik's eyrie badge. "Jotan, sir."

"You know that the Seraph King loves all of his subjects, don't you, Jotan?" Piprik continued. "He wouldn't want any of them locked away. There's a new treatment facility south of the heights. We're taking all of the reds there for testing."

He passed the guard a set of orders he'd prepared in case this happened. "Take this scroll to your captain. Some reds may stay behind. Find them a place in Reevesport to wait for their kin."

The guard looked from his own cut foreleg to the sick opinici. Lei went through his harness pockets and offered an aneda-treated bandage.

"Yes, sir," the guard said.

Piprik let out his breath only when the guard was gone. He'd only filled out one more stamped set of orders with the royal seal. He was saving the third, blank stamped scroll for a future project.

His plan had been to try to sneak away with Mally's subjects first, but that no longer seemed reasonable. Instead, he had Lei and Olan rush to the refugee camp, where Kia's parents should do the rest of the work of getting the reds moving once they saw the fate that awaited their loved ones.

In the meantime, Piprik went searching for his wagon. It was gone, but there was a piece of parchment offering him payment should it not be returned in a fortnight. That wasn't ideal, but nothing ever was. They'd have to fly back to New Eyrie.

First, however, it was time to test his costume. With everyone behind him, he walked up to the southern gates.

"Without an order from Hi-kun or a reeve, I can't let you leave," the gate's overseer said. "The army will be here at any moment, then you can take it up with them."

Piprik didn't speak. He went through his harness, pulling out his second piece of parchment with the royal seal on it. It'd taken some work to make it look as though the seal had gone on top of the words and not the other way around, but he didn't expect anyone to challenge him.

The guard's eyes grew wide when he saw the name Piprik on the paper. Piprik had no idea what tales were told of the real Piprik nor what was said about his disappearance, so he'd made up a cover story.

"Sir, this says you'll be taking the reds with you, too?" the guard prompted.

Piprik nodded. Behind him, Lei shepherded the refugees into a line. They walked past the guard, beyond the spiked barriers, and took flight.

Kia's parents gathered Olan and went with him. No one made eye contact with the guards. A hundred refugees went past the front gates and took to the air. Two hundred. Piprik couldn't breathe the entire time.

Finally, only Lei and Piprik were left. "You understand that the king does not wish it to be known that I still live, yes?"

The guard nodded.

"Tell no one," Piprik continued. "If anyone asks, this order came from the reeve."

Piprik and Lei made their retreat. It was a long journey to New Eyrie, but he was feeling pretty good.

"I told them to gather the last of the food from the stores," Lei said. "Without the wagons, it seemed like we'd need supplies for the trip. The army isn't going to be happy when they find out."

The morning was unpleasantly warm, and Piprik was grateful they weren't in the desert right now. Lei wanted to make a detour to grab his things from the abandoned Crest-fall raftworks. Piprik would have forbid it, but they were limited in speed by the slowest refugees. A good number of them hadn't flown in months. Some of the largest eagle opinici carried the elderly.

It took about four hours for Lei to fetch their things and catch up again. During that time, the refugees had their first chance to sleep near a creek. When Lei returned, his face told a worrisome tale.

"When I got my old harness, I noticed someone had fixed up the raftworks," he said. "I could be crazy, but I would have sworn I saw some Crackling Sea opinici on a raft off the coast."

Piprik frowned. That was much farther north than the Ashen Weald fishing rafts went. Nobody wanted to be on the sea with the reeve's pet around, either. He wasn't sure what to do with that information except pass it along.

"There's more," Lei continued. "We're being followed."

In a perfect world, Piprik would have had a full day's head start. "The army?"

"No—or, at least, not yet. Some of Silver's hawks," Lei

said. "There are just a handful coming here. Not enough to fight us."

Piprik didn't know if the refugees would raise talons against any kind of military force. Having seen what had happened to the kin they had been told were living the high life in Reevesport had convinced them to come home, but they wouldn't stand against organized troops.

"Hey, what's going on over here?" Olan asked. "Everyone's anxious to get back in the air again."

Piprik looked at Lei, then to Olan. "Can you gather the strongest refugees? We have a few silver hawks that need dissuading."

As the rest of the refugees left, fifteen eagle opinici gathered around Olan, Piprik, and Lei.

The silver hawks landed, and one of them stepped forward. "You're not Piprik. And even if you were, you're no longer the Eyes of the King."

"Look at my harness," Piprik said. "No one who knows me would say I'm anyone different."

When the silver hawks stepped forward to look at Piprik's badge, the redwood refugees leapt forwards, managing to catch three of the five.

The last two went into the air shouting curses. One left to return north, but the other kept watch from a high altitude.

Olan carefully stripped the primary feathers on the captives, then released them. The silver hawks glared as the Redwood Valley refugees returned to the sky to head south.

"Do you think they'll send the army after us?" There was a brightness to Olan's eyes in spite of his white feathers and red beak.

"I'm sure they won't," Piprik said. The fact that the

argent opinici had focused in on his identity worried him. They very well might.

Several more hours of flight and Piprik's wings started to ache. The refugees were doing their best, but they'd had to stop several times.

He kept doing the math of how far they'd traveled, how fast an argent hawk could fly, how fast the military could be redirected. His calculations moved from idle worry to real fear when lightly armored white opinici appeared in the sky to the north.

"How far away is New Eyrie?" Olan asked. "We only flew this route the once, and I wasn't watching then."

The Crackling Sea stretched long to the east. The Jadebeak Mountains were west. The land below them was mostly salt flats. They hadn't reached the start of the sawgrass marsh, let alone where it dried into plains and ranches.

"Greyfeather Pip?" Lei looked worried.

He returned to the question he'd been asking himself for hours. Would the army chase the refugees? Or were they more concerned with Piprik and Lei? They'd borrowed the royal seal. They were holding the last of the vials of purple salt. They had Piprik's badge.

"We need to split up," he said at last. "They're not going to risk me getting away. I think we can keep them off your tail long enough for you to get home."

"How?" Olan asked. "Water, mountains, or back the way we came. Where would you go?"

"The Jadebeak Mountains are more like hills," Piprik said. "And on the other side..."

"...the Emerald Jungle." Lei was wide-eyed.

"We have several things they want." Piprik turned to Olan. "You lead your opinici to New Eyrie. They'll take you in. Lei, do you still have Henders's badge? Give it to Olan so they know we sent them."

Olan accepted the badge. "You said my sister is ranger lord. Is she there?"

"No, Blinky said the Ashen Weald's leaders and military are all on the east coast of the sea practicing war games," Lei explained. "Though if the Seraph King's forces really do follow you there, that might be a problem."

When Olan looked unsure, Piprik encouraged him. "We'll be fine. We make for a great diversion. Besides, we have friends on the other side of the mountains."

Lei's face betrayed the fact that he believed their friends might tear them apart for crossing the border.

"You'll do great!" Piprik said. "Follow the coastline. We're going to head west and see if they follow us."

"It's not me I'm worried about," Olan said. "You two are crazy."

Piprik's laughter was nervous and brief. He considered sending Lei with them, but he'd given up on controlling his apprentice. If beak came to claw, he'd tell Lei to flee. There was always a chance they'd get lucky.

As the Jadebeak Mountain range came into focus, he could see the first of the emerald trees peeking over the low hills. If his sense of direction wasn't too off, his old campsite was directly west of them right now. Under the emerald broadleafs, a shattered vat that once held purple elixir was probably buried beneath fallen leaves and megapedes. In its shattered pieces, he wondered if there was a Blackwing Eyrie badge with the name Khalim on it.

Behind them, the Seraph King's forces pulled west, focusing on two wayward fisherfolk impostors instead of the refugees.

32

THE BATTLE FOR THE RUINS OF CRESTFALL

B elatedly, Cherine realized he didn't have a plan beyond escaping to the ruins of Crestfall Eyrie to find his pride of sand gryphons.

"We need to disappear into the hideaways and dens," he said as they landed outside the stables. "Sand gryphons are good hiders. What do you think?"

Hoppy shook his head, his crest wobbling from the motion. "No. My eyrie now. Fight."

"Sorry," Kia said. "I don't mean to be impolite. But they have metal talons and these nasty things called flechettes. They even have an opinicus in full metal armor."

"Not problem!" Hoppy chirped. "Have our own metal opinicus."

It took Kia a while to realize he meant Cherine. "He's great, but he's not army-stomping material."

"Stomp thunder bird," Hoppy said. "Stomp flat. Boom! No more thunder bird. Metalbeak stomp Metalworks. Big fight! Boom. We help."

Sponge flew down after them with a coo.

Hoppy nodded. "She say defenses ready. She protect

eyrie. She champion of Padfoot Pride. You and brown gryph hide if scared. Sand gryphons protect you."

Zeph was lying across a patch of six sandgrouse gryphons, soaking up their moisture and purring. The sand gryphons who weren't providing a nest of water for Zeph were building small sand sculptures that resembled their general shape along the roads and between the walls of the canyon. Others pushed together rocks to get the same effect. From the sky, it would look like the base of the canyon was full of them.

"Come, metal sand gryphon," Hoppy said to Cherine. "We prepare like last time. Understand?"

Cherine did not, and he wouldn't get time to.

"What about the flechettes?" Kia asked. When Hoppy and Sponge both looked blank, she explained. "The metal spikes that fall from the sky and kill things like at the glassworks."

Sponge cooed. In the skies above, the flamingos and Metalworks had arrived.

"Oh!" Hoppy said. "We hide for those. Run inside!"

With Hoppy's call, the sand gryphons all fled into the abandoned homes of the eyrie. Zeph followed the wet gryphons, Kia followed Hoppy, and Sponge pushed Cherine right back into the same home he'd been captured in. They fled into the back and pulled the curtain closed.

"I don't like hiding here," Cherine said, but more and more hoopoe gryphons slipped in. Soon, the entire curtained-off nesting area was full. There were gryphons on top of gryphons on top of gryphons. They were surprisingly stackable.

Outside came the sounds of iron flechettes crashing against stones and gryphons made of sand. He worried for any live gryphons who may have been caught out there, but Hi-kun's bellow helped ease his fears.

"None of them?" The Metalworks shouted. "You didn't harm a single vermin? Go into the city. Go home by home if you have to, but I tire of these obnoxious, sand-covered squirrels. Purge the eyrie. I expect a hundred gryphon corpses at my feet by sundown."

While Cherine would have liked to believe that the Crestfall military didn't usually wear glass trinkets into war, these had been awoken by an explosion and hadn't had time to change. At least, that was the only explanation he had for the jingling sounds of the opinici searching each room.

While they spread out, The Metalworks returned to the same location he'd captured Cherine, possibly following Sponge's wet paw prints for a second time. The sand gryphons looked under the bottom of the curtain and whispered back up to Cherine.

"He inside. Coming this way. Shaking head. Seems unsure? Not sure? Somewhat sure. Wait, not coming. Okay, your turn, Metalbeak!"

From the back of the nesting area, Sponge pushed Cherine's hindquarters. The tip of his metal beak broke the curtain.

"Oh, he saw!" a sand gryphon whispered. "Coming this way."

Sponge squeezed between the other gryphons and slipped out the bottom. She cooed something that had the same sound and cadence as Hoppy's *We have our own metal opinicus!* and then pulled the curtain open.

It took two seconds for the look of confidence on The Metalworks's face to drain as thirty pointy-beaked sand gryphons flew at him, sticking their beaks between the joints in his armor.

He let out a cry and leapt out of the building. Cherine followed after, expecting the sand gryphons to need help. Instead, he saw that a similar scene had been re-enacted in every room.

Sponge cooed, and one of the hoopoe gryphons translated. "Say they call in all sand gryphons from across desert. Lots of thunder bird to eat. Lots of room in eyrie to nap after eating. No just Padfoot Pride now."

Cherine shook his head with amazement. He was looking for a place to do the most good when he saw some late arrivals to the battle fly overhead.

Mally the Nighthaunt landed atop the canyon with a screech. His cry echoed into every cavern. The moment Cherine felt the sound hit him, the Nighthaunt turned and looked at the headmaster's journal strapped to Cherine's harness.

Cherine had forgotten about it on the flight over, but when he reached to untie it, he remembered Rybalt's warning that the pages probably had pitohui poison on them. Now would be a bad time to afflict himself with a deadly neurotoxin.

Mally slipped between sandgrouse and flamingo, hoopoe bird and white-tailed kite, Metalworks and Hoppy, in his pursuit of the journal. Cherine fled for the southern gates.

The Nighthaunt's red talons closed around Cherine's tailfeathers as Sponge and her compatriots knocked Mally out of the sky. Where one sand gryphon was small, a dozen together hit like a wet rock.

Cherine knew he should stay and try to fight, but instead, he found himself headed for the guest cave. It had kept him safe from the blackwings; it should keep him safe from Mally.

He pulled himself inside the dark maw and his sense of safety changed to the same dread he'd felt last time he was here. The thunder bird meat Hoppy had ordered brought here was gone. Only sauce stains at the entrance hinted that it had been here at all. Had a sand swimmer come by and eat it? Drag marks showed the meat being pulled into the cave. Hopefully the lizard wasn't still around. The turquoise had also disappeared. It seemed unlikely lizards cared about the color of pretty rocks.

On the thought of *pretty rocks,* he recalled the strange black gemstones set into the walls of the cave. As he crawled in, he didn't see the stones, just the usual brown and grey rocks with their strange feather-like pattern. Perhaps the Padfoot Pride had traded them to the other sand gryphon prides?

Outside, the screeching cry of Mally came closer and closer to the cave. Cherine went deeper, turning the corner he'd traversed before. This time, hidden from all but the barest of light, he saw two of the same black gems and settled in next to them.

"I can smell him." The clicking screech of the Nighthaunt constrained itself down into something resembling opinicus speech. "He's in here. I need the book. You may kill the scholar."

Cherine tried to slow his breathing, but he was starting to hyperventilate. He didn't know why he kept going into caves. Bad things always happened to him there. He'd lost his beak in one weald cave. He'd spent months in another listening to strange sounds in the dark.

Mally's unusual feet, neither paw nor bird talon, tapped against the cave floor. Cherine didn't risk looking out from his hiding spot, but he could see the wall of hematite that had been missing earlier. The black orbs had all returned.

The beginnings of a panic attack gave way under the sheer force of curiosity. He was certain that wall had been brown and mottled minutes ago. Now, pairs of black gems decorated it.

As the sounds of a dozen flamingos entering the cave reached his ear holes, he turned to look at the two that had brought him to his hiding place. The hematite looked wet.

"I don't see him," a Crestfall accent said. "I've got a flint and tinder. Does anyone have a portable brazier?"

"Why would anyone have that?" A new voice.

"Over here," a third said. "Looks like this cave already had one, stolen from the glassworks. Light it, and we'll bring it with us."

All of this was background noise to Cherine's inquisitive mind. He stared at the black gems, trying to figure them out. The last piece only clicked into place when he reached a talon towards one to touch it.

They blinked.

In that moment, Cherine could make out the outline of a gryphon roosting against the rocks, its fur and feathers perfectly colored to look like cave wall.

Also in that moment, one of the flamingos lit the brazier.

The wall of pure black eyes let out a screech. The same way bats might explode from a cave, the gryphons of the abyss attacked the opinici around the brazier.

Cherine didn't want to be torn apart. The clicking, he now realized, was the same sound he'd heard in the depths of the cave systems under the weald. It was the same clicking the Nighthaunt made.

He edged along the wall and made his way towards the entrance. Several flamingos escaped, similarly terrified, but the cave gryphons had eyes only for one opinicus: Mally the Nighthaunt.

He screeched and slashed, but they pulled him into the depths.

Cherine thought of the painting of Mally, pre-Nighthaunt, that had once hung in the headmaster's study. He'd once been a beautiful peregrine falcon. The artist was supposedly Headmaster Neider himself, a gift from back when Mally first made tenure.

Somewhere in the world, he'd lost that beauty. Somewhere in the world, he'd gained his black eyes and long body. If Cherine had to guess, Mally had gained his black eyes from the depths of the earth, and the earth had come to reclaim them.

Cherine shivered and headed towards the eyrie before either of the Crestfall opinici thought to net him.

HI-KUN, THE METALWORKS
ALABASTER EYRIE OPINICUS

33

MAGIC ROCKS

During his time frozen atop a plateau of glass and pools, Cherine had considered that Crestfall's eyrie was too big for just the Padfoot Pride. Seeing it now, every home was swarming with small gryphons.

In a sea of orange and cream-colored fur, Zeph and Kia both stood out. His copper hawk friend was stationed under a bridge-like walkway, and whenever an opinicus flew under it, he'd pounce.

Kia had gathered enough flechettes to fill her pockets. When she saw Cherine, she flew over to him. "I don't know how to use these without hitting the sand gryphons, too."

A cry from the north sent both opinici into the air. The Metalworks, his armor stained with blood from all of the pin-prick hoopoe bites, was gathering a fresh group of the Seraph King's forces who'd just arrived from Whitebeak—fresh being a relative term after their desert flight.

Cherine wasn't watching the reinforcements. Instead, he saw Hoppy chirping to him from atop the section of the canyon where they'd ambushed the thunder bird. A new set of rocks had been pushed to the edges, ready to go.

"Are you still a good flyer?" Cherine asked Kia.

"Better than you," she replied.

He grinned. "If you can get their attention and fly them through that pass over there, the sand gryphons will take care of the rest."

Kia pulled out the flechettes she'd been collecting. "As long as we go now, I can get their attention before they get into the air. Are we good?"

Hoppy let out his *hoo-poi* call.

"We're good!" Cherine went to the end of the canyon to give the sign to attack while Kia flew into the sky.

The gathered white opinici must have noticed Kia's vibrant plumage flying over them. She was hard to miss. That none of them called out with alarm meant they never considered that after Crestfall and the glassworks, someone might use their own weapons against them.

Even from his perch in the pass, Cherine could see Kia empty her pockets. The flechettes were sinister and ingenious—the fins on one side righted them immediately and started the spike spinning as they fell. Gravity did the rest of the work.

They were just heavy enough to puncture armor. Of the reinforcements, six were killed where they stood and another thirty wounded.

Kia dove low, gaining speed, and went into the pass. The rest of the white-tailed kite opinici chased after her. Just when she passed over his head, Cherine shouted up to Hoppy and the rain of boulders and rocks came down.

Fortunately for the sand gryphons, Kia had wiped out a good number of the reinforcements and held their attention. They didn't think to look up until it was too late. Unfortunately for Cherine, who was sitting at the end of the pass, The Metalworks had flown a little slower than the rest and hit the pass after the last of the boulders had been pushed over the side.

He did not look happy to see the Redwood Valley food scholar.

Sponge called out a warning from one side. Hoppy shouted "Fake beak, magic rock! Fake beak, magic rock!" as they flew by.

Thankfully, Cherine had spent enough time with the sand gryphons that he knew what that meant. It was time to lead The Metalworks into the Crestfall armory he'd been searching for since the eyrie fell.

Cherine looked up at the floor markers. He dashed to where the armory should have been and dug with all his strength.

The armory had, in fact, been hidden exactly where it was. When the sandstorms hit, the Padfoot Pride simply moved around the floor markers to make it look like the second story was the first. That was why all the *ground floor* homes had balconies.

Cherine had just managed to dig his way in, breaking through several wooden planks used to keep the sand at bay, when The Metalworks caught up to him.

"Come back here, scholar!" Hi-kun shouted. "I should have killed you when we captured you. Had I known the trouble you'd put me through, I'd have killed you twice!"

"That doesn't make sense!" Cherine called back as he squirmed through an incredible amount of metal, weapons, armor, statues, and ornaments. From above, he could hear scratching as the sand gryphons dug more holes down into the armory, breaking apart swaths of the ceiling, which let light in. Almost everything down here sparkled.

Paw prints marked where the pride had come to fetch magnets for him to transform them into necklaces. Except for water, all of their treasures were stored alongside the eyrie's armor and weapons.

The armory turned dark again as the large figure of The Metalworks shoved himself inside. He hadn't brought backup, which was good for Cherine, probably figuring he could kill one scholar on his own. Bad for Cherine was the fact that the Metalworks was probably correct in that assessment.

The high commander made a show of unlatching a pair of white metal talons and securing them over his own. He stalked towards Cherine, circling past the weapons and armor. "I wondered where these had gone."

Cherine considered trying to find a pair of talons of his own, but he thought back to his capture by the Ashen Weald. It had been a mistake to think he could outfight or outfly Merin, let alone The Metalworks.

Instead, he very calmly continued backing up, weaving his way through Hoppy's stolen treasure.

"I don't suppose if I give you the book Mally's after, you'll leave me alone?" he asked.

No reply from Hi-kun. Sand gryphons spilled into the room, but there were only ten of them. With The Metalworks's weapons and armor, that wasn't enough.

One of the gryphons who burrowed in was Hoppy. He nodded to Cherine, who recalled the advice: fake beak, *magic rocks*.

Cherine led the Metalworks past a pile of glass and next to the far wall. The seal of Crestfall University was on most of the objects on this wall, and said objects had all been secured into nooks and crannies or tied down. He could feel the pull of the magnets against the metal buckles on his harness even from here.

Cherine stopped walking. The Metalworks pushed

towards him. Just as Hi-kun raised his talons, the ten sand gryphons rammed into him, pushing him against the wall.

Had there been a more confused look on the face of an opinicus, Cherine hadn't seen it.

The Metalworks struggled to break free, but the combined force of the magnets kept him in place. Both of his back legs, his foretalons, and even the metal in his helmet kept him from using his beak or claws to untie any of his outfit. "You think you can stop me like this? When I get out of here, my metal talons will tear all of you apart!"

The sand gryphons clicked their beaks in anticipation, and for one moment, Cherine was worried he was about to see a grisly murder. Then he realized it wasn't violence he saw in their orange plumage; it was avarice.

While The Metalworks was stuck against the wall, the sand gryphons began to steal his metal talons and everything precious on him, working as a team to liberate them from the magnets.

By the time they were done, Hi-kun would be left naked —but finally free of the magnetic fields that held him prisoner. Cherine wanted to be somewhere else before then.

34

THUNDER SPONGE

Zeph hung upside-down from the bridge across the canyon. Every few minutes, Sponge flew by with several flamingos in tow, and Zeph would pounce, crushing at least one of them.

As the number of flamingos thinned, Crestfall's forces lost confidence. He was fairly certain they would have fled before now, but one of their captains kept rallying them again and again to send after the sand gryphons.

The head opinicus wore several glass necklaces that chimed when he struck, so in the manner of a weald gryphon, Zeph had nicknamed him Captain Jingles.

When Hi-kun and Mally had vanished, Jingles had taken over leadership. Crestfall's forces had weapons. They had armor. They were tired from the flight, but they were determined to win back their homes.

"Do not stop until every vermin is dead!" the captain shouted. "We will reclaim this eyrie or die trying."

The next time Sponge flew by, Zeph reached out from his upside-down perch and grabbed her out of the air. "Hey, you. We need to take the captain out. If we do that, I think the rest of the flamingos have had enough."

Sponge looked at him with an expression he'd only seen on pigeons. As best he could tell, it was complete disinterest. She cooed, a sound half pigeon and half frost chicken, but said nothing else.

"I don't understand," Zeph said.

Sponge blinked.

Then she turned and went hurtling straight towards the Crestfall captain, making a sound that, while still half pigeon, was also full battle cry.

All of the sandgrouse gryphons turned and converged on the captain, who honked in alarm.

One of the hoopoe gryphons poked Zeph. "She consume thunder bird. Invincible now. We follow Thunder Sponge into battle."

None of what the sand gryphons said made sense, but Zeph flew after them, hoping to get some height and dive at the captain if he saw an opening.

Sponge flew at Jingles's face, but the captain batted her away, sending her flying into the canyon wall with a splat.

Not the splat of real damage or a dead gryphon, however. It was the splat of a wet taiga tail against hard ice. It was the splat of a hairball against a redwood.

Sponge and her lookalikes bounced off the walls and continued attacking the captain. While he was busy protecting his head and neck, the small hoopoe bird gryphons snuck in low and pulled at his tailfeathers and wings.

Several little sandgrouse gryphons flung themselves at Jingles at the same time, and Zeph saw his opening. Right as the captain twirled to dislodge them, Zeph's dive caught the opinicus in the chest.

They crashed into the sand, and only Jingles's fast reflexes kept Zeph's beak away from his neck. Where Zeph had agility, the flamingo had size and strength. He rolled Zeph over and pinned him. Zeph tried to kick, but his dewclaws caught on the captain's leg bracers, narrowly missing the bladed edges.

Jingles pulled out a long, pink glass knife and was about to stab down when Sponge's dive—which was more like if someone dropped an eggfruit from a great height than anything one might see from a falcon or hawk—hit Captain Jingles in the back of the head and knocked him unconscious.

Zeph pushed the opinicus off of him and thanked Sponge. "You did great! Thanks for saving me."

Sponge cooed and another sand gryphon translated. "She say you nice, but she wish you taller."

"Me too!" Zeph said, and they slow blinked at each other.

The copper hawk gryphon shook off the sand and went looking for his friends. Cherine was using pieces of paper to detach a book from his harness. Kia flew above several flamingo opinici, chasing them off and threatening them with flechettes if they turned around. She only backed down when one took a swipe at her and shredded a few of her feathers.

While the sand gryphons looked after their wounded, a naked and bleeding white-tailed kite pulled himself out of the sand, grabbed Captain Jingles unconscious body, and escaped west.

Whether the desert and thunder birds would let Hi-kun make it all the way back to Whitebeak, Zeph didn't know. He wished them luck, so long as they never returned here.

Hoppy chirped orders to different groups of sand

gryphons. They were indistinguishable from each other to Zeph, but he gathered they were different prides who lived in the desert. They collected the bodies of the dead and moved them out into the dunes.

"No want thunder bird here," Hoppy explained. "Nor sand swimmer. Bad lizards."

"I know monitors," Zeph said. "It's good thinking. I guess that's why you're pride leader."

Hoppy purred, and Zeph went to check on Kia and Cherine.

Kia glided back in, hitting the sand off balance. "One of those flamingos didn't like being followed. He got a few feathers."

Zeph inspected her missing wing plumage. "You should be okay. We can imp some new ones on once we get home. Hatzel always keeps a few of my feathers around. She's very sentimental."

Kia rolled her eyes but returned his grin. "All things aside, I really didn't think we were going to get out of this one alive. I thought we'd finally lost Cherine."

"I'm good!" Cherine called out. He was rubbing the book in the sand, which Zeph decided not to question. "I was saved by cave gryphons."

Kia and Zeph laughed.

"What?" Cherine asked. "No, really. Cave gryphons. They came out of the guest cave and ate the flamingos attacking me and pulled Mally the Nighthaunt under. Also, I think they were the ones making the clicking noises in the weald caves. You said you heard clicking at Hoarfrost, too, didn't you, Zeph? And they probably stole the forger's lunch when we were in prison. I'm going to see if Sponge speaks cave gryphon. She's supposed to know thirteen languages."

Zeph and Kia watched him go.

"Is he okay?" Zeph asked. "It's just that I can't tell. He's always in crisis mode or trying to solve a problem or figure out some equation. But out here, he seems, I don't know, relaxed and crazy at the same time?"

Kia chewed at one of her smashed feathers, getting it ready for imping later. "This is kind of what he was like as an apprentice. I've missed this excitement. Maybe getting away from the Redwood Valley is what he needed. There's no Ashen Weald here, no one who wrongfully blames him for the fires."

"What's Ninox going to say?" Zeph wondered. "Is she going to want him so far away?"

"That's not her call anymore, is it?" Kia rifled through her pockets for some aneda bandages and began fixing up Zeph. "Gryphons don't mate for life."

"They can if they want. It's not a law or anything," Zeph explained. "Just look at Pink Paw and Xavi. But you know, if there's one thing I've learned about Cherine, it's this— nobody can hold him. Not Merin's pride, not the Ashen Weald, not Crestfall, not the Seraph King, not the Reeve's Bane, and not even Ninox. He's like a slippery fish; he always gets away."

"Mmm," Kia agreed. "Have you ever thought of settling down? Come to think of it, I don't think you've ever had a mate in the time we've known each other."

"In the single year we've known each other?" Zeph said. "Last mating season I was... in a frozen mountain being chased by rabid starlings. The only gryphon around then was a frosty pink Younce. I'm not as into that *pretty but grumpy* thing as Tresh seems to be."

In the distance, Cherine had gathered several sand

gryphons together and was telling some sort of story. As best Zeph could hear, it was something about the daughter of a Crestfall reeve.

Hoppy and Sponge made their way through the crowds to Zeph and Kia.

Sponge cooed.

"She say Cherine stay here a while," Hoppy explained, "but you send message south. Metalworks saw treasure. He return. I no have other place to put shinies, so I trade. Blackwing treacherous. Seraph King even more so! Who rule south? Is it Metalbeak's owl?"

"There are a few rulers, but we all work together," Kia explained. "I'll bet Satra and the Ashen Weald would love to have a glut of metal to put to use. What would you like in exchange?"

Sponge cooed. Hoppy cooed back at her, and they continued their exchange for some time before Hoppy switched to speaking common.

"Protection," he said at last. "Me reeve. Let you use glassworks. You protect from thunder bird. Make trade happen. You good, we no trade with blackwings or white wings."

"I think that can be arranged," Zeph said. "Everyone has been worried about the northerners taking an eyrie in the south, but with Poisonmaw and now Crestfall, we'd have three-quarters of the sea to ourselves."

Kia pulled out a quill pen and began writing everything down. "We should get Satra to visit. And some kind of military outpost. Figure out how to get water here. Maybe Triddle has some ideas for changing salty sea water into something fresh and drinkable."

Hoppy and Sponge nodded along.

She handed Zeph a letter explaining the situation. "Well, go on."

"Me? I just flew across the desert." He looked at Kia's torn feathers. "Okay, okay. I'll do it. If you can get me some water and food, I'll head out now. With any luck, everyone is still at Sailfin point, and I won't have to fly to the kjarr."

35

VICTORY

Cherine led Kia to the guest cave. The walls that had once looked brown and grey with the plumage of cave gryphons were now covered in Padfoot Pride glyphs. The roosting cave gryphons must have covered them up because the chalk-like markings were faded and old.

"It's beautiful in here," she said. "Are these everyone they've traded with? There are so many eyries and prides."

He looked at the sketches of the gryphons, locating the black eyes and long whiskers of the cave pride. Despite him trying to explain, Kia laughed it off.

"There've always been rumors of cave gryphons in the weald," she said. "Even when I was a chick. If you want me to believe they're real, you're going to have to produce one. Those're your rules for bats, aren't they?"

They spent several hours with a lit brazier, copying down the glyphs and stories that had been hidden on his last visit. Once they'd finished, Kia headed north to the eyrie to get started cooking. The city of Crestfall was full of sand gryphons again, and they'd need to figure out food for whatever forces the Ashen Weald sent up here. The thunder birds killed by the Crestfall opinici were being chewed into pieces and flown here by teams of hoopoe gryphons.

Cherine stared at the cave. He didn't know how long he'd been out there, but Sponge and Hoppy finally came to fetch him.

"You okay?" the Padfoot Pride leader asked. "You no stay in guest cave. You sand gryphon now. Part of pride. Cave for guests only."

"Who were they?" Cherine asked. "The cave gryphons."

Hoppy shrugged. "I say already. Guests. I no speak language."

Sponge made several prolonged coos, which Hoppy translated. "She say they search weald for Nighthaunt, no find. Find you. Like you. No sure why you sit in cave and can't see. Sponge tell them you sweet but dumb. They no steal your food in forest cave."

Cherine couldn't help but feel vindicated at the source of the clicks in the weald.

"They go back. To Ashley Nose," Hoppy said. Sponge cooed several times at him. "To Ashen Navel? To Abyssal Naze? Yes? Good. Go home to Abyssal Naze. Were planning to leave. Good guests. Like to trade. Stay in cave all day, only come out at night. Make pretty song. Sad they no say goodbye."

The two sand gryphons left their large, metal-opinicus sand gryphon friend behind when the smell of roasting thunder bird reached the cave. Cherine took a step inside. Without anyone here with him, the cave felt like a more dangerous place to be. He struck a rushlight. He was half expecting the walls to be brown and grey again, full of black eyes, but the glyphs remained. He searched through his harness and took one of his last three inkwells and dipped a talon in as he was still missing his pens. He started drawing the glyph for Hatzel's pride in honor of Zeph's part in the battle. Cherine wasn't sure what he should draw for Kia. Redwood Valley didn't seem right, and she didn't spend much time at Swan's Rest anymore.

He settled on a new design. He had blue, red, and green inks to play with—the perfect combination. He combined them together to create a new crest for her. In the green and red, he worked in a verdant branch of juicy red rimu olives. In the blue, the scales of the fish Kia sent north to nourish the weald refugees. Scholars had a bad reputation, well-earned by their worst members, but Kia represented the best they had to offer. Thanks to her efforts, everyone had stayed fed, and he wanted to honor that.

Once he was finished, he stretched his wings. He wasn't brave enough to go deeper into the darkness to see where it went, but he took a look at his old hiding spot where the eyes had blinked at him.

Behind the same rock he'd used for concealment were all of his stolen feather pens. Well, not all—a few were missing. It took him a moment to notice because there were the same number of feathers.

What had changed, however, was that there were grey and brown cave gryphon feathers mixed in with the old ones.

He grinned. No one back home would believe him, but he would turn both feathers into cave gryphon pens.

He packed up his things and went to the eyrie to wait for the arrival of the Ashen Weald.

36

JADEBEAK, REVISITED

As the white king's forces drew closer to Piprik and Lei, they moved from the Jadebeak Mountains to flying just over the Emerald Jungle. Piprik kept his eyes peeled, but he didn't see any starlings, infected or otherwise.

"Just when you need a horde of starlings, they're nowhere to be found," Lei echoed his thoughts. "Is there a way to call out for them?"

Piprik looked back. It was a small blessing there were no argent hawks chasing them. The last one had turned back when the army arrived. "The catch is that if we call and too many starlings come, we could be in trouble, too."

They were now south of the Crackling Sea and approaching the Jadebeak River. It was too late to turn and try to catch the Ashen Weald, and it felt like a cruelty to lead the army into the Heart of the Bog. Black Mask and the crone's wingtorn wouldn't stand much of a chance against a fully armed flight of opinici.

Piprik's wings started to give before Lei's. "I need to stop. I never knew an opinicus could fly for this long."

"Hang in there, Greyfeather Pip," Lei said. "I see the

Jadebeak River. Erlock and Wendl will be by the waterfall waiting for us, right?"

Piprik hoped so, but he had his doubts. Even if they were, could they hold off an army? One of his wings lost strength, and Lei had to catch Piprik's harness until he righted himself.

He caught his breath and went for the cave. There were several landings he was ashamed of, and the one through the waterfall was among the worst he could still walk away from.

They rushed inside, but no one was there. He swore. "Do they just come back at night? I didn't think to ask."

Lei leaned against the cauldron but squawked when his talons touched the metal. "It's hot!"

Through the den's entrance, Piprik could see the shadows of the Seraph King's forces landing along the waterfall and cliffs. He took the vials of salt and tried to hide them behind Wendl's cassia-laced nest. Even if they were captured, she would be able to put them to use. He visualized what the waterfall looked like outside. There were bog blossom glyphs on the northeast side of the river, the violet crone variant on the southwest side. Had there been any starling glyphs? Or would any starlings who arrived just watch them die?

"Did you see any pride glyphs?" he asked Lei.

"I don't remember," Lei said. More opinici landed outside. "Wait, there has to be one. Remember when Henders told us about the dig site? He said they saw starling marks. We're west of there."

An opinicus in metal armor stepped to the front of the cave. "Piprik the Imposter, you and your co-conspirator are under arrest by order of the king. Put down your weapons, remove your harnesses, and come out. Otherwise, you will be harmed."

Lei reached for the pouch where he used to hold his mother's talons, forgetting it was now empty. "I think we're going to be harmed either way."

"How hot was the cauldron?" Piprik asked.

"Very." Lei held up his talons. They throbbed red where he'd touched it.

"This is your last warning!" the captain shouted. "If we go in there, we will kill you both and return with your bodies."

Piprik took off his harness. "You stay here. I'm going out. With any luck, it'll buy us time. No matter what happens, do not tell them about your mother."

For once, Lei listened to him and stayed back. Piprik walked outside. His wings drooped down at his sides, overextended from flying so long.

"What's your name?" the captain asked.

"Piprik," he bluffed. "The order for my capture is part of the ruse. I've been secretly working as a double agent for the king, sending back information from the Blackwing Eyrie. I insist upon speaking to Hi-kun. Harm me and my contact at your own peril."

The problem with captains, he thought, was that they lacked imagination. If their orders were to capture someone, they generally did that without entertaining the thought that whomever they captured was secretly a double agent.

It was, counterintuitively, easier to trick someone who was a scholar. Their minds would often fill in the blanks, and they were willing to look at something crazy—such as a prisoner claiming he was a double agent—and consider the possibility it was true.

One of the soldiers produced a modified goliath bird

hood with a collar and chain. Piprik couldn't imagine flying back north blind. With his wings aching the way they did, he couldn't imagine flying north at all, but he didn't think the Seraph King's forces would want to stop and rest on the edge of the Emerald Jungle and bog.

From the top of the waterfall, a few rocks fell down. A pebble struck Piprik on the back of his head. When he looked up, he recognized the thick beak and long tail of Erlock.

"It's Chartail," he called out behind him as he slowly backed into the den.

"Is she alone?" Lei asked.

Piprik shook his head. "I have no idea. Help me get this harness back on. Be ready to fly."

Lei stretched his wings. "Fly where?"

"I'm going into the bog," Piprik said. "But if we get separated, I want you to fly straight to the Flower and rally every Ashen Weald ranger you can find. Tell them what's happened here with the white opinici. Have them send whoever can be spared to watch but stay back if there are starlings."

Lei nodded. "Okay, I'm ready."

The captain outside had stopped watching Piprik and Lei. He was now looking up at Erlock.

37

ERLOCK CHARTAIL

E rlock's arrival back at the mountains had been met with a crowd of starlings preparing another incursion into the bog to search for blossoms and pumpkins. Despite her warnings about causing a war and the upcoming peace treaty, the Jadebeak Pride was indifferent to a weald half-starling and her wishes. Until the pridelord ordered them to stay west, they'd continue searching.

Oddly enough, the justification they cited for being allowed in the bog was that Jun the Kjarr's smell had faded from the northern glyphs. It seemed it was the scent of the Kjarr specifically that held the pact in place.

Hence Erlock was in the middle of arguing with a flight of starlings about how they could not cross the mountains when she heard the Seraph King's captain issuing commands on the other side.

Wendl came through the trees. "I couldn't fly. There are white opinici here. The Seraph King has found me!"

"Or Piprik and Lei got caught stealing the elixir," Erlock said. She followed Wendl and crawled out of the cover of the jungle and looked over the ledge. She counted forty opinici panting and drinking outside Wendl's hidden den. They shouted at someone inside.

"Go tell the jadebeaks they have my permission to enter the bog," Erlock told the starling opinicus. "But tell them to arrive claws-out and ready to fight."

"That's the only way they show up anywhere!" Wendl scurried back between the emerald broadleafs, and Erlock perched atop the cliff and looked down. An unharnessed opinicus who looked like Piprik was fifty feet below her. He exited the cave alone.

Erlock tightened her paws, letting her wicked claws extend. A few small rocks fell down, catching the attention of the opinici. They didn't seem sure what to think of her on her own.

Her long tailfeathers flowed down the cliff face. She was larger than most of the starlings. Her plumage was a mix of greens and browns, her beak much thicker.

Erlock Fantail, feathers regrown, leapt from atop the waterfall in a dive. She pulled her wings in close. Her tail streamed behind her.

The captain leapt back, and Erlock spread her wings, twisting and catching the top of his harness with her back paws and sending them both flying off the ledge. She pulled him close and caught his wings with her front paws.

Two snaps later, she leapt off his body and beat her wings to gain altitude as he fell the full length of the water-fall to the rocks below.

One down, she thought. Thirty-nine white opinici took flight to chase down the gryphon who had just killed their captain.

A horde of starlings erupted from atop the waterfall in their own dives, catching the army off guard.

In between the chaos, she saw Piprik and Lei slip out of

the cave. The starlings, all of whom were ostensibly looking forward to the medicine, goods, and treaty, locked onto the fisherfolk as they came near. Their green wing altruism was unwavering even when their self-interest was at stake.

"Wendl!" Erlock shouted.

The scholar flew above the battle, afraid to get her talons dirty. With Erlock's call, the opinicus saw her old friend and flew interference, trying to keep the jadebeak starlings away from Piprik.

Erlock found herself nudging diving starlings off course. There was no helping it. It was like a light had been ignited inside their brains.

Nighteyes came out of the den. On her beak was the orange elixir that suppressed green wing altruism. She flew towards Piprik and Lei.

At first, Erlock thought Nighteyes was attacking them. She turned to dive and catch the purple starling, but as she drew closer, she realized that Nighteyes was just flapping her wings so it looked that way.

And it was working.

So long as it appeared as though a starling was attacking the fisherfolk, the jadebeaks locked onto the Seraph King's forces instead.

"Take them to the dig site," Erlock called to Piprik. "I'll meet you there, okay?"

Piprik shouted an affirmative.

Wendl started to turn back, but Erlock nipped her tail.

"Not you," the fantail said. "You stick close to Nighteyes. If your alchemy wears off, you need to send her away."

Erlock pushed herself to fly faster, gaining altitude, and surveyed the chaos below. The starlings fought like they were infected, instinct overtaking tactics. The Seraph King's forces knew what they were doing and worked as a team.

Unfortunately for them, they were only thinking of fighting a frenzied horde. When several opinici grouped up to watch each other's backs, Erlock's posture changed. She pointed her beak towards one flying below her, folded her wings, and began diving from the sky above them.

They shifted several times, forcing Erlock to make small adjustments as she dove. At the last moment, she changed her position, pulling her beak back and reaching out with all four paws.

Her back paws caught her target across his chest. As she flew past, she managed to grab hold of the back legs of another opinicus with her forepaws, pulling both of them down.

Erlock kept her wings folded for impact. While her claws were sharp and her aim was true, the real damage didn't come from her paws.

When the opinici tried to spread their wings to slow their fall, they did so in a panic. Erlock could hear the first opinicus's wings break from the force.

She let him go, not bothering to watch him any longer.

The other opinicus's wings held. Erlock's forepaws pulled her opponent close, and she grabbed a beakful of feathers and yanked them out, then disengaged. Armor was nice, but it didn't protect wings.

The opinicus would be able to glide down, but she wouldn't be able to get airborne again. In a battle like this, that was as good as having been killed.

Erlock returned to the high sky. The advantage of being a fantail in any sort of fight was that she could fly higher than other gryphons or opinici, and her eyesight was without parallel.

Once she'd forced the opinici to break ranks, the starlings were doing a good job of mopping them up. She caught sight of an opinicus who had removed his armor and was making his escape. He was some sort of fast hawk, and in a fair fight, he'd have survived. As it was, he made it over the fields of sawgrass before she caught him.

With Erlock so high up, there was nothing fair about this fight. No one could fly faster than a fantail could dive.

She wasn't without mercy, and she spread her wings before she connected, catching his harness and flinging him towards the ground.

He squawked in surprise but managed to right himself. Only quick reflexes and a sturdy beak allowed her to catch his back leg and bring him all the way to the sawgrass.

They crashed among a flock of goliaths, startling the birds away. She was twice the opinicus's size, and she stood on him, keeping her paws on top of his wings and legs so any pressure would break them.

She turned to one of the startled ranchers who'd narrowly avoided being caught in the stampede. "Do you have rope for the birds?"

"Y-yes?" the rancher responded.

"Good," she said. "My name is Erlock Chartail of the Fantail Pride, and this opinicus is under arrest for crimes against the Ashen Weald. If I hold him down, can you tie him up and take him to New Eyrie?"

Several of the ranchers secured the prisoner, and Erlock flew back south. She didn't think this particular white opinicus realized how lucky he was. The starlings wouldn't leave survivors.

PIPRIK LET Nighteyes and Wendl guide them to the abandoned dig site. They took shelter in the overlook above the pools where the mummy had been found.

The burned wagon that had once housed the seraph was gone, though the ground was still scorched in a wide radius around where it had once been. New grass was starting to reclaim that area. The tower was similarly charred, with its lower levels black and the roosts up top in better shape. After the battle between the Night Haunt and Reeve's Bane, the Ashen Weald had burned the clay jars stored nearby to be safe.

Piprik and Lei took shelter in the thick underbrush. Wendl and the Nightsky pride leader took turns keeping watch. The starlings seemed satisfied with the excitement by the waterfall and didn't go into the bog.

"I think you're in the clear," Nighteyes said.

Her dark blue eyes with specks of white in them prompted Lei to ask, "How did your eyes get like that?"

"Wendl," the violet starling replied. "I would have lost my sight entirely had she not cured me. It's why I'm willing to endure her strange brews where others will not."

"How much did you take?" Piprik asked. "When will it wear off?"

She shook her head. "Wendl made enough to last me a long time. She said you wouldn't break your promise to her, so I've been taking a bit of the elixir every day in secret, and I brewed enough to bring with me. I'm coming to your weald to meet the new Kjarr."

It was dark and also speckled, so Piprik had missed it, but Wendl had made a harness for Nighteyes and strapped vials to it.

"She said you would know how to make more." Nighteyes looked at him expectantly.

"Yes, of course," Piprik said. "We'll get you set up with Biski. She can give you as much as you need. I believe the kjarr gryphons can find most of the ingredients here."

Lei pointed down at Nighteyes's sharp claws. "You may want to trim those just in case you forget your dose."

"Would you have me muzzle my beak, too?" the starling quipped.

Wendl landed. "Erlock's on her way!"

The fantail pride leader soon followed. Her first question was directed to Piprik. "Did you get it?"

He nodded. "I put it in Wendl's crate beneath her pressed flower collection."

"Excellent." Her second question was directed to the starling opinicus. "I know the pridelord won't want me back in the jungle, and even if he invites me back, my pride is probably on the edge of mutiny at this point, but we need to figure out a way of communicating. Short term, let's use the waterfall. The Ashen Weald will leave messages there during the day; the starlings can leave messages at night. Once a week, we'll have someone check it. Good?"

Wendl nodded. "I should go and dissuade the rest of the starlings from coming in here."

"Wendl," Piprik began, but before he could finish, she hugged him. Even with her gryphon ears and green plumage and tail, he could tell it was her by the way she wrapped her wings around him.

She let him go. "You look so old, Khalim. All of your friends are in the Emerald Jungle. Why not join us? We can find a cure together. We can put alchemy to good use and make up for our time with Mally."

He shook his head. "You know I can't do that."

She didn't respond in front of the strangers, for which he

was grateful, but she handed him his old badge, retrieved from the ruins. It read *Khalim.*

Someday, he wanted to see his mate and son again. If he became a starling, there was always a chance he'd see them and the green wing altruism would take over. His talons went to his harness before he remembered that Lei was holding his medicine bag—and the vial of purple elixir he'd brought with him when he fled the jungle. It was one of the same batch that had changed Wendl and himself.

"You two can find time to chat at the waterfall later," Erlock chastised. "I need to get to Satra. And what the hell happened with Urious, Biski, and Tresh in the bog?"

Piprik and Lei shared a look. They flew back—slowly, for Piprik's wings—and he let Lei explain about the bog pride joining the Ashen Weald, the peace with the fisherfolk, Quess, and everything else—including their own run-in with the seraph and Reeve's Bane.

They were nearly to New Eyrie before Erlock softened. "It'll be good to see everyone hale and whole."

"That I'm sure of." Piprik thought back to the last time he'd seen Erlock. She'd been surrounded by starlings then, too, though only the infected variety, and those were in cages. After all the adventures in the swamp, the final member of the expedition was returning home.

38

THE ASHEN WEALD

It had been a few days since Zeph left, and Cherine was helping Hoppy itemize the armory while Kia read through Headmaster Neider's journal.

"It's weird, right?" she said. "He talks about us like we're still sitting outside the botanical gardens at night, talking philosophy and theories. Like he's not responsible for much of what happened back home."

Cherine didn't disagree. "You can call yourself a full scholar now, though. The head of your university has awarded you that status—moments before dying."

"Something I learned from Biski," Kia countered, "is that the moment you start calling yourself a medicine gryphon —or scholar, in my case—everyone starts treating you as one. I don't need his blessing. But I am going to run his research and recipes by some food scholars I know and see if they're viable."

"I know food scholar," Hoppy said. "Let you borrow for fee."

"For free?" Kia prompted.

Hoppy shook his head. "For *fee!*"

Kia sighed and looked to Cherine. "I miss the days before you were famous, when I could just show up at your little grove and have you work on problems for me."

Cherine took a bow. "I'm the model of the adventurer-scholar. I shall seek out the cave gryphons and establish the cultural exchange of ideas."

Cave gryphons led to bats, and soon they were back to arguing like they had in the old days outside the botanical gardens. They were headed outside to find someone to drink when a new arrival landed.

"Zeph!" Kia shouted. "Is everything okay? Where's the Ashen Weald?"

Cherine cooed for one of the sandgrouses to come rinse the sand off of their copper hawk friend. "You didn't find any trouble, did you?"

Zeph shook his head while he caught his breath. He drank one sand gryphon and rubbed the other over his face. "Why is it so hot out here?"

Cherine and Kia shared a look, then both began to describe how deserts were made in their best scholar voices.

"Enough, enough!" Zeph pled for mercy. "The Ashen Weald is coming. They just want to show up all official-like. I came with a few feathers. I think these'll fit?"

Kia laughed when she saw them. "Are these from Mia? You didn't pluck my sister, did you?"

He shook his head. "She says all rangers carry extra feathers, just in case."

"Of course they do. There's just one problem." Kia did a little twirl, showing off a set of imped blue feathers.

"Where'd you find blue feathers?" he asked. Then a look of alarm took over his eyes. "My hat! You *plucked* my hat! I flew all the way back here just so you wouldn't be stuck any longer than you had to and this is how you repay me?"

She laughed and gave him a hug. "We'll make you a new hat if you really want one."

"Who'd you get a hold of?" Cherine's mind went to Ninox. He didn't want Sponge and her in the same place, especially since the sand gryphons continued calling Ninox his mate, which she may not appreciate.

"Basically everyone." Zeph held onto Sponge like she was a pillow, but the little sand gryphon didn't seem to mind. "I don't know who'll come, and you won't believe this, but Erlock was there."

"Did her tailfeathers grow back?" Kia perked up.

He nodded. "And she brought a purple starling with her."

Cherine tried to act similarly surprised. His time in prison had left him woefully unaware of pride politics, something he'd need to remedy if he was going to serve as the sand gryphons' trade ambassador.

When dark shapes appeared in the sky, his first thought was that the Ashen Weald had missed the ruins of Crestfall and circled back around. But the shapes were dark-plumed.

Reeve Rybalt Reevesbane landed atop the outer rim of the canyon, looking worse for wear from his time escaping the palace. Beside him was Impir the Mad, the Redwood Valley peacock prisoner responsible for the destruction of New Eyrie and the assassination of Grand Reeve Ivess.

Bario perched nearby, his bright red plumage with black markings nearly the opposite of the small force of blackwings behind him. His saltpeter and flameworks technology had fundamentally changed warfare in the south, and his explosive escape from the Crackling Sea had killed many opinici, including most of Brevin's children.

Iony and Ellore joined them, followed by another twenty

shaved glacier gryphons. Many of their long ears were sunburned.

Rybalt's eyes were on Zeph, Kia, and Cherine. After everything that had happened, Cherine feared they were about to lose control of the eyrie to the blackwings. With the leftover thunder bird eaten, many of the sand gryphon prides had returned to their desert hideaways. Only the Padfoot Pride remained to guard the eyrie.

Zeph crouched. Kia's talons were in the harness pocket where she kept the flechettes she'd picked out of the sand. Cherine found himself reaching for his pen and journal out of habit.

Before Rybalt could make his demands, a new set of gryphons and opinici appeared in the southern sky. Looking from the blackwings to the Ashen Weald, Cherine didn't know if any eyrie had ever housed such impressive individuals at the same time.

Satra the Kjarr's golden crest rivaled Hoppy's orange. Cherine recognized Pride Leader Grenkin from his eye patch and prosthetics, the metal talons of which glistened with jelly toxin. Askel and Triddle landed side-by-side. Askel's forelegs held two metal bracelets, while Merin's other three were on Triddle's back legs and tail, which was wrapped around Askel's back paw out of habit.

Zeph nodded up to Hatzel, who cast a shadow like a thunder bird. The same saber beak that had kindly welcomed Cherine into her nesting grounds when he found himself homeless after the fire looked fierce in the desert sun. Erlock and Soft Paws flanked her.

Just when Cherine thought he'd seen it all, the fisherfolk settled in on the bridge over the canyon. He recognized Tresh from her shark tooth markings. She looked no less ferocious standing next to Rorin the Hunter, his chest splashed red.

Ninox landed her gryphons behind Cherine. Her eyes never left Rybalt. She hooted something to Grax, and the brown owl put herself in front of Cherine to protect him from danger. Even Younce, looking as miserable as, well, a taiga gryphon in a desert, was present, though none of his kin had come with him.

Behind them, Quess, Mia, and a dozen other gryphons and opinici made famous by the wars led the combined Ashen Weald, fisherfolk, and free pride forces. Orlea, Naya, and a parrotface—possibly the elder, Cherine wasn't sure—gathered behind the more ferocious members.

Rybalt issued an order and the glacier pride retreated. Moments later, the blackwings and other opinici disappeared, leaving only the pitohui reeve alone before the might of the south.

The Reeve's Bane inclined his head and wings in a bow to Satra, but he turned and winked at Cherine, Kia, and Zeph before fleeing back to Blacktalon.

Satra the Kjarr glided down from the top of the canyon to where Cherine and Hoppy were. She didn't acknowledge that the last time she'd seen Cherine, he was locked up in her dungeon. "I understand someone is willing to trade large quantities of metal and weapons in exchange for protection and food?"

Cherine bowed to the Kjarr. "May I introduce you to Pride Leader Reeve Hoppy Padfoot, ruler of Crestfall?"

EPILOGUE
BLOOD

Birds and megapedes scattered from the screeches coming out of the moss-covered rock that marked the entrance into an elaborate cave system spanning a third of the continent.

By beak and talon, Mally the Nighthaunt pulled himself out of the darkness and into the blinding light. If he'd guessed correctly, this was one of the roads the abyssal gryphons had been attacking.

A long smear of blood followed in his wake, both his and that of his assailants. To what would certainly be his future regret, he'd only managed to wound the gryphon whose eyes he shared.

His body screamed in pain and hunger. He let out another screech, startling more wildlife. In his flight through the caverns, he hadn't eaten in days. His body needed iron, needed blood. He dug all four of his talon-claws into the earth and screamed again. The sound echoed back from every direction, confirming what he already knew: he'd frightened away any prey.

Far in the distance, he could just make out the clomping

of a goliath bird with reinforced shoes for road use. He pulled himself along the ground and into the middle of the path.

Silver stopped the caravan and ordered the opinicus workers to go back and look the other way, but Mally didn't have time to wait. He leapt on the lead bird, killing it in one go and feeding upon it like he was an animal.

The less iron his body was able to process, the more he needed to consume. While he was covered in blood now, by the time he was able to wash it off, more of the iron's red tint would fill his plumage and talons.

He fed until his stomach and crop were full and the screaming in his head had stopped, then turned to consider Silver.

"Mally." She inclined her head slightly.

When he opened his beak, the sound that came out was the click-screech the abyss gryphons used to echolocate. It took a few tries to force that into the shape of common. "What word from your argent hawks."

Silver patted a free spot on the wagon behind her, and he slithered up and curled in a loop to heal and groom while the guards returned to butcher the dead bird into portable pieces and calm the live ones.

"Crestfall has shattered," she said. "The blackwings' lead phoenix has refined saltpeter into something called black powder. Your pools were poisoned. A significant number of flamingos and our forces were killed by a combination of thunder birds, sand gryphons, and, on the southern front, starlings. Scouts say the Ashen Weald is reinforcing Crestfall Eyrie as we speak. Hi-kun and the pink reeve still live, but there's no crossing the desert the way things stand now. And Piprik, the old Eyes of the King, has returned from the dead."

Mally didn't comment on any of that, having already known about Khalim from their encounter in the bog. The rest were issues for kings and reeves, commanders and captains. With a large enough army, he could reclaim what essence salt remained in his first workshop from the abyssal gryphons for one final set of trials. There was only one thing he was concerned about, one thing the Seraph King was concerned about.

"And the king's prize?" he asked.

Silver inclined her head towards the crates he sat on. They smelled of the bog but had the Crackling Sea Eyrie's crest on them. All ten wagons were full of stormcloth.

"You really think this'll work?" she asked.

He closed his black eyes against the oppressive light of day. "The king will have his ascension. Wake me when we reach the capital."

A QUICK NOTE

Thanks for reading *The Ruins of Crestfall*! If you're enjoying the series and want to help other readers find it, please consider leaving a review. Reviews help new readers find the series and encourage authors and publishers to keep a series going.

Need more gryphons while you wait for *The Crackling Sea* to come out? Sign up for my newsletter and receive a free ebook copy of *Blue Eyes and Other Tales*, a short story collection set right after *Starling*. This book is currently only available to newsletter (kvalenagle.com/gryphonlist) and Patreon (patreon.com/kvalenagle) subscribers.

Blue Eyes and Other Tales includes "Blue Eyes," the story of Satra and Mignet, a lesbian beak-cute gryphon love story full of terror birds. "Connixation," where it's one small gryphon against the end of the world as we find out the fate of the Williwaw Pride. "Silver Eyes" follows Deracho and Thenca as they enlist the aid of a young bog witch to save a friend. And "Blue-eyed Festival," a holiday stories that ties together the previous three starring Younce, Satra, and Zeph.

AUTHOR'S NOTE
SAND

The desert is full of wonderful animals—lizards who burrow through sand like they're swimming, magical flying sponge birds, scorpions, and even bats. So how does an author choose who gets to be a gryphon or opinicus and who doesn't and what wildlife to populate his imaginary desert with?

It's pretty simple. Aesthetics and adaptability (which we'll call awesomeness). Sand cats and hoopoe birds look like they were meant to be combined into Hoppy. Sand cats exude sassiness. Hoopoe birds provide a certain self-absorption that compliments the sass. Put simply: they look cool, especially for the hoopoe bird half.

Sandgrouse are awesome, where in this context, *awesome* means that they're well-adapted for the environment they live in. The male sandgrouse will fly twenty miles through the desert to locate water, puff up his feathers to soak it up, then fly twenty miles back to share it with his mate and chicks. That's a pretty amazing bird.

Flamingo opinici, while quite the aesthetic, have their own level of awesomeness. I grew up with the Everglades variety of flamingo, but there are some species who live in toxic pools at high altitudes where little vertebrate life can survive. They actually freeze into the pools at night. And as anyone who has been to a zoo knows, they aren't born pink but a grey color. Their diet of aqueous bacteria and the beta-carotene they get from their food allows them to secrete a special oil, which they then rub through their feathers to stain them pink.

I talked about the sand cat's sass earlier, but they're also well adapted to live in deserts. They have thick fur that covers the soles of their feet, allowing them to survive extreme heat and cold, even far from water. They love playing in and drinking water, but they don't need it—they get enough moisture from their prey. They're well-adapted for hunting hoopoe birds, desert monitors, sandfish, and sand vipers. They're also good about burying anything they don't eat for later.

Can you tell I was excited to get to write desert gryphons? So many fun birds and cats! There's one more animal I've been geeking out over, but if you read back through the series, you've probably seen hints of them as far back as the first clicking and cave gryphon comments in *Eyrie*.

Tell me if this sounds familiar: a nocturnal creature that eats fruit and sometimes bugs. It has incredible night vision. It hangs out in caves and makes clicking sounds to echolocate.

As Lou Diamond Phillips from the movie *Bats* might say, it sounds like we need "some sort of bat-ologist." But I'm actually talking about oilbirds, which the gryphons of the Abyssal Naze are based on. With their black eyes, cave-camouflage plumage, and long whiskers, they already look like a fantasy creature. They're the only nocturnal fruit-eating bird in the world—well, I should say they're the only *flying* nocturnal fruit-eating bird. Let's not forget our friend the kakapo ground parrot.

They also unleash a hellish screech when they're hanging out in their caves, which is one reason why their Trinidadian name is *diablotin* or "little devil." Supposedly, its cave cries sound like tortured men.

The English name of oilbird comes from—oh, hold up. You may want to skip the next paragraph. It's probably what you're thinking, but go on and read ahead a little. Pretend this next paragraph doesn't exist. I'll catch up with you in a moment.

Okay, the name oilbird comes from the fact that the chicks are full of fat. They're chubby and full of oil, so it was a common practice to sneak into caves, steal the baby birds, and boil them down to make oil.

Welcome back! Prehistoric oilbird fossils suggest the first of the species to become nocturnal ate the same types of fruits and berries, but they hadn't yet evolved to be able to hover or roost in caves. You didn't read the previous paragraph, did you? Okay, good. Baby oilbirds are called squabs, and they're very cute. Don't go back and read that paragraph.

If you made it this far, you're probably wondering if hoopoe birds just looked cool or if they have any amazing desert adaptations I ignored. And, well, they do, though their gryphonic counterparts lack them.

They're really gross.

"Grosser than that paragraph you told me not to read but I read anyway!?" I can hear you shouting at your signed, inscribed hardcover edition of *Crestfall* that I tried to draw an adorable gryphon in but it ended up looking like a pigeon. For those who needed another dose of cute, here we go.

The name *hoopoe bird* comes from their *hoo-poi* cry. They're really cute and bring gifts of food during mating season. And when they need to sunbathe, they find a patch of sand and do this kind of old-timey "fetch the smelling salts" faint so their face and wings and tummy are exposed to the light. And they're little swordswains with their beaks, using them to fight off predators or catch large bugs.

But they're also kinda gross. They're one of the few bird species that never cleans their nest. And those oil glands birds have to keep their feathers waterproof? The hoopoe bird's glands are full of nasty bacteria. And they also use those glands to coat their eggs in the same nastiness.

In fact, their eggs have grooves in the shell designed to make it easier. The bacteria then infects the chicks when they hatch. And if you're wondering: *But why? Why would anyone do that?* The answer is that it gives them an evolutionary advantage.

Scientists decided to go around shooting hoopoe birds in the glands with antibiotics to see what happened. The answer is that the birds seem fine. In fact, they raise the eggs that hatch the same way as the bacteria-filled birds. But fewer of their eggs actually hatch.

It seems that having bacteria that doesn't harm the hoopoe birds covering their eggs stops other harmful bacteria from getting in. For anyone who really wanted me to put all of that in the book—sorry! You should definitely go write your own bacteria-gryphon book, though. The world always needs more gryphon novels, even if they're kind of gross.

Writing a hot desert novel in January has been an interesting experience, though I did write my frost snow novel in

June, so maybe that's just my writing process. I've been snowed in for about a week now, and food and coffee have run out. I think I've attempted to shovel the driveway six times just for the sun to disappear and the snow to return within a few hours. I'm rethinking the life choices that put me here without snow tires, extra firewood, or coffee.

Still, it put me in a situation where I had nothing to do except write, and write I did. I've been battling Catastrophic APS for a while now, and this is the fastest I've ever written a novel from zero to second draft. I'm about to go through, do some edits, get it to draft four, and mail this off to my editor. Then I'll put on my snow boots and head out to the store.

If you don't hear from me again, I'm not frozen. I just decided it's warmer inside the grocery store, and I'm living there until things thaw out.

-Vale

ABOUT THE AUTHOR

K. Vale Nagle is alarmingly hard to kill. While he's written his entire life, after surviving a pulmonary embolism and multiple organ failure, he began to take his writing more seriously and worked to get a degree in creative writing while recovering.

During that time another embolism struck and failed to kill him, at which point the doctors discovered an undiagnosed autoimmune disorder and patched him back up. Having used up two of his nine lives, he began publishing short stories and novels. When the doctors said that lung surgery was a 95% certainty, he dyed his hair dark blue, which is when he discovered that he was so unwell that his hair wasn't growing. A year later, and a switch from dark blue to teal, and his hair has finally started growing again (albeit silver instead of its pre-embolism black) and he's writing like a fiend.

Now, Vale writes feral fantasy—books with mythological creatures and nature-based settings, often involving gryphons and conflict.

He can be found online at kvalenagle.com, via his newsletter, or on Patreon.

 facebook.com/kvalenagle
 twitter.com/kvalenagle
 bookbub.com/authors/k-vale-nagle

Use Telegram? Need to express your emotions via adorable stickers? You can grab the Sand Gryphon Telegram stickers at https://t.me/addstickers/Crestfall and always have a scream_gryph emoji handy!

ALSO BY K. VALE NAGLE